MW00353846

MATRIARCHY

By Monica Joshi

© Monica Joshi 2020

ISBN e-book: 978-0-9939384-2-9

ISBN Print: 978-0-9939384-1-2

© Cover Design by Ebru Sonmezisik
https://www.ebrusdesign.com/

This is a work of fiction. Names, characters, businesses, places, events, locales, and incidents are either the products of the author's imagination or used in a fictitious manner. Any resemblance to actual persons, living or dead, or actual events is purely coincidental.

To Jason and Priyanka —

PROLOGUE

"Are you ready?"

"*Born* ready."

"Here's your speech."

"Let's do this thing."

She was ushered out with six strong male bodyguards by her side. They pushed the crowd back with the weight of their forearms.

November 4th, 2024.

She sported her proud smile for the cameras that were all pointed at her.

The votes were in.

She had won.

The democratic process had succeeded in putting a woman in charge of the United States of America.

"And here she is, the first female president of the United States of America," the CNN broadcaster said.

He boomed into his mic over the cheering crowd, trying his best to introduce Jessica Alberton in the simplest words he knew: the first female president of the United States of America.

The crowd cheered as she tried to make her way to the stage.

Her shoulders shifted slightly into a forward hunch, mimicking Atlas with the weight of the earth on his back.

After a long, drawn out campaign that had spanned eighteen months, she had finally succeeded.

This is when the world would *change*. Everyone knew it deep inside their gut.

It radiated through all the corners of the earth. This was the moment that they had *all* been waiting for.

The live stream logged seven billion people and counting watching her win. Each one, individually, taking pride in this democratic decision of the greatest, freest country on earth.

"Who are you wearing, Mrs. Alberton?" one of the men asked, shoving a microphone in her direction.

From tennis pros to politicians, the media was interested in this *one* mundane thing: what, or rather *who*, they were wearing.

"I'm wearing Target!" she said in a French accent, pronouncing it *Tarjay*.

The crowd gasped.

"Just joking of course. I'm wearing Prada," she said, quickly scanning the media crowd for nods of approval.

She heard the reverberations of a long deliberate sigh. *None* of them wanted her to be like them. That would be too close for comfort. They needed her to be on a pedestal.

"I need to make my speech now," she said.

The broadcaster stepped aside and let her pass as she quickly stepped onto the stage.

The crowd cheered again.

She raised her hands up and brought the crowd to silence.

"Ladies and gentlemen, we are gathered here today to witness the biggest event unfold in the history of the world."

The people in the front row craned their necks to look up at her, their eyes glimmering with the stage lights.

"Never before has this sight been seen by mankind. A woman shall be the Commander in Chief of the free world."

This called for a standing ovation, and one she was given.

The drums beat in the background as her heart beat in rhythm.

The crowd silenced itself, desperate to hear more.

"I stand before you today and vow to make this country great, make the world bow at its feet, and lead this country to prosperity."

She paused and smiled into the blaring white light that blinded her from seeing the enormity of the crowd.

"For years, women in this country have fought amongst men, learned amongst men, taught amongst men, ruled the businesses and the masses alongside men, but never have they seen the Oval Office as a space that they, too, could reach."

She paused and looked into the crowd, seeking any face in the abyss. They looked back at her with eyes of hope, sincerity, and earnest. She didn't see their expressions.

She turned the pages in front of her upside down so that she couldn't read from them anymore.

"My parents told me that I could be anything, as do all of yours. I wanted to be president, so I married a man who would stand by me as I reached this podium."

She was no longer speaking like Reagan.

She felt empowered by her voice echoing through the crowd in the large expanse of the auditorium.

"I want to thank him and my family for supporting my campaigns, enduring my long hours, and letting me pave the way for a wave of women to hold the Oval and seek justice and freedom for all those fighting to live the great dream in this country that we call the United States of America."

She paused.

Took a breath.

Looked into the abyss and smiled.

She heard them cheer back.

"My comrades in this journey, all of you..."

The crowd silenced themselves as their egos were stroked. This was just as much *their* victory as hers.

"... have spoken via your votes today and have chosen me to lead this country to greatness."

She focused on the outlines of some women in front of her. She saw their hands moving in unison to the orchestra playing the national anthem during a long pause in her speech.

She raised one fist in the air, smiling and showing all her teeth.

"Yes! Yes! My campaign promises still hold true…"

The crowd cheered for a good long minute and a half. All eyes around the world were still glued to their TV screens.

She turned her pages once again to read what she had written.

"Our health care system will protect the poor. Our welfare system will be revised to not allow for any misuse, and our peacekeepers and soldiers abroad and at home will be taken care of as they should be, after protecting our rights and freedoms with their lives."

She paused, clearing her throat.

"I know this in my bones: America was *not* great. It was *never* great. But *now*, we will *make* it great. *Together*."

The crowd cheered, screaming "USA! USA! USA!"

The camera man turned his lens towards a woman who was texting inattentively. The camera quickly shifted to another woman who smiled and jumped along with the crowd.

There was a different expression on her face; some would even call it sinister when the clip was replayed ad nauseam for days to come.

"To all the women in the crowd, I promise you this: the government will no longer work against you. It will work *for* you, *with* you, and only *because* of you."

This was the line that would stay with the crowd.

Bang! Bang! Bang!

Her body hit the ground.

The Revolution began.

CHAPTER 1

This wasn't the first time he and I had been together.

Me, Althea.

Him, Michael.

I was waiting for him to come into the bedroom again.

How did we get here?

I kept asking myself that.

When he walked back in with his espresso in his hands, I stared at the veins in his forearm.

I wondered how they got to be so prominent.

No other person I had ever been with had had arms that made me catch my breath every time I looked at them.

He strutted to the window.

His bare ass shapely and round, glistening in the morning sun.

I stared shamelessly.

Damn.

If anyone saw us right now, they would think we were in the same kind of world that existed fifty years ago.

A world where women were wooed and strong men did the wooing.

Men like the one in my room right now had been *long* relegated to the books of the past.

The books that we were discouraged from reading, for fear that we would be wistful of the humans in them.

Now, most men were *glad* if we dominated them in the bedroom and elsewhere.

I had been with those kinds of men before. *None* of them compared to the one in front of me right now.

I couldn't remember a time when men were in charge.

Not in my life time, that was for sure.

He must have known the consequences.

He must.

I *thought* I knew what was at stake. And yet, I sought him out anyway.

That's what I told myself when *this* began.

He needed my body and I needed his…everything.

I looked at his beautiful chiselled back as he sipped intensely on that aromatic black liquid.

Gawking.

Damn.

"Michael, do many women stare at you like I do?"

"Yes."

He didn't bother turning around to look at me.

A man of few words. Even if you got to know him as closely as I had.

He knew what he was getting himself into.

He was intently staring out of the floor-to-ceiling windows.

I felt helpless with desire.

My eyes travelled back to his body.

I let them climb up slowly from his heels to the top of his head. Admiring every muscle along the way.

He turned around to look at me with concupiscent desire and I just wanted to taste the coffee off of his lips.

He put the espresso cup on the floor near the windows and inched closer to the bed.

My heart leapt up in my chest as he began climbing on the bed, on top of me.

He hovered there, above me, looking longingly into my eyes for what seemed like years.

Damn.

How did we get here?

CHAPTER 2

This wasn't me *two months ago*.

A secretive, chivalrous-man loving woman.

Sitting here on the subway, relinquishing the subtleties of our passionate lovemaking made me realize that I was completely smitten by Michael.

I blinked to keep from falling sleep.

It was just past three on a Sunday morning.

Safe for me to leave his apartment for a subway ride home.

Not safe for Michael to escort me back to my place.

The subway came to a screeching halt, jerking me awake, just as I had begun to slip into a coma.

"Next stop, Carlington."

Five more to go.

I gripped hard onto the pole that obstructed my view of two women holding hands in the subway car across from me.

Each minute jerk of the car made them appear in full view for a split second before the red head disappeared behind the pole again.

What would they think of me if they knew I had just been intimate with a *man*?

I saw the redhead nuzzle into the brunette's neck.

I could fathom what it would feel like to be in that relationship.

I could feel the brunette's hair grazing against my nose. I could imagine smelling her day-old shampoo and just a hint of day-old perfume.

The brunette giggled.

It was that time of night.

I knew what their dalliance would amount to, but could they imagine what *mine* would?

I bent over to tie the laces on my boots that had come undone.

I glanced over to my right, into the rest of the subway cars.

One long, never-ending strip of womanly pairings.

No man in sight.

I felt *safe*.

CHAPTER 3

Waking up the next morning was a chore.

The hangover from great sex intermingled with the dreaded list of things I had to do in the recesses of my tired brain and resulted in a throbbing headache.

9 A.M.

Shit.

No, seriously, shit.

Only six hours of sleep.

I hadn't slept a full night since I started the tradeship with Michael.

No nights of eight consecutive hours.

Shit.

When I had moved out of my moms' place, I hadn't realized that all the grocery shopping, laundry, and cleaning would fall on *me*.

Marriage would solve that.

I would have another person to share in those mundane tasks.

Especially if the person was as maternal as Ma.

Argh!

I missed that.

I missed the homey feel of an apartment.

Even a year after I had moved out, I hadn't quite nailed that feeling.

Even with Felicity's help.

My place felt like a hotel room.

Cold.

Calculated.

Minimal personal touches.

It had the bare minimum.

But it was my own space.

Before getting off the bed, I checked my phone.

No new messages.

It was still early.

He slept hard.

Into the afternoon.

I closed my eyes and savoured the last memory I had of his hard body against my back as we spooned.

The moment I opened my eyes again, I returned to the humdrum of the rest of the day.

I got up and walked over to my fridge.

Beer.

Some olives and mushrooms.

Shit.

What was I supposed to make with *that*?

I threw on a sweatshirt and my jacket over my pyjama tank, grabbed my keys, and headed to the nearest convenience store without having brushed my teeth.

They should at least have fruit.

Even if it was a dollar and a half apiece, it was still better than coffee and olives for breakfast.

Especially before I had to sit through lunch with my moms.

Shit.

CHAPTER 4

Walking to the store, I noticed the ever-increasing number of homeless men on my street.

The women had all been taken off the street *years* ago.

All the men looked sickly thin, some swaying their heads from side to side to match the songs that played in their heads.

One wore army green cargo pants and a trench coat with a hoodie inside.

He didn't sway.

He sat still, with the hood covering so much of his face that I could barely see the colour of his skin.

His extended palm bore a deep gash.

No gloves to cover the frost-bitten fingers.

I had seen him a hundred times before, as I had been walking down the same street, to the same Quickie Mart.

I felt helpless as I walked past him and his minimal possessions — just a deflated grey backpack that had acquired visible patches of discolouration from being covered in snow so many times.

On the side of his winter toque was a pin, showing an eagle taking flight.

A veteran.

I walked past him, certain of the next few actions I had to take.

I bought some fruit and almond milk, said hello to Macy at the cash, and walked with purpose towards the man.

His outstretched palm was blue from the cold.

I put a cold piece of fruit into it.

"I hope you like apples."

"Thank you," he said.

"Thank you for your service."

He didn't bother looking up at me.

A bit of pride and sympathy swelled up in the pit of my stomach.

An act of kindness that made me feel like I had done something to alleviate the man's suffering, if only for a moment.

I smiled to myself, huddling deeper into my jacket and crossing my arms trying to keep warm.

I heard a crunch as I walked away.

Passing more men swaying their heads, I wondered what had made me give the apple only to him.

CHAPTER 5

I think it's time I properly introduced my complication: Felicity.

I call her Fess.

Meeting her off of the Women Empowerment Bank's carefully curated profile-matching system was a blessing.

Of the thirty women I had been matched with, she was the *only* one who I had believed was beautiful and intellectually stimulating enough for my twenty-five year old self.

And she was soft-spoken enough for me to want her more than *any* of the other men and women I had casually seen in the past.

She had never been with anyone before me.

On our first date, we talked about all the things we had wanted out of life — travelling, working abroad before we turned thirty-five, sky diving, and even what we wanted in our sex lives.

It escalated fast.

Before I knew it, she had come back to my place, taken off her clothes, and we had made love.

That was the night that I knew she was the one I wanted to marry.

She didn't resist the obvious trajectory of our relationship, either.

I was swept up in the comfort of it all.

The entire relationship came easy.

We knew how to work each others' bodies, so the orgasms were easy.

It was with the same ease that we began to leave our clothes, then our jewelry, then our stuff at each others' places.

She gave me her key, but I steered clear of giving her mine.

I kept telling myself that I just didn't want to succumb to the chore of making a duplicate, but really I was just resistant to the commitment.

At first.

Then, I started to notice the lack of passion.

I loved her.

I could *say* that.

I could say that to both her and myself convincingly.

But I couldn't say that I loved her enough to know that she was the *only* one I wanted to be with forever anymore.

A year and a half after I met her for the first time, I met Michael.

He was the missing piece of the puzzle in my increasingly comfortable relationship with her.

He gave me the passion that I had been so desperately craving.

Then, I started to have a life outside of Fess.

I could be a better partner to Fess with him in me.

In my head and my body.

He stimulated me in ways she never could.

And because we weren't life partners yet, I could still justify my lack of commitment.

CHAPTER 6

The encounter with the homeless man had left me feeling uncomfortable in my own skin.

I thought my act of compassion would have alleviated the occasional guilt I had about the privileges in my life.

I had listened to the droplets fall from the melting icicles onto the balcony railing for the rest of the morning and into the early afternoon. It had helped me meditate and quiet my thoughts before dinner with Moms.

I had been down this street a hundred times before.

I knew it like the back of my hand.

Why did I have to endure the weekly monotony of needing to see my moms?

They pay your rent.

Oh, right.

I looked around at the billboards with a newfound curiousity.

Had that perfume bottle barely covering that man's junk *always* been there?

It was so blatantly sexist. It hadn't seemed that way before Michael had introduced me to the idea.

He called it objectification. I called it reparations in advertising.

That's what they had taught us.

I just parroted what they had said.

I waited to cross the street.

On the pole, a simple poster hung by two staples.

Herstory: The 1900s Under Her Eye

The annual charity gala to preserve women's literature from the 1900s at libraries across the city.

Join us for dinner, drinks and dancing.
April 23rd, 2075.

NO HETS ALLOWED

Typical.

I'd probably be going with Felicity.

It was in hushed tones that Granny, Ma's mom, had told me about how she had lived her life before Alberton became president.

That was before she passed away six years ago.

I never pressed. She wanted to talk, and I let her.

I had always thought that women were the more inquisitive ones. According to Mrs. Grant in 10th grade literature class, we were always asking the "right" questions.

But when I had asked Mrs. Grant why my grandfathers' version of history wasn't legitimate, she had gone into an hour-long lecture about why men, history's greatest oppressors, couldn't be trusted to write the truth.

Her beatdown in class, and my classmates telling me to stop asking questions that would get me into trouble, shut me right up.

I only asked the "right" questions after that. At least in school. *Definitely* around Moms.

I asked questions about what problems women faced while having to be leaders. I asked about how we could make the men of today pay for the crimes of their past.

Perhaps women had just been *conditioned* to do what they were told since the beginning of time. As my moms put it, women had usually been told to shut up and sit in the back. Before Alberton made it so that women would have to sit in the front.

We did it.

The men sat in the back of the classrooms now. *The men* got to ask questions at the end. *The men* were told to shut up or were ridiculed out of the room if their questions were not appropriate.

We did that to them.

Obey or else.

And yet, somehow, *this* was a woman's world.

Where women were free to do whatever we wanted.

Except ask the wrong questions.

It was just one straight road from this signal light to Moms'. The road seemed so straightforward, and yet I felt more confused than ever before.

When had we stopped thinking for *ourselves*?

When had we become so biased in favour of women?

It was justified.

They *owe* us our time in this world.

And until two months ago, keeping my curiosities in check had been just fine.

I wouldn't have reignited the desire to ask these questions until…

Michael.

He was…something else. He amazed me with his profound knowledge of the world's rich *history*. A word he taught me. We had been taught it was *herstory*. He said that this *herstory* was a word introduced to protect women's fragile egos. His words, not mine.

Like my Moms' egos?

Maybe.

A bold judgment on my part.

They lived through the inequality.

How could *I* ever question their lived experience?

CHAPTER 7

The doorbell rang and echoed.

I waited.

Someone opened the door. One of my moms, I don't remember which.

I was frazzled by the time I got in and removed my coat and boots.

"How's work?" "How's Felicity?" "How's the apartment?"

I answered with more than just a few monosyllabic words. "Fine" and "great" would never cut it with them.

I've tried. I know it.

When I got tired of the mundane, I sat still until they finished buzzing around me as they tried to get lunch on the table.

Then they began their barrage of "you should…" lectures, as I sat there with my arms folded across my chest waiting to cram a few sandwiches in my mouth.

Their expectations were never-ending.

They wanted me to be different.

Marry the right girl.

Better the world.

Or something.

My stomach began grumbling with the sight of all the sandwiches on a tray in front of us, some iced tea with precisely three ice cubes in each glass, and napkins on our plates.

That was Ma's doing.

Mom wouldn't do any of that.

When we had finally served ourselves, we settled into conversation.

"So, work is good?" Mom asked.

Natalia, Mom.

Ma's Magda.

Mom asks all the practical questions.

Ma asks all the emotional ones.

It works.

"Work is, you know, work. Rita says hi, by the way."

"Oh, Rita! I can't believe she still works in admin. I thought she'd have surely moved up by now."

"Well, not all women want to climb the money ladder, Mom."

Shit.

A sideways glare from Mom as I kept eating my sandwich.

Ma's chewing echoed in the uncomfortable silence that followed.

Mom cleared her throat.

"So, how *is* Felicity?" Mom asked.

"She's busy. Work."

"You should think about asking her to be life partners already," Ma said.

"She has plans on how she wants to propose, Ma. I'm not going to ruin those for her. She *does* want your ring though."

"The Hayworth ring?" Mom asked.

"No, the Chatthum ring that Granny gave Ma."

Mom chuckled.

"That girl has her eye on the prize. I like her."

They both laughed at the insinuation that my future wife was a gold digger.

So far, so good.

Everyone had returned to a state of contentment. My quip forgotten.

"Did you read the New York Times today?"

Shit.

"I only got through the headlines."

"Well, if your generation could read a little *more* than the headlines, you'd be more outraged by the protests outside of City Hall for the past week."

I didn't want to respond to snide with snide. But I couldn't help myself.

"Better to be a duchess of all news than a queen of a few articles."

Ma touched my wrist.

A warning.

Another glare.

"The men were campaigning for proportional representation in the Senate. *Ha!*"

"What's wrong with that?"

I *instantly* knew I had put my foot in my mouth.

"Well, *dear*, asking for proportional representation is what *we* did, forty years ago. And that got us *diddly squat*."

"But that was *grandma's* generation, not ours. We want women *and* men to have a voice in making the laws of this country. Don't we?"

Ma abruptly got up. Mom put a hand on her wrist.

"Mags, sit down. It's okay, we won't get into it."

"Ma, it's fine. We were just talking."

Ma sat back down in silence.

"So, Al, who is the 'we' that you're talking about? Which 'we' wants women *and* men to have a voice?"

I cleared my throat and swallowed the last bit of crust that I had crammed into my mouth to keep myself from talking.

"I thought *we* said we weren't getting into it."

Mom slammed her free hand on the table, sending the second half of her sandwich flying onto the floor.

It was almost cartoonish.

I had to stifle a laugh.

The look in her eyes warned me that I shouldn't let it out.

I covered my mouth instead.

"Let's get into this, Althea."

Shit.

The next several minutes of back and forth concluded in Ma walking away and Mom yelling in my face.

How had I even gotten myself into this mess of a conversation?

Oh, right, my attitude.

"That's *just* the way the world is, Althea. It's *just* the way it is," Mom said.

She only said my full name when I was being a handful.

"You mean, women control the men, and I'm just supposed to *accept* that?"

"Yes, *they do*. And they do because now they have power in every possible way you could *dream*. Our vaginas make men fall to their knees. Men worship them because they know there can't be a future race without them. We're in children's minds from the second they're born until the day they die, because they grow from the food that *we* produce in *our* bodies. Then, they have to *beg* us to deviate from our original desires to *be* with other women, to *comfort* other women, to *raise* other women, long enough to fuck our brains out so that we can produce the world's legacies. Ever since we learned how to do that with a syringe, it's gotten even easier to discard them to the side, to use them when we see fit. They have become our *toys*. They can't live without us, because we've made them *dependent* on our existences. They are *nothing* without us."

She was talking *at* me.

I shook in my socks as though the cold outside had entered my body, crept into every bone and decided its desired place of rest was my feet.

"What if I don't want to live in that world anymore?"

"*That* is our reality. Believe me, you wouldn't want it *any* other way."

She was pointing a finger straight into my face.

"I can think of a *million* other ways I would want to live," I said defiantly.

She pushed her finger into my nose and then drew it back, only to smooth the loose strands of hair back into my ponytail.

A useless endeavour.

"The alternative, is that men take over. Again. They take *our* hard-earned, rightful place in society."

"I think…"

"What *do* you think, exactly?"

She was egging me on.

I folded my arms across my chest again.

Defensive.

"I think they just want *equality*," I fought back, not even knowing why.

"Ha! Oh, do *I* remember when *we* wanted equality. They gave us *nothing*! They told us that having a right to vote and a seat at the table in the corporate offices of rich old men was supposed to keep us from wanting more."

"So, what, it's *our* turn now?"

"*Yes*, Althea. It's *our* turn."

Patronizing.

Just like that, she turned around and walked straight out the door, before I had the chance to protest.

I had been parented.

She went back to her job, and I was left there twiddling my thumbs while I heard muffled crying coming from the other room.

Shit.

I knew she was right in a way. It was the way the world was. The women control the men. I had better get used to it.

My thoughts raced back to all the crazy things that Michael had been saying to me for the past few months.

Was he right?

Or did moms understand this world better?

Was I even a womanist if I didn't believe this was the right way?

The only way?

CHAPTER 8

Mom's outburst left me helpless for more answers.

So, here I was, once again.

An overnight date.

At Michael's.

How did we get here?

I can pinpoint the day I began to listen to Michael, *truly* listen to him when he spoke instead of just craving his body.

I'm trying to be chronological, but I can't quite tell when the shift happened in my mind.

Or had this desire always been there?

Was he just my excuse to start asking the wrong questions again?

Laying here, next to him, I wondered if it had been *that* day.

It had been another one of those mornings where we had been engaged in deep conversation that led to passionate sex.

Had it been *that* particular day that had caused the drastic changes in me?

Or was it all that time that I had spent engrossed in the books he had encouraged me to read?

My head was spinning.

Where was my head, anyway?

I had been immersed in *this man* for just over a month and a half at that point, and it had felt like everything I had been told about men had been extracted and replaced by doubt.

The beginnings of a relationship, they called it.

Except we had been going at this for two months now and the feeling hadn't gone away.

The dalliances I had had with men before, all paid at the gigolo houses on Fredricton, had never made me feel this way.

I had even stopped taking the hormone stabilizers that would have otherwise allowed me to think more clearly.

That was just a month ago.

It made this "love" feeling that much more opaque. The hormones, mixed in with the lack of sleep, the intense conversations and the sex had me feeling like I was on a different planet.

Nothing changed with Fess.

I maintained my cool with her.

I looked at the man next to me basking in the afterglow of our bodies colliding.

The way his eyebrows symmetrically divided his face right down the middle made me want to cup his face in my hands to accentuate his perfect lips before I kissed them.

I could be playful with him.

I had to be more assertive with her.

She liked being dominated.

I liked being dominated.

Just not by her.

I recalled asking him the first few times we met,

"Have you thought about calling a woman a *cunt* before?"

I kept my eyes locked in with his.

"Yes," he had said.

"Aren't you afraid of what might happen if someone heard you say that? Out there?"

"No," he said.

He had looked at me, meek, helpless, as though I had held his life in my hands.

His raw vulnerability had conjured up protective sentiments in me.

"I'm not going to tell anyone what kind of words you like, if that's what you're wondering."

"I didn't think you would."

"It would be the end of *this*. Of *us*. And really, I don't want you permanently silenced. I *like* bold men."

I had raised my eyebrows towards him, playfully biting my lip.

"I would love it if you called me that when we are fucking."

"Of course."

It thrilled me to know that he would comply with my basest whims.

I must have made him feel safe enough to use such callous language to describe such an intimate act between us, because he did it now.

Every time I asked him to, he did it.

It was precisely this desire to push the boundaries of what was acceptable between a man and a woman that electrified every bone in my body.

He was a man who oozed what we had been taught was toxic masculinity.

He was silent in the way he would voice his sentiments.

Guarded, strong, and sturdy.

I brushed his eyebrows with my thumb.

Perhaps he was just defeated and broken in by me.

While I was just reading my own biases into his manner a little too much.

CHAPTER 9

Althea's transgression against her very being was still weighing on Natalia's mind as she stormed into her office. She had had the *audacity* to make her Ma cry, talk back to both of them, and then give them the silent treatment for two days.

Spoiled little girl!

How had that girl gotten these ideas into her pretty little head?

Before she could follow that train of thought to a conclusive place, she heard a distinctive ping on her phone.

A notification of a new blog post from Draven Alec's blog.

He was a *spectacular* intellectual adversary.

He was the type of man that she wanted to hunt, break down, and *torment* until he became so *passive* that he turned into a house-husband to some woman or man that the WEB had picked out for him.

She read the title and couldn't stop until she hit the end.

CURBING THE CURFEWS

Last week, in a desperate attempt to control men's movements more than ever before, the *Late Night Act* was proposed in House to be discussed for the second time in the last fifty years.

The *LNA* suggests that men ought to have a nightly curfew of 7 P.M. to protect women who are afraid of men's beastly urges and incurable desires for sexual deviance. Specifically, men whose animal instincts have not been tamed by voluntary use of estrogen pills.

The last time the act was proposed, in 2031, men were able to win their freedom for movement past 7 p.m. as it was still the case that men held the majority of the late night shift jobs.

There was much debate in parliament and in homes about the practicality of such a curfew: how would men be able to sustain themselves or their families if they were bartenders? What about lawyers and doctors who had to work at all hours? What about construction workers on our beloved highways who could only work from 2 a.m. to 5 a.m. with no interruptions during the rush hour insanity of early mornings?

With no good answers to the practical hindrances of such a motion, the act was tabled and hadn't resurfaced until last week.

The workplace has changed now. Fewer and fewer men work the night shifts, let alone *any* shifts. The government has made it easier for men to just stay home, collect welfare, and have only part-time jobs, mainly to protect the women.

The proposal of this Act comes on the heels of the newest report in the Daily Guardian regarding the rates of violent crime increasing between the hours of 9 P.M. and 3 A.M.

The genders of the perpetrators have not been released, however it seems unlikely that these perpetrators would be mostly *men*, seeing as women have made it virtually *impossible* for us to leave our homes after 7 P.M. without a female companion or chaperone in most localities around this country.

The victims are over 70% male, and transgender men make up another 18%, while women are only a tiny minority.

We have been harassed on the streets, leered at, catcalled, and groped to the point where most of us have even *willingly* chosen to no longer set foot outdoors past 7 P.M. or whenever it gets dark.

The earlier it gets dark, the earlier we stay home.

And well, men, winter is here. We are already resigned into our apartments by 5 P.M. and there we stay until daylight.

I guarantee you they will still find a way to say it's male on male violence that has increased violent crime against men, even though all I have seen lately are blonde bimbos walking around past 9 P.M. trying to harass any unsuspecting men.

Hide your husbands, hide your boys, brothers.

Until next time, for liberty, equality, and the brotherhood,

Yours,
DA

Underneath his inane diatribe, a series of women commented that DA was a complete misogynist who did not understand the *first thing* about what it meant to have to pay for the actions of other men.

Natalia liked one comment in particular:

Women, for *years*, probably before you were even *born* (seeing as you post these stupid blog posts like a child that doesn't know or understand history), had to burden themselves with useless thoughts like — should I wear that? Will I give men the wrong impression? Should I go out wearing that past 9 at night just in case some *ape* decided that he could take advantage of the situation? They had to burden themselves and police each other and make dress codes in their minds that they strictly adhered to, any deviation of which they were told made them "slutty". These burdens are now rightly being put on *men*. Thank *goddess* you're made to feel what our predecessors have felt for *years*. This toxic masculine debauchery needed to be curbed with a curfew a LONG time ago. I'll be *glad* when men have a curfew put on them, self-imposed or otherwise.

Natalia had responded:

I appreciate the female perspective on such a close-minded man's disgusting post. Using the fact that more men have been victims of crime compared to women is *not* a reason to eliminate discussion of the *LNA*. In fact, it will *protect* men to have to stay indoors, seeing as DA here is concerned that men have been the most harassed. *Useful* for the men, I say!

Natalia was exhilarated by the positive reactions that her comment received almost instantaneously.

She spent a good twenty minutes in her office chair reading through all the comments and going through the entire spectrum of human emotions.

CHAPTER 10

Being with both Michael and Fess felt like *infidelity*.

We didn't use words like that anymore.

It was just *normal*.

Michael was my *side piece*.

He and I were in a *tradeship* - it was consensual and usually started by the woman.

My grandma would have been confused, my moms less so, but my peers not at all.

The fact that they would call what I was doing *horrible* instead of just a necessity for sanity made me appreciate being born in the 40s.

The problem, and this was the *real* one, was that I was hiding my side piece from Fess.

So, it *felt* like infidelity.

After leaving work at the university on Friday afternoon, I waited for Michael by the front door of our usual cafe.

The hustle and bustle of the place always made it easier for me to feel safe.

In here, *anything* was possible.

In here, I could have a dalliance with a forbidden man, forget about Felicity, and just *be*.

Two mature women sat in the plump velveteen armchairs two feet from me.

The atmosphere was monotonous.

I was impatiently waiting.

For *him*.

Boredom necessitated eavesdropping.

"I always figured there was a reason why women looked so lonely and desperate even though they were with other women. We were all *missing* something," the one with the white strand in her deep auburn hair said.

"We were missing that *testosterone*. A little bit of *competition*. A little bit of *adventure*," the one with the crisp grey hair slicked back into a bun said, almost jumping out of her seat.

"God, *adventure*, how I miss that exhilarating feeling that men would give us. Remember when too much of our time was spent pretending to be emotionally mature and adequately masculine to make up for the lack of men in our lives? Especially when some of our dads and brothers were sent off to Fangsel?"

"I was told since I was a child that to become a woman, so completely feminine and beautiful in my own right, I had to reject my innermost desires to be with a man. If I wanted to be with a man… well, it was just completely *unimaginable*."

And so they went. On and on.

"Who needs a *man* these days though? Everything you want you can get in a *woman*," the one with the white strand quickly retracted her position just in case someone listening had heard her crave a man's company.

She shifted uncomfortably, but she pushed on, "I do mean *everything*. Have you seen the *strap ons* these days? They are *perfect*. Longer and harder than anything a man could ever offer."

They both nodded in agreement.

"Men even want to *become* women. There's been a rise in the number of transgender men, who are desperate to find that estrogenic burst of happiness," I insisted, out loud.

Oops.

They didn't care that I had interrupted. They just added me into their conversation seamlessly.

"Some of them actually have the condition in their minds, but others are just looking to play with fire. They will never be respected as much as women who are *born* women," the one with the grey bun adamantly said.

I pushed my chair towards them.

Intrigue.

"I can respect them for not wanting to be like our historical oppressors. It takes a lot for them to want to make that change. It's *still* not easy," I added.

"They will *always* be known as the oppressors. The ones who took from women their power and their voice. They will never successfully change the minds of Gen Zs. The younger ones, maybe, but us and our mothers, they will *never* change our minds."

"We will *always* be wary of the Y chromosome that separates us."

"Men just have a different nature," one of them resigned.

They both sighed.

I sat there wondering if that was even true anymore.

Hadn't we beaten the Y out of men?

CHAPTER 11

Across the street, someone was watching me.

I could feel their eyes on me through the ice-stained glass.

I didn't think anything of it at the time, but now, looking back, I should have been more careful.

I was reckless.

As soon as Michael walked in, dragging the winter cold in with him, I broke away from the two women intent on keeping me entrenched in their womanist woes.

Their reminiscing about the "good old days" made me crave Michael more than I could admit, even to myself.

In that moment, I was helpless with desire.

His arms.

He looked absolutely *dashing* today.

I noticed that he had shaved but left a little scruff.

Most men these days didn't grow out their facial hair. They meticulously groomed themselves until they were bare.

Nary a hair in sight.

Even a little scruff made him all the more attractive.

I smiled shyly and looked at my half empty cup of foam.

"I didn't know what you wanted, so I didn't order for you," I said.

"Okay, I'll get something," Michael said dryly before kissing the crown of my head.

That was a sign that he could be a brother or a relative.

It kept us safe from prying eyes.

The two old women seemed not to notice.

It didn't fool the woman in the dark burgundy coat leaning against the side of the building across the street, smoking a cigarette and looking intently through the window of the cafe.

CHAPTER 12

"Have you been waiting long?" Michael asked me once he settled in with his coffee.

"Just long enough to have a chat with those ladies," I said.

I nodded over to the women who had resumed giggling and chatting. Neither of them nodded back in acknowledgement.

So much for craving men.

They hadn't even noticed this handsome piece in front of me.

He whispered, "so maybe we should go back to my place, then?"

He was always so flighty.

I never understood it.

He had said once before that it was because he didn't want me to get into trouble, but I always wondered if this was his way of holding on to some control of the situation.

If he told me that we should leave and I *did* leave, then it might seem like he had more control over the situation.

I wanted to hold on to my *own* sense of control.

"Maybe finish your coffee first?" I said, looking straight into his eyes.

He pinched his nose trying to get the blood back into it, pursed his lips, and then drew the mug towards them.

One sip.

"So, what's been new, anyway?"

Second sip.

"It's been the same." He seemed particularly cagey today.

"When can we go see James and the others? I want to know what the fuss is about." I was at the edge of my seat.

I couldn't deny it.

This danger of knowing what the men were thinking and talking about enticed me against every instinct of self-preservation.

"Next week. Sometime."

Third sip.

"You seem more interested in your coffee than in talking to me," I said without even realizing why I was being so quippy.

Fourth sip.

Pause.

Fifth sip.

He looked at me intently and stuck his tongue out.

"It's just so cold right now," he said with a lisp.

Then, he laughed.

Then, I laughed.

I suppose the awkwardness was over.

I knew he felt freer when we were at his place.

When I drove us back there, we stayed awake for hours into the early morning listening to music from the 20s and 30s.

His touch.

All man. All amazing.

I felt like I was floating.

The wall of books that he had accumulated.

The piles of CDs all over the floor.

His carelessness.

The newspaper clippings of all the terrible things happening to men all over the country.

His empathy.

All that he really wanted to do was help them.

All that stopped him was fear.

In this room, with me, he felt free to not fear a damn thing.

I wanted this.

I wanted *him.*

He was grateful for that.

I was grateful that he was grateful.

We were melting into each other.

I remembered Ms. Swanson in health education telling us that these were the symptoms that we would experience if we were in an unhealthy relationship:

Moodiness.

Frustration.

Lack of Appetite.

Loss of sensibility. (Rare, but she said it happened when we stopped being logical.)

Feelings of obsession.

Euphoria.

Check. Check. Check. Check and check.

Sadly, this meant that I was in the wrong relationship for me.

That's what I had been told.

The right partner for me had to be a *woman,* according to my moms.

The right partner for me had to be someone who would just stimulate me *intellectually*.

Michael wasn't a woman.

Michael stimulated me intellectually.

When we slept together, I felt like I was with the right person.

One by one, like the leaves falling to the ground in the midst of autumn, so were the folds of my sanity coming undone.

I should ignore him and focus on Fess.

She would be thrilled by the sudden spike in my interactions with her.

I should make it a point to take her to dinner with moms one of these nights.

Next weekend, I swore to myself as I lay beside him hearing his soft snore.

CHAPTER 13

Mom requested, over text, that we reschedule our weekly dinner this weekend.

The lack of a phone call from Mom, insisting that I apologize to Ma, meant that I had been forgiven.

I hoped.

I was grateful.

I didn't want to see either of them.

I needed space and time to think about what I was going to do next.

With Michael.

With Fess.

I curled up into my bed in reminiscence about all the times I had committed lies of omission.

Not telling Fess about Michael was a lie of omission.

What would I even say?

"I'm sorry. I found a more interesting human than you. He happens to be a man."

Shit.

I wouldn't exactly call her the *jealous* type, but she was definitely the type to emote a little too much.

Even in public.

It was a few months ago that I had refused to stay at her place overnight because of work the next morning.

What started as a simple nudge and flirt slowly devolved into her crying into my shoulder, in the middle of dinner, at a five-Michelin-star restaurant.

"I have never felt so completely in love with anyone else before you, Al," she had said.

I had felt cornered, like I had to say something just as hyperbolic in return. I had decided that remaining silent and looking into her eyes was a better bet.

"I just wish, you know, I just *wish* you would come home with me tonight and every night."

That night I had been guilted into escorting her home, but I had refused to stay.

My desire to be alone, and focus on myself, was more important.

She didn't speak to me for a week.

She did send passive-aggressive texts, however, letting me know what an asshole I had been.

It was exhausting.

The making-up part. *That* was even more exhausting.

For the past little while things had settled down between us.

Why ruin a perfectly content woman's blissful ignorance?

Settled.

Down.

That was *supposed* to be me.

Settled.

Most of my friends from college had been engaged for months or were already married to the loves of their lives.

All women.

All *married* to women.

The WEB had done its job well. At least when it came to my circle of friends — now acquaintances, as is what tended to happen after many of us got married. We eroded and whittled down to a few and then, it was just me, myself and I.

There had been one friend who had disappeared when she was twenty-two. No one had asked questions then, but we all knew she had fallen in love with the janitor. Everyone suspected that they had eloped to Canada or Mexico to get married because no state would do it anymore.

"What's the point? Most men are on welfare anyway. They don't need to get married to be stable, the state takes care of them. The ones that have jobs are usually working in menial labour, making enough, why do they need to get married? What protections can marriage give them? Our taxes pay for their existences. Hopefully, with WEB, they'll die out soon enough," Mom had said about the matter once.

My mind wandered back to one name: Maya.

Maya.

The one who left with the janitor right out of university.

I wondered where she was now.

What happened to girls like her?

Anxiously, I put my thumb to my lips, only to realize that they were dry and chapped.

I picked at the dried skin until it bled a little.

I pressed my thumb down on the wound, licking the blood away.

I hoped Maya was happy.

CHAPTER 14

A lunch date with Fess, before I had to go back to work.

It would be quick.

That's why I said yes.

Mondays were always rough.

Too many tedious tasks needing my attention in the administration at the university.

Too many people sending their prosaic, annoying questions that they could have answered using a quick internet search on their own.

A lunch date would be a good break from the mundane.

I looked over to my assistant typing away at her desk. I could only make out half of her left eyeball.

She looked Picasso-esque.

An artist whose work I had only just been acquainted with because of Michael.

I got up and made my way to the door to leave.

"Polly, I'm out for the hour," I said.

She just nodded in my general direction.

I walked down the stairs to the main floor.

I could see the back of Fess' head as she sat on the couch in the reception area.

Her big, black, beautiful curls sat still on her head. She had an earpiece on and was animatedly chatting away.

Yet, her hair didn't move.

Hairspray?

The smell of which nauseated many but turned me on.

Shea.

I tapped her left shoulder and slunk down beside her on the right.

She smiled as she continued chatting.

I looked at my phone.

No new messages.

No Michael.

"Miss Mitchell, I'll call you back regarding all the details about the artwork," she said.

Her voice was as smooth as silk.

I had briefly forgotten that.

I touched her bare shoulder and felt goosebumps.

I loved the way she always took off her jacket inside a room to show off her shapely arms.

She smelled like cocoa and shea.

I kissed her neck.

She giggled and pulled me into her neck even more.

"Of course, of course, not a problem at all," she said, trying to keep still.

"Tell her you'll call her back," I said.

"I'll call you back, Miss Mitchell. Okay, take care! Bye!"

She was enthusiastic.

That was her personality.

Bubbly when she wanted to sell, cool, calm and collected when she was just hanging out.

"Sorry, I totally had to take that and…"

I cut her off by kissing her deeply.

I pulled away and looked into her eyes.

"Is that a new flavour?"

"Lemon. You like?"

"Love."

She giggled again.

"So, where to eat?" she asked.

"First, I need to talk to you about something," I said.

"Okay, spill."

I locked my fingers in with hers.

It was time. I had to ask her to be more committed.

"I want to invite you to dinner with my Moms, this Sunday."

"Your weekly dinners?"

"Yeah! They would love to meet your parents too, but I know your moms are busy for the rest of the year. I think it's time, Fess."

She looked at me with a sparkle in her eyes.

"Really?"

"Serious. I'm almost twenty eight. It's time to get serious about us and take the next steps."

"In a month, I know."

I was a December baby. Hence, I loved the winter.

"So, summer of twenty seventy six sounds reasonable."

She nodded enthusiastically and kissed the back of my hand deeply until her lemon scented lipgloss made a mark on it.

"It's just time, don't you think? I'll ask Ma for the Chatthum ring. It only makes sense for you to have it."

I held my left hand up and examined it.

"What ring should I get?"

She frowned.

Her parents didn't come from money and she wouldn't have been able to afford anything more than a silver band.

I knew that.

"Fess, I didn't mean it like that. I meant it like, should I get a silver or gold band?"

"Silver. It suits your skin tone better."

She smoothed the stray strands of hair off of my cheek and tucked them behind my ear.

Her touch felt as soft as a baby's butt.

My emotions were supposed to match hers, but I felt numb.

The timing made sense in the grand scheme of things.

Yet, I felt nothing.

I cleared my throat and looked at the ground.

"So, about lunch?"

CHAPTER 15

By the time Fess and I had finished lunch, we had discussed her going to the WEB, getting all the paperwork in order, how many kids were in our future, and then some.

I was back to feeling overwhelmed.

I *wasn't* ready.

I *was* ready.

I didn't know anymore.

Kids were the plan. I knew that.

Fess would quit her job and stay home for at least a year with the kids.

It made sense.

We would have to solidify that trajectory with the WEB's results on our parental skills.

On the off chance that I had more of a maternal inclination than she did, I supposed that I could be the one to stay home with the kids.

Yuck.

I hoped not.

I checked my phone.

No new messages.

I wasn't expecting anything from Michael, but I thought that he would have at least reached out to make plans.

I wasn't going to message first.

He liked the chase.

I liked to *be* chased.

Especially by him.

What if he was with someone else?

Unexpectedly, a pang of jealousy crawled up and into my throat.

I called him on impulse.

One ring.

What the hell am I doing?

Two.

Shit.

Three.

Beep.

"It's Michael, leave a message."

Beep.

"Hey, it's me. I have Friday off. Want to meet?"

Beep.

I sounded like a giddy little girl.

Shit.

CHAPTER 16

Against my better judgement, I met Fess again on Friday.

I was in a testy mood.

Seemed like my conscience was insinuating something.

Best to just ignore it.

Instead, I focused on my agitation that grew with each day that Michael didn't respond to my voicemail.

This time, she was flustered with the stress of something at work.

She was taking it out on me.

I was barely paying attention.

"Can you, *for one second*, understand that this deal is *important* to me? The commission is *huge* and it could pay for an actual *ring*, that I would like to *actually* buy for you?"

"Mhmm, I understand, but you asked *me* to lunch, remember? We didn't *have* to meet."

She was still wearing that lemon lipgloss.

This time, her hair was in a loose bun atop her head.

She looked beautiful when she was mad.

The fury made her cheeks flush with hues of red.

I was frustrated with the sexlessness of our relationship.

How long *had* it been?

I let my eyes wander to the tables around me.

Every couple looked as bored as the next one.

I rolled my eyes.

She caught that.

Shit.

"What now?"

"My eyes were just tired," I said.

"Not really an apology, Al."

We ate quietly for the next ten excruciating minutes.

"I don't want to fight, Fess."

She sighed audibly.

I touched her hand, gently stroking my thumb over the back of her hand.

Smooth as a baby's butt.

Not that I knew what a baby's butt felt like.

"It's just work. I'm just *annoyed*. I don't mean to take it out on you like this. I'm sorry."

"I'm sorry too. You really don't need to worry about the money. Soon, we'll be family and what's mine will be yours."

Except Michael.

"Yes. Yes, I know. Do you want to walk by the docks for a bit?"

"Definitely. But I thought you had to get back to work fast?"

"I can make time," she said cheerily.

She turned off her phone.

Shit.

I gestured over to the waiter - the first man I had seen for a while.

"The bill. Thanks."

I couldn't wait to get out and breathe in the fresh winter air.

CHAPTER 17

We had both been stupid.

"It was a terrible idea to get ice cream in this weather, Fess," I said laughing.

She pointed to her lips.

"I think you'll have to kiss them to make them warm again."

Subtle.

I tossed the leftover ice cream onto the ground and pulled her towards me.

"You just littered!"

"The gulls will get it."

I kissed her deeply.

We stayed there in the warmth of each other's embrace for what seemed like eons.

It felt like I was sipping a warm cup of tea in a cozy sweater indoors while watching the snow fall outside.

Except that we were *outside* and the snow began to fall on our uncovered heads.

I kissed her again.

We then walked hand-in-hand to the bench near the dock and sat there in silence, basking in each other's warmth.

She felt like that hue of green paint that every landscape needed to complete it.

She *fit.*

That's when my phone beeped.

One new message.

It read:

Al, meet me at our usual. I want to show you something. 3 P.M. today?

Finally.

"Who was that?"

"It's not important."

I shrugged it off and pulled her in deeper.

I looked at a bird flying overhead, swooping dangerously close to the half-frozen waters near the parked boats.

It was hungry.

There would be no chance of fresh fish to eat for at least another month.

It kept taking off, circling, and gliding down until its little body grew tired of being blinded and weighed down by the falling snow flakes.

Eventually it perched atop a garbage can near us.

Fess shifted deeper into my coat.

I kissed the top of her head and watched the bird peck through the garbage to find whatever edible food it could.

Two more hours.

I could hardly wait.

CHAPTER 18

Parting had never quite felt so bittersweet to Felicity.

Her dark, tight curls barely moved an inch in the crisp winter wind as they said their goodbyes.

She brushed her shoulders against Althea's on their walk back to the subway station.

"This was an awesome date, Al. Let's walk down by the docks more often.".

"Of course, baby. I'll see you Sunday, right?"

"I'll be there at six sharp!"

She wanted to solidify their relationship with rings on their respective fingers as quickly as possible.

She could hardly wait.

They kissed.

"Yes, of course. I love you," Althea said, looking into Felicity's eyes.

"I love you too," Felicity responded like every other time.

They held each other for what seemed to Felicity like a lingering second before she knew that Althea had to leave.

When Althea walked away from her, she almost always felt the same. A little bit of loneliness, a little bit of joy because she knew that absence made the heart grow fonder.

She sat down on the bench ready to make some more phone calls in a desperate attempt to get her commission back.

It was right then that Felicity saw him. He was in a line up with all the other boys ready to be shipped off to goddess knows where. He had big, curly, bushy black hair very much like her own. There were signs of age on his young face.

She felt an instant enchantment. A tenderness growing in her heart that she had never felt before. She felt it burrow into the hollow of her chest.

He couldn't have been much older than five. He kept picking at a scab on his knee, barely browned over.

She worried about the infection that would ruin his otherwise flawless skin.

Why was he in this line up? Wasn't he fit to be shipped off to some parents that could raise him properly?

"*Hey!*" she screamed.

"*Hey! Hey! You there!*"

She ran up to the woman who was urging them onto the bus, trying to get her attention.

"Yes, ma'am?"

"Where are you taking them?"

"Oh, you know, probably to the ports, some to the rich houses to be door persons or some other thing."

She pointed at him, feeling instantaneously guilty that she had used the same language that all the other women do to talk about the boys that don't belong.

"What about that one?"

"Oh, that one, that one…" she paused, looking around to make sure the other boys couldn't hear. "He's set to go to the Fangsel."

"*Fangsel?*"

"Oh, yes ma'am."

"But he's so young."

"Oh, no ma'am. He's the right age. Just about six now ma'am. But they say he's no use to anyone with the one leg being like that and all that."

"Six! He's so young!"

An awkward pause followed.

"Can I keep him?"

"Oh, for amusement, ma'am?"

She hesitated. She knew that if the woman knew her *real* intentions, she wouldn't be okay with the arrangement.

"Er...well, yes. I'll find work for him."

"Oh yes, ma'am, yes, of course you can keep him if you can get some use out of him ma'am."

"Thank you...Yuka," she said, glancing at the woman's badge. It was probably a name she used only on the job. There was no way that was her real name.

A real name would expose her to all sorts of vitriol from the men's rights activists who had been very vocal about little boys being shipped off to Fangsel to be worked until they died.

"Oh, but you will have to talk it over with a lawyer, ma'am. Valentina, perhaps? She's the best there is in these types of matters, ma'am."

"Okay, but can I take him *now*?"

"Oh yes, yes ma'am."

The woman unchained the boy's frail arms. The others just watched. They all looked so helpless. There was no doubt in her mind that a lot of them were going to end up in Fangsel. She couldn't save them all, and he was who she wanted.

"Thank you. Thank you *so* much," she said to the woman.

To the boy, she said, "come on now, we shall get that cleaned up. At *home*."

He smiled at her. A broken, sad smile.

His eyes were glazed over.

She didn't know what he had seen in his brief time on earth, but she wanted to make it so that he could at least *try* to forget.

Her heart broke into a million pieces when she looked at his face. It was only when she thought of the peace and comfort she could give him that she felt her heart mending itself.

"Time to take you home, then hopefully see Valentina and finalize this," she said, more to herself than him.

She knew it wouldn't be easy.

CHAPTER 19

This case.

Valentina had been dreaming of the day when the proceedings would be over so that she could *finally* relax with yet another win under her belt.

And there was always the money.

A huge factor in her deciding to take the case.

She had fifteen minutes to get in a smoke and a sandwich.

The sandwich cart was a ten minute walk there and back.

She settled on the smoke.

There was no smoking allowed ten feet from the entrance of the courthouse. This was the one place where no-one would dare break the law. Unless, of course, you were Valentina Nebraska, a nationally celebrated women's rights lawyer who had earned the privilege of this rule-break.

She check her phone as several people and their lawyers raced past her.

She lit her cigarette.

Breathe in.

The first puff in always went down smoothly.

Twelve new messages.

She beeped through each one.

Breathe out.

The third one caught her attention.

"Val, it's Felicity, Natalia's soon to be daughter-in-law. I need your help."

Valentina checked her watch - twelve minutes to go.

She puffed through the rest of the cigarette as quickly as she could.

Before she pressed on Felicity's number, she quickly spat out the tar that had coated her throat.

A couple of prissy-looking women stared at her in disgust as they passed by.

She flipped them off.

Fuck 'em.

She dialled, waited, and smoothed out her bangs with her free hand.

"Hello, it's Felicity Galliers for Thornton Enterprises, how may I assist you?"

"Felicity, it's Val returning your call."

"Oh, Val, hi!" She sounded chipper.

"So what do you need?"

"I have a boy, about six or seven or so…"

"I can't help you."

"Just hear me out."

"Natalia is my good friend and I don't need this complication. What about Althea? I thought you two were a done deal."

"It's, well, yeah, we *are* a done deal. He was headed for Fangsel and I don't want to say too much on the phone, but look, can we just meet?"

"If you can get in writing that Natalia is okay with this arrangement, then *maybe*," Valentina said, about to click off.

"It's *my* decision. I am doing it on my own."

Valentina paused.

"Then it'll be five grand. No more, no less."

"I can do three now, two after Althea signs the paperwork," she said.

This woman *really* wanted the boy, but Valentina still hesitated.

"I can give you another number, she's just as good…"

"No, Val, I need to get this done, *fast*."

Against her better judgement, Valentina agreed and clicked off.

She checked her watch: one minute.

She shook out her bangs and adjusted them to the right side.

Her stomach growled.

Goddessdamnit!

Just like that, her fifteen minutes were up and she raced back into the courthouse.

CHAPTER 20

I had been restless with desire since I had gotten his message to meet up.

Just like that, here we were, hands clasped together in insurrection of all that I knew to be good for me.

I wasn't quite sure what to make of this place. After an incredibly long subway ride, walking through what seemed like a *million* alleyways, Michael took me back to a familiar neighbourhood.

Near my workplace, a dingy, abandoned club, just under the bridge, two block down from the university.

I was wide-eyed with the knowledge that there *was* such a place so close to an architecturally intricate web of academic buildings.

It was stranger that I had never noticed such a place *existed*, despite having been around this neighbourhood five days a week for almost two years.

It had been said that academic institutions would be the first to want equality for men and women.

Or was it equity?

They *did* try. Fifty or so years ago, when Alberton was president, they had tried to achieve equality.

They set up a series of laws that allowed visible minorities and women to succeed in the workplace.

They called it affirmative action.

Alberton had begun to enforce a fifty-fifty distribution of men and women in all workplaces.

Then, there were more women than men in the workplace.

Then no men at all.

At least not in universities.

"What are we doing here?"

He just held my hand and rushed me down the stairs into an old room that smelled like beer, piss, and testosterone.

Does testosterone even have a smell?

Before I could utter any sort of disapproval at our new meeting spot, because *anywhere* but here would have been better, I was being shoved into a room with twelve of the most terse men I had ever seen in my entire life.

Some with deep lines on their faces, others with lines only on their foreheads, and a couple of fresh-faced ones with pink cheeks who looked barely a day over eighteen.

"What is this…? Oh! Look! It's James!" I waved at the man closest to the screen.

He nodded back in acknowledgment.

None of the others glanced my way. None of them moved. None of them cared that we had slunk into the back. They were all engrossed in a video narrated by some man with a distorted voice talking about the effects of suppressed male potential.

Of course it was projected onto the wall.

"You said you wanted to be thrilled," Michael said as a matter of fact.

Well, consider me stunned.

The video kept buzzing in the background. It was white noise to me. I wasn't keen on knowing the facts. I just wanted to hear their opinions.

"… women have taken away our rights to be *leaders*. They have waged their war against masculinity and succeeded in making it out to be so *toxic* that so many of us don't even want to be men anymore."

That's true.

"They have told us again and again for *decades* that we men, at our core, are just *monsters*. Heartless, unfeeling, cold, *monsters*. They stripped us of our ranges of emotion. Our biological difference from femininity."

I glanced over at Michael, knowing that he had no interest in me right now.

This is why I admire him.

The stern way in which he looked over at the screen, absorbing every little bit of information, made me want to know him even more.

All these men around the room.

All of them battling their own inner demons.

All of them with brains that went underused, and dreams and distinct personalities that the world refused to acknowledge as a source of untapped talent.

"If all the women could, they would *eliminate* us this instant, but they would rather keep us as slaves: doing the mundane labour, the mining, the building, the opening of the doors to the fancy restaurants…"

The man on the screen paused and took a breath. He had been at this rant for the past twenty minutes.

At least that's how long *we* had been there for.

He ranted more than a PMS-ing woman ranted, and believe me, even with the hormone stabilizers given to women of any age, without discrimination, women were still off the charts *neurotic* at times when they were PMS-ing.

But, I digress.

"…they don't care if we want to live for our own sake. They only care that we are alive to make their lives as *easy* as possible. So what happens if we are all gone? What happens when they suck us dry for our sperm and then kill every last one of us?"

Ay, there was the rub.

I watched in horror as a few men around the room nodded in approval of what that insane man was preaching as *gospel*.

CHAPTER 21

The sound of a loud car honk woke me up.

It was the morning after my first introduction to the men's rights group that Michael and James had wanted me to see for myself.

I was still reeling from the fallout.

I had met James and Fernando before, briefly. I had walked in on them having an intense conversation with Michael about the proportion of male to female suicides.

They had been kind but *adamant* that they had the right facts.

This was a month ago.

My head pounded.

I was dehydrated and out of fresh tears and anger.

7 A.M.

I slipped deeper into my bedsheets. Right at this moment, I would have *loved* to have been born as a rich woman's spoiled cat.

My blinds were open, as always, so that I could feel the day seep in through the little slits and wake me up with the sunrise.

7:01.

The alarm would ring in exactly forty-four minutes.

The pillow was so soft. My eyes grew weary. I had stayed up crying and journaling in anger.

Now, all I could feel was the weight of my head crushing my eyes and drawing them closed.

It was hard to process a damn thing through sleep deprivation and my thoughts running wild.

*"How can they say these things about **all** women, Michael? And YOU! You just stand there and absorb this propaganda like some dumb mute who doesn't have a brain or an opinion of his own?"*

"Draven gives them his opinion. And I fundamentally agree with him."

*"What the hell! You actually **believe** this loon? Who thinks that **all** women want to control men, by doing what? Do you believe that about **me**? Removing the destructiveness of traditional male behaviour? Which for so long made women afraid to even leave their **homes**…"*

*"He's just trying to push back against this rhetoric that **all** masculine traits are inherently bad. That **men** are inherently bad."*

"Even if they aren't - it's better to be female than male. We are more empathetic, more nurturing, more giving. What's so wrong about that?"

*"And who taught you that **all** women are like that? Who molded it to push a particular narrative? Are the men of today responsible for the mistakes of our forebears?"*

*"But we **all** want men gone though? Right? So much for generalizations! Maybe **you** are not responsible. But how can you be trusted to not overpower us again?"*

*"What about me? Do you trust **me**?"*

"We're in a tradeship. I don't have to trust you!"

I remembered going on and on, in a heated frenzy.

A few eyes on us as they passed us by in the street.

"Shh, Al, quiet down."

*"Why? Because I'm pushing back? Does that make you feel like you're less of a **man**?"*

He just stood there, overwhelmed, unable to even get a *word* in as I raged on like raving lunatic.

I opened my eyes wide, trying to see through the fog of sleep.

I was met with blaring, digital red numbers.

7:16.

It wasn't like I could sleep anyway.

I threw the comforters off my body.

My head screamed bloody murder.

Back under the covers I went, shut my eyes as tightly as possible, and snuggled into the last twenty minutes of uninterrupted sleep, suddenly dreaming of falling and landing on the ground unscathed.

My legs jerked me awake.

7:45.

The alarm went off.

Great. I had to pretend to give a shit about this day until I had to deal with Moms and Fess this weekend.

CHAPTER 22

When Michael woke up, he had been sweating through every pore in his body.

Yesterday hadn't gone quite as smoothly as he had hoped.

Tick. Tick. Tick.

Focus on the clock. Focus.

As with any other time when he was stressed or worried, he had had the dream again.

The scalpel piercing into the tender flesh in his inner thigh.

Digging and digging.

Digging for something.

Then, the Q-tip.

The soft little bud, trying to soothe the pain.

The Q-tip cleaning the little spatters of blood in the most precise way so that there was only raw pink flesh left.

The rest of his body couldn't protest.

It was numb.

Focus.

Tick. Tick.

He pulled his legs closer to his chest.

He squeezed his thighs together until his knees turned white.

The resulting numbness turned the sharp throb into a dull ache.

His manhood became a squishy gelatinous substance.

He released his knees just a little.

Focus.

He took a breath in.

A drop of sweat fell from the top of his bush onto his balls.

The memory of the scalpel crept into his conscious mind.

He flipped over into the fetal position.

First on his right side.

Then his left.

Before he knew it, he was rubbing his knees together.

Squeezing his thighs shut until he couldn't feel anything from the waist down.

He clenched his entire body until the skin enveloping every joint turned a bright white.

His teeth clattered even though the sheets on him were thick.

Focus.

Tick.

Tick.

His whole body shook with a fitful shiver.

Fuck this.

He threw the sheets off himself.

He spent the next hour grooming his crotch.

Plucking every hair off.

He ran his fingertips over the smooth skin as freckles of dark, thick hair formed a cloud on the white tiles of the bathroom floor.

Bare.

Focus.

CHAPTER 23

Today was the day when Fess would ask Moms, in person, for the Chatthum ring.

That meant that an engagement was imminent.

I was numb to the prospect.

She had already made plans to have an intimate dinner with me at Le Chat Rivière on the sixth.

A week *before* my birthday.

Classy.

At least she was going to spare me the theatrics of a birthday proposal.

I kept the looming heartache I felt about Michael at bay.

I had cried into my pillow for long enough.

I couldn't afford another row with my moms.

Even though it was the dead of winter, perhaps a yellow flower print dress would make the most sense for this occasion.

I yanked the dress off of the hanger in my closet.

The hanger snapped in half as the dress came tumbling down.

My phone buzzed in my back pocket.

Can't wait for tonight, xo Fess

Oh Goddess!

Did she have to remind me every chance she got?

Why was I getting *so* agitated?

Maybe it was time to go on those hormone blockers again.

Quitting them had been a terrible idea.

The family doctor would ask questions. So would the WEB before they dispensed them out.

I could say it was wedding nerves.

I picked the dress up off the floor and realized it had several dust stains on it.

Shit.

Three hours to go and I would have to rewash and dry this stupid thing just to look like little miss sunshine.

Better get on that.

I had an image to live up to: a happy, soon-to-be fiancée.

CHAPTER 24

I got there before Fess.

That gave me time to give Moms a heads-up about the nature of this dinner.

"Mom, Ma. I just want to let you two know that Felicity is going to ask Ma for the ring tonight."

"Oh, sweetheart! That's wonderful news! We're so happy for both of you!" Ma said.

"Don't get too excited yet. She still has to actually *propose*."

"But you've made plans to meet? And what about the WEB? Have you had a chance to go and make arrangements? See about all the future daughters?" Mom asked.

"Mom, we're not even *engaged* yet!"

Ma laughed as my face rouged in response.

"You need to consider these things, Althea. Marriage is not something *casual*."

"I know. I just want to give us a chance to *enjoy* being engaged first."

The doorbell interrupted me.

"I'll get it," Ma said.

"No, Ma, relax. I'll get it."

As I walked towards the door, the walls in the entry way started to close in on me.

I put my palm against the wall with the jacket hooks.

Breathe in.

What if I just smashed my palm straight into one of those hooks?

Breathe out.

I opened the door to Fess' beaming face.

Breathe in.

I blinked rapidly, trying to regain focus before pecking her on the lips.

Breathe out.

"I brought Ma some flowers. And hey! They match your dress. You look beautiful, Al."

She kissed me again.

I tuned her out.

It felt like she was talking a mile a minute.

I let her go past me into the living room.

"Felicity!" Ma said.

Fess slid off her boots and ran into Ma's arms as though she were already a part of the Hayworth family.

Shit.

This is what I was signing up for.

Forced niceness and amicability amongst the four of us.

Ma escorted her into the kitchen.

I saw her pull out a flower vase from under the sink.

She and Fess were chatting away like they were old college roommates meeting after a decade.

Mom pulled out her phone.

We weren't needed.

I pulled out my phone too.

No new messages.

Had Michael officially shut me out?

I looked over at Mom scrolling away on her phone, looking at goddess knows what, then at Ma and my future wife laughing at some inside joke.

Was this *it*?

I would get married, have some daughters, and…*that's it.*

I felt the walls narrow in on me.

I put my hand on my stomach, feeling it cave in as I held my breath.

I heard my heart beat faster in my ears as my vision narrowed into a tunnel of black abyss.

Before I could delve too deep into my sense of despair, Ma called me and Mom to the table.

My legs felt like they had iron weights attached to them.

Each step I took towards the table should have sounded like a thud.

After what felt like a million years, I settled into the chair next to Fess.

My legs began shaking under the table uncontrollably.

What if the last day I had seen Michael was the day that we had a fight?

I looked at Fess' smiling face wanting to say, "I love a man! I love a man!"

"Can you pass me the garlic bread?"

"Sure, Al. Here, take some butter too."

After Ma had served the soup to us, Fess cleared her throat.

I tucked a pleat of my dress between my legs and clenched them together in anticipation.

"Natalia and Magda, Mrs. Hayworths, I feel as though this should come as no surprise. It's almost two years in the making, but Al and I are ready to take the next step."

Felicity reached for my hand on the table.

The gesture made me feel suddenly calm.

I returned the favour.

"Mom, I know you saw a certain future for me, and I can assure you that Felicity is a part of that *certain* future."

Mom and Ma sported huge smiles towards us.

"Sweethearts, we are *thrilled*! Felicity, from now on, you call me 'Ma' and Natalia 'Mom', okay?"

She started crying as she got up to hug each of us.

Typical.

Ma wouldn't pass up *any* opportunity to be overly emotional.

Felicity wiped her eyes.

"Mag...Ma, I would like to ask you for the Chatthum ring to give to Althea. I know it means a lot to you and it symbolizes the tradition that Althea and I would like to carry on."

"Felicity, you can have *anything* you want! We're going to be *family* soon, and what's ours belongs to you and Althea and our granddaughters," Ma said.

I saw Fess' face fall.

She cleared her throat.

I saw the pulse in her neck quicken.

Was she just as apprehensive as I was about the speed at which everything was happening?

"I...I'm not so sure about grand*daughters*," Fess said.

Mom dropped her spoon into her soup bowl.

"What do you mean, *you're not sure about granddaughters*?"

Fess looked at me for back-up.

I didn't know what she wanted from me, so I stayed mute.

"Mom..." Fess started.

Mom glared at both of us.

Best to proceed with 'Mrs. Hayworth' from now on.

"Mrs. Hayworth..."

Noted.

"...I did not mean that as a slight. I meant that while *daughters* would be lovely, I would love both a girl *and* a boy equally."

Ma and Mom stopped moving entirely.

I stared at Fess' head in astonishment.

When had she changed her mind about this?

A year ago it was all about the baby *girl* names. Rosalee and Amelia.

The WEB tried to encourage the birth of girls, but they hadn't yet manufactured artificial sperm that would only produce *females* to the contentment of their Board of Directors.

Abortions of boys were encouraged. The ones that *were* produced could easily be put into foster care, put to work, or be abandoned without repercussions.

"I also think that if we were to adopt..."

"Let me stop you right there, Felicity. *If* you were to adopt, I would prioritize *girls* and not boys. The boys, if useful, can still make for good manual labourers, but the *girls* need good mothers with respectable homes to rear them into strong women."

"Mom, there's really no need to discuss this yet," I finally interjected.

Mom pushed her chair back and stood upright.

Ma let tears fall down her face.

"Mrs. Hayworth, with no disrespect to either of you, I think it's a mistake to dismiss the plight of boys in the State's care."

"And what about the plight of the *girls*! They ought to be our *only* priority!"

"I agree that it *is* more important, but we can care about *both*, can't we?"

Mom grabbed Ma's hand with such brute force that it *shocked* me to not see Ma even flinch.

"*We*, the Hayworths, *including* your future wife, will *not* stand for a grand*son*."

The disgust with which she said 'son' left a bitter taste in my mouth.

What would she do if she knew about Michael?

What would she do to *me*?

Gulp.

"Mrs. Hayworth, this is a decision that *Althea and I* would need to make. While we would take your opinions into consideration, we wouldn't let that stand in the way of us giving a child, of *any* gender, a loving home with two mothers who love each other."

Fess looked at me with determination.

"We both love you, Mom. But this is a *personal* decision. We hope you understand our point of view, but if not, we hope that you won't take it out on your future grandchild," I said.

Mom scowled and clutched onto Ma's forearm even tighter.

"I'm going upstairs. Magda, give the girl your ring before they leave. See yourselves out. And congratulations, again."

Two meals, in a row, that had gone against Mom.

Shit.

After she and Ma had gone upstairs, I stood up and grabbed Fess by the shoulders.

"What was *that*!?"

She looked defeated.

"I don't know what came over me, Al. I'm sorry. I'm sorry I ruined our celebration."

I pulled her face up to mine and kissed her deeply.

"*Stop.* Stop talking. That was *amazing*! You surprised the *hell* out of me, and I am ready to *commit*, Fess. I am so *completely* ready."

I meant every word without a single shred of doubt in my mind.

Ma left the ring on the table in the hallway.

Just as quietly as she had slunk in to place it there, she had climbed up the stairs and disappeared into their bedroom again.

Fess grabbed the box before we left to go back to my place.

We made passionate love that night, and then again before she had to go back to hers.

She didn't stay the night, but I didn't care.

Perhaps there was a chance that she would come around to the kind of ideas that Michael and I had been discussing.

Perhaps there *would* be a way to satisfy my *Michael* cravings with a woman who could give me everything I needed.

CHAPTER 25

Magda and Natalia waited until the front door slammed shut.

They sat in complete silence for ten minutes while relishing the echo of the front door slamming.

Magda lay on the bed and placed her palms on her eyes.

Natalia began to unbutton her blouse before Magda could let her tears flow.

"Was that *really* necessary?" Magda asked.

"Do you really want to love and dote on a grand*son*?"

Magda sat in silence at the edge of the bed, watching Natalia take off the many layers she had put on herself.

When Natalia had stripped down to her underwear, she threw her clothes across the room towards the walk-in closet.

"Fucking, fuck, fuck, *fuck*!"

"Nat, baby, just sit with me."

Magda tried to motion her toward the bed.

"No."

Natalia flung her arms around to air out her armpits instead.

She had to move.

She could feel the adrenaline rushing through her veins, making it impossible for her to sit still.

Magda scooted further onto the bed until she could slink down with her back perfectly cushioned by the throw pillows.

"I can't deal with that girl's *insolence* anymore. First, she talks about how *men* deserve some sort of *equality*, and now *this*. Not *once* did she even *object* to Felicity saying that they would love a male and female heir *equally*. Absolutely *absurd*!"

Natalia was waving her arms in the air like a penguin.

Magda tried to stifle a chuckle, but she couldn't get the image of the fat, chubby Arctic animal out of her mind.

She burst out laughing.

"Look at you! It's impossible to take anything you say seriously right now, Nat."

Natalia inched menacingly closer to Magda's side of the bed.

Natalia had a crazed look in her eyes, like a wild animal knowing it had been trapped and cannot get free.

She clenched her right hand into a fist, looking dead into Magda's eyes.

Magda sniffled.

"Watch your fucking mouth," she said.

Magda looked at her incredulously.

"I'm so…"

Natalia punched the wooden headboard. The old wood split where she had punched it.

Magda winced and covered her face with her forearms.

Natalia wrestled Magda's arms away from her face.

She brought the same violent hand towards Magda's face.

She examined her own hand for a brief second, before dragging the bloodied knuckle across Magda's forehead.

"You really shouldn't laugh at the woman who puts this roof over your head."

Shell-shocked into silence, Magda looked up at the woman she loved, pointing at the ceiling with her cleavage in Magda's face.

She had tolerated the arm grabbing, the occasional fingerprint bruises, and the yelling for some time now.

But not this.

This was something new.

Magda got up from the bed, maintaining eye contact with her wife.

She shoved past Natalia, trying to wipe the blood off her forehead.

Natalia followed her wife into the walk in closet.

When she was behind her, she wiped the rest of the blood on Magda's white skirt.

She pushed Magda's hair to one side and kissed her neck.

"Get cleaned up."

An *order*.

She slapped Magda's behind as she went back into the bedroom.

"Okay," Magda whispered to herself.

CHAPTER 26

While Magda cleaned herself up in the bathroom and got ready for bed, Natalia sat on the bed waiting for her to bring the first aid kit.

She examined the intricate lines on the back of her hand, now matted with blood.

Her life line, her blood, her family name would *not* be tainted by Felicity's whims.

She unhooked her bra and threw it onto the pile with the rest of her clothes.

Natalia looked down at her tits hanging out.

They had gotten softer with age.

She pinched the skin just above her nipple.

Her breasts were just a mound of flesh under non-elastic skin.

The wrinkles were settling into her face and her body.

The suppleness wasn't quite what it used to be, but at least never giving birth meant that she had not lost the fullness as much as Magda had.

She cupped her breasts and looked down at them in admiration.

Even if these breasts hadn't fed the damn girl, there was no way that she was going to sit idly by and let Althea defy the values that she had tried to instil in her.

Who was putting these ridiculous ideas into their heads?

Was it just Felicity who had them?

Althea's values *had* to align with hers.

If it came to it, she would take back her initial blessing of this union.

She had to do something, *anything*, not to have the Hayworth name tainted by a male.

Only one name came to mind: *Olivia*.

CHAPTER 27

Olivia read the text twice.

She recognized the number.

It was the same style of text as all the other times this client had wanted something done.

She put on her trench and waited for further instructions.

Ten minutes later there was a new message: Done.

Their usual location would have an envelope waiting for her.

It was a location that they had decided was the safest drop spot over ten years ago.

She walked down the stairs of her four storey walk-up.

Out the door and behind the building to the car park.

The package was a neat, crisp, brown envelope.

A sticky note inside the envelope read FIRST PAY.

As long as there was cash, Olivia didn't bother to harass the client until there was information to share.

And cash there was. A solid eight thousand.

She scrolled back to the first text: My daughter. Bring me something good.

Alright.

Easy.

The client wouldn't have asked unless there was dirt to be found.

She would find it.

CHAPTER 28

After his leg had healed and she had settled on a name, Felicity took Aibek out for the first time.

She decided to buy some parenting books.

The woman at the register gave her stomach a look of longing.

"You're barely showing! Have you picked out a name?"

"Well, I decided to adopt, actually!"

"Oh! That's amazing too! I'm so happy for you and your wife. What's her name?"

"It's Aibek."

"What a unique name! What does that mean?"

"Messenger."

Felicity caught a glimpse of him playing between bookshelves.

"Aibek! Come here and say hello."

"Oh my! It's a little *boy*!"

"Yes, I got him a week ago. He's still learning his name."

Felicity plastered the biggest smile she could muster on her face.

She *knew* that she would get this reaction.

Maybe she should be telling people that he was conceived.

The questions would still persist.

"Why didn't you get rid of him?"

"Was it necessary to bring *another* oppressor into this world?"

"What if he decides to become a het?"

"Are you sure that you can raise him to be respectful of women?"

"Will he grow up to be a womanist, or will he try to overthrow all our progress?"

The woman interrupted her thoughts. "I hope the books help. It's a rough job raising boys to be excellent men. You should also pick up 'Feminize Your Boys' by Judy Trooper."

Felicity had been grateful for her curt reaction.

It was better than her imagined diatribe.

She *knew* that she could care for a boy.

Wasn't acting on pity the first sign of being selfless?

And wasn't selflessness a maternal instinct towards the innocent?

Wasn't Aibek *innocent*, after all?

He was still young. He could be tamed and molded.

That's why she would read all the parenting books she could get her hands on.

She had acted on impulse.

Impulse was another maternal trait.

A trait that the WEB and all her tests had deemed to be a *positive* one for raising a child of her own. The tests that she had taken just yesterday, with Althea.

She was happy she had been impulsive.

No one could take him away from her.

He *belonged* to her.

He was hers and hers alone.

CHAPTER 29

I felt that it was appropriate under the circumstances to ignore Michael for as long as I possibly could.

Besides, Fess had subverted my expectations.

She had stood her ground with Mom.

My Mom.

Damn.

And yet, I missed him.

So, almost two weeks after my very public screaming match with Michael (well, more *my* screaming than his), I texted him the most innocent-sounding greeting I could muster.

Hey!

It was the week of my birthday, after all. I deserved a bit of male attention.

I could keep him around until the wedding.

Right?

He eventually brought up revisiting the MRAs.

One more time and then I *swear* I won't say another thing.

Fine, I'll give it another shot.

I should have listened to the nagging voice inside my head that told me to ignore him and just focus on my newfound rhythm with Fess.

His boyish and ecstatic **Yes! Yes! Yes!** in return had made me realize that he had been practicing his persuasive speech for days.

I was glad for the experience too.

This time was different.

This time we got deeper into the heart of things after the meeting.

"Draven believes that women are only keeping men around to satisfy their *own* needs..." I said, trying to understand.

"Yes! Exactly!"

"Why do you care so much? I mean, why do you care what *I* think?"

"I just want you to know *what* I think, and *why*."

"Fair enough. So what was that thing about men...going their own way?"

"He thinks that the movement at the start of the century about men going their own way and creating their *own* intricate society made the most sense for male progress. Of course, they would ideally also have some women come along with them who haven't been completely *brainwashed* by this only-women-in-power lunacy," Michael said, walking at a brisk pace.

"How do you fathom that you'll be able to break out of *this* place that you are so against?" I asked, half-amused.

He stopped and grabbed me by the shoulders.

"*Complete and total anarchy*," he said, with a glimmer in his eye.

I did all I could not to laugh, but it was uncontainable.

His smile vanished.

"Why are you laughing?! It's the *only* political system that we haven't tried yet! We've tried men on top, we've tried women in power, and neither of those have worked. At least with anarchy, maybe we can *finally* have some equality?"

"Anarchy would result in us being killed in *hoards*. The crazies out there want any excuse to wield weapons of mass destruction with complete freedom," I said, shrugging his hands off of my shoulders.

I pressed on, "Violent anarchist men killing children is the reason why we banned guns in this country. That was how women got into power, remember? The tragic death of the hundred and forty nine school children during Alberton's electoral race is what made her such a sure pick. *No one* wanted that to happen again. No one *wants* that to happen again. The entire country was *stunned*. How can you possibly condone a political system that gives people the unchecked freedom to own *killing machines*?"

He pulled me close to him.

"You have an innocent mind."

Way to diffuse the situation.

"And *you* have a wild one."

I felt the warmth radiating from his body.

It was cold. He was rugged.

Here was a man who emitted more body heat than Fess and I could produce *together*.

It suddenly felt a little *too* comfortable.

He looked me in the eyes.

"Okay, okay. I'm not talking about anarchy right away. First, men could fight for proportional representation again. We've been steadily declining in population since the 30s, but our population is *not* miniscule. We're still thirty eight percent of this damn country!" He stopped holding my hand and stuffed his hands into his pockets.

I looked at him intently.

The tips of his ears, bright pink.

The tip of his nose, bright red.

His cheeks were flushed.

Goddess, he looked good.

I knew I shouldn't go back to his place for another night in a row.

But we also *couldn't* end this discussion with him getting on the R going west and me getting on the 105 going east.

I kissed him hard.

"Let's go back to yours," I said earnestly.

He smiled and snuggled me into his navy peacoat.

"So, you *really* are attached to this idea of anarchy, huh?"

"Yeah, I think it's the best way. The *only* way. Haven't I convinced you yet?"

He smirked.

I chuckled a little.

"Well, I'm willing to let you *try* to persuade me."

I was amazed by my willingness to put myself in harm's way.

No one could ever find out that I was *willingly* exposing myself to these radical ideas.

Especially not Moms.

What if he corrupted me? What if I let myself be derailed from a wonderful life with Felicity that would ensure my happiness?

Or at least, the happiness that my *moms* wanted me to have.

'Do I contradict myself? Very well, then I contradict myself, I am large, I contain multitudes at almost twenty-eight years old.'

Shit.

CHAPTER 30

Darrin tucked his journal back under his mattress.

He used to hide it under the floorboards, before he had come clean to James about his past.

While James was at work this morning, he decided to bore himself by flipping through it.

2069.

What a year that was.

Darrin's breathing had been composed before he started reading it.

He had a tic.

The result of his brain forcing him to push out more carbon dioxide than one normal exhalation would allow.

It usually happened when he was excited or stressed, or when he had had to pleasure some woman who had paid him for his body.

He flinched at the memory.

He hadn't had to do that in a while.

Those meetings with all those women had always been nerve-wracking.

He would have much rather just stayed a cam model.

But the worst tics happened when his nervous system had been shot to hell by the heroine.

His addiction had started with the misguided idea that a blunt could cure his tics.

It hadn't taken long before the blunt had lost its charm, and the needle had become a necessity to get the high.

He had been sober for four years, going on five, because of James.

He had been sober *for* James.

Sobriety, for Darrin, didn't mean that he hadn't snuck in a snort or a needle here and there.

His brain *needed* it.

He told himself that when he went on a bender anytime James was away on one of his activist excursions, but he always made sure that he had sobered up by the time James got back.

They both kept their secrets, but overall, their marriage was a happy one.

Here and now, staring at the ceiling, his breaths came out in twos.

Revisiting old dalliances on Fredricton, in that grotesquely lime green painted room in that dingy old house, made him agitated to be in his own skin.

A needle would have helped his mind go blank.

His eyes grew tired of staring at the same two spots on the ceiling.

Blank.

He could have amounted to something.

Blank.

He pulled out his current journal again and restarted his thoughts on a brand new page. At the top he wrote the date again:

March 3rd, 2075 —

And that was the day before I met Althea. The day before I became a stranger to myself —

All he wanted was a needle.

Blank.

CHAPTER 31

Feverishly, I walked over to the kitchen sink and poured myself a drink of water.

It wasn't until the Advil kicked in that I realized I had slept until the middle of the afternoon.

Three o'clock in the afternoon, to be exact.

Well, I had gotten home at four in the morning.

I was irritated with myself and felt hung over.

I recalled drinking a beer with Michael before…

One beer wouldn't do that to me, but this felt different; almost like the exhaustion after sex and having my mind blown by an intellectual equal (a *man*, no less) was just too much for my body to handle.

I reached for my purse and pulled out the book that Michael had given to me

He was telling me things that I still wasn't convinced I should believe.

He told me that there were books that had been pushed to the back shelves in the thirties, simply because they were written by het men. Some had even been burned in the streets by radicals, claiming that it would solve the systemic oppression that women had faced over the past several millennia.

They were no longer read in schools.

They promoted misogyny and male supremacy.

Words that I had learned about while studying about the Revolutionary War of 2026.

There had been book burnings in several states. That was before they hung a lot of the men in power at the time. Mostly old, rich men.

I looked at the cover of the book and wondered why a book titled 'Nineteen Eighty-Four' could create such an intense reaction.

Any book that went against the matriarchy, found in the rubble after 2027, had been put in the Library and Archives building in Boston.

I had only read literature by female authors.

Michael was the only one I knew who had managed to develop a collection of books from both men *and* women from before the revolution.

He said he had found them at a used book store on ninth avenue.

I said I wanted him to take me there one day.

But for now, it was time I read something that *didn't* have a female author.

Hopefully get into a little bit of trouble if I brought it up at the dinner table with Moms.

So I began to read about a man's futile struggle.

Big Brother. O'Brien. Winston.

I could relate the most to Julia. I understood her desire to fall in line.

And yet, I could empathize with why Winston would want to rebel against the Party.

I was hooked. I only stopped reading well past when the sun went down.

An entire day lost in the throes of a man's mind.

More.

I just wanted more. I needed more than just one book, one man, or one point of view.

I craved the minds tainted with the Y.

CHAPTER 32

Perhaps it was right after I was done reading *Brave New World* that Michael's views on the fucked up ways in which we treated men began to resonate with me.

Or maybe it was after I finally read Draven Alec's blog post: WHY WOMEN WANT WILLY WONKA *and* HIS CHOCOLATE FACTORY.

Or maybe it was during the library's annual gala in April of '75 with Felicity when I observed all those women in happy life-partnerships.

I felt like I didn't quite fit into this place anymore.

I was dancing with Felicity to the early century throwbacks.

But my secret rendezvous with Michael just hours before the event kept me from being completely in the moment.

This gorgeous woman was right in front of me with her crazy curls bouncing on her head as the music played, and yet I wished I were here with a man.

Mom would have said that I should have my head examined.

I *should* have my head examined, but why wasn't this normal?

Why didn't I have the freedom to love whoever I wanted?

Why did I have to *pretend*?

I took a long hard look at Felicity's face, dewy from dancing.

This woman loved me.

She *loved* me.

She loved me and I could barely even look at her.

I had sex with a man on my mind, and then our post-sex conversation replaying in my brain.

"I'll be right back," I said, barely audible.

"What?" Felicity said over Grande's 'Break up with your girlfriend, I'm bored'.

"I'll be right back!" I yelled.

I pushed away from her and into the crowd.

Just like that, with the essence of her far in the distance, I breathed as deeply as I possibly could before pushing open the front door of the library.

I felt beads of sweat roll down the small of my back.

The nylon blend of my dress wasn't helping the situation.

I took in several more quick, deep breaths as soon as I got to the bottom of the steps.

The moment I got into the crisp spring air, I could feel the zipper attach itself to my skin as the sweat began to dry.

My chest heaved, but I could barely feel myself breathing in.

The people around me felt like blips in time.

My neck itched.

The thin silver choker necklace dug softly into my neck as I played with the hook trying to get it off.

Air.

It felt like a thick noose had replaced the fine silver strand that had once adorned my neck.

I heaved and slumped onto the bottom step.

Inhale.

Breathe in.

Exhale.

Slowly.

I tried to focus on replaying the conversation that Michael and I had had last night.

Inhale.

Ever so gently, his voice crept into my conscious thoughts and took over my anxiety.

> *"Al, women leaders weren't exactly angels in the past. Thatcher, back in the 90s, was a **lunatic**. 'Iron Lady' was too kind of a nickname for her. She wanted to bring back capital punishment and she absolutely destroyed England's manufacturing industry, even though she claimed to be 'working' for the working class. She outsourced jobs that were predominantly held by men. She left those men who used to work in the factories completely hopeless and jobless. Those men lost their hope and sometimes even their **families** because of that wretched woman. I mean, really, all that you need to know about her is that she wanted to kill those who killed. Where's the humanity in that?"*

I had nodded.

I had been taught she had been monumental in the development of Europe's compassionate welfare state.

He had said that the welfare system kept men feeling like victims, like they didn't have autonomy over their own existences.

Exhale.

Breathe, Al, just breathe.

Focus.

I could hear Michael's voice, clearly pressing on through my audible heaving:

> *"Then, just before Thatcher, there was Indira Gandhi in India, who was so smitten with the Russians that she wanted to bring communism to India. Something they couldn't afford because of colonizers. But, of course, she had her supporters too. She was despised by the Sikhs and loved by those who wanted lavish vacations on the tax payer's dime."*

I had been taught that achieving equality of outcome was a brand of success.

Inhale.

I tried to concentrate on his words and the way he spoke about the people in history with theories that I had never been taught were plausible.

"What about Jacinda Ardern? She was an amazing role model for young women everywhere. Even had her baby while she was the Prime Minister of New Zealand," I remembered retorting.

"One example of a decent leader. But, the country was small."

I remembered frowning.

*"Merkel was around when Alberton came into power. Did they teach you that? They had pretty similar ideas of 'united we stand'. Merkel wanted all the countries in Europe to become one and the same. European Union, she called it, so she made it difficult for a country to leave and maintain their trade agreements with other countries in Europe. We still have the European Union. And Alberton, she just wanted, well, you know what she wanted. You learn all about it now. And isn't it odd how we've **only** had women in power in the west ever since? Even though nothing else has changed? We **still** go to war with countries in the east, we **still** pay tax, and fundamentally, we're all **still** just following a single person's whims and wishes."*

It was odd.

It was odd how we were never told about this opinion on women in history. None of them were strict saints from his perspective. Nevertheless, we were taught they were *revolutionaries*.

I had retaliated even harder after that.

"But, those examples no longer apply. Women leaders only went to war back then because they were trying to compete against men in the game of 'who's got the biggest ego'. Slowly, but surely, we developed international peace. Less wars, no more guns produced in our country,..."

*"Exactly Al, **less** wars. Not none."*

I furrowed my brows, recalling that the conversation had stalled after that.

I had gone silent with reflection.

Exhale.

I felt a soft hand touch my shoulder.

"Al, you okay?" I heard a familiar voice.

Not Felicity.

I turned around to see a face that I had seen on countless news channels before.

"Val? Hey!" I said, taken aback.

What had she heard?

I stood up as quickly as I had sunk onto the step.

As soon as I had composed myself and smoothed out my dress, I gave her a polite peck on the cheek.

Her bangs grazed the side of my face as I inhaled her rose-scented shampoo.

"So you came to this facade of a ball too?" she asked, pulling out a cigarette from her clutch.

"Didn't have a choice. Felicity…"

"Ah."

She widened her eyes, then looked down at the ground.

We stood there in silence as the little hairs all over my arms and upper back stood up.

"You want a smoke?"

"Why not?" I shrugged.

Something to keep me warm.

Inhale.

"How's Nat?" she asked between puffs.

Exhale.

"Mom's, you know, a workaholic," I said nonchalantly.

Inhale.

"And Maggie is still home now? What happened to her Etsy store?" she enquired dutifully. It was just as dutiful as the same time last year, when she was forced to make polite chitchat with me at the gala for women's reproductive health.

Exhale.

"It's still there," I said, enjoying the feeling of the smoke gently passing through my nostrils.

She tossed her half-smoked cigarette onto the ground and crushed it with her heel.

"I better get inside, kiddo, or my date will start to wonder if I ran off to another client," she chuckled, patting my shoulder.

She stretched her lower back in her sleek, black jumpsuit and pointed her fingers suggestively towards her tight rear.

Valentina was *quite* a woman.

I shook myself out of visibly *gawking* as she climbed the stairs back to the front hall of the library.

My cigarette still lit and the night still young, I just smiled.

Sometimes, I shocked myself.

Did I have a wandering eye?

Perhaps.

But how could I not?

With so many amazing women in the world…and men?

It felt like the smoke had gone to my head. Or maybe it was just the menthol.

Inhale.

This was turning out to be an *insightful* evening.

Exhale.

I frowned.

By the time I went inside, I was calm again and ready to resume my role as Felicity's dance partner.

She hadn't noticed that I had been gone for over half an hour.

She did, however, notice the smoke on my breath, and I was chastised for my lapse in judgement all the way back to my place.

CHAPTER 33

She had managed to keep Felicity's son a secret.

Somehow.

Valentina patted herself on the back for that.

She could have given in to the desire to at least inquire about that *child* to Althea at the gala last night.

She had smoked away the tension in the air instead.

Saturday didn't mean that she had the day off.

So here she was, pacing outside Judge Heidelbaugh's office.

She and Karyn had been friends since primary school.

Karyn was her mother's friend's oldest daughter.

They had once had a babysitter-child relationship.

Now they had a judge-district attorney relationship.

She hadn't had a smoke yet.

The man was guilty, yes, but not of what he was being charged.

Valentina knew that she didn't have a case, but Karyn was adamant that he be put behind bars as quickly as possible.

They had a quota to fill.

"Judge Heidelbaugh will see you now," a pointy-nosed woman said, opening the door to the judge's reception area.

She maintained a consistent pace as she walked through Karyn's door.

She cleared her throat.

The nicotine patch hadn't been working all that well.

She smoothed out her bangs while Karyn shuffled the papers in front of her into her neat pile.

"I'm glad you came, Val," Karyn said.

She didn't bother standing up or even glancing in her direction.

"I think it's time to consider a lesser sentence in the Bulsheivik case," Valentina said. "There's no way for me to prove that he *was* in fact — "

"He's *got* to go to Fangsel. And he *did* initially refuse to give his sperm to the WEB."

"Yes, but I can't *prove* that. They have his sperm at the bank now. They have the DNA tests to confirm it. And there's no record of him fighting the anal electrocution. There are no cameras allowed inside the Collection Rooms, so what can I do? My hands are tied."

Karyn sighed loudly.

"Any messages on his phone regarding the matter?"

"A couple, but they all show a bit of hesitation, as is natural given the situation."

Valentina scratched at her nicotine patch from outside her blazer.

Nothing she did satisfactorily itched the area on her forearm.

She would eventually resort to ripping off the patch and smoking again just to keep from fucking *itching*.

She looked directly at Karyn, noticing that age had not been kind to her former babysitter.

She had lines of age prominently denting every fold in her forehead.

"*Find* something on him. The asshole is already in jail, so you might as well slap him with another suit. Has he screwed a woman the wrong way? He seems like the type."

Karyn pulled out a chocolate bar from the drawer in her desk.

She noticed disapproval written all over Valentina's face.

"Not all of us are a size *two*, Val, and some of us need to go on obscene diets. In my case, the *chocolate* diet."

"I'm not judging, believe me! I'm trying to ditch the cig. The patch makes me crave sweets. It's not you, it's me."

"Alright, alright. Just find *something* on this guy to keep him locked up. Find a nurse who will testify that he *didn't* actually go in voluntarily. A brain defect like that could still persuade the jury that he's a menace," Karyn said between bites.

"I'll — " Valentina was cut off by the sound of Karyn's phone ringing.

"Alright, now fuck off," she waved Valentina off and barked into her phone, "Yeah?"

Valentina walked out with her head spinning with possibilities.

Women he had slighted.

Something.

Anything.

He wasn't innocent. *None* of them were. She just had to find out *how*.

Resistance to female authority was enough cause to be thrown in prison.

She was happy to live in this world. But when she thought about the consequences of what she was doing, it sometimes gave her pause.

But only for a second.

In any other world, she wouldn't have the kind of rewarding job she had.

Putting assholes away, ensuring the success of womankind, *swelled* her heart with pride.

She held her head high and swooped the bangs off of her face.

Taking away the freedoms of insane men was *worth* this power.

CHAPTER 34

Darrin sat in his chair, pondering the complexity of the task that he had set for himself.

Chronicles of a Man on Fredricton.

America *deserved* to know what he had gone through as a toy for women.

After yet another night spent frantically pacing back and forth in his ten by ten apartment with just one small window overlooking a parking lot, he was fed up.

All this introspection made his head hurt.

The number of pages in the journal would be inadequate, and that bothered his OCD more than anything.

He ripped out the last page from his notebook.

Breathe.

One.

Two.

He started again.

April 25th, 2075

At first, I had hoped that she would be gentle. But after we began, I just wanted her to finish as fast as she had strolled in and picked me. Althea Hayworth — she took my virginity. I knew she would never live up to my ideal. She had this long, braided, coarse dark hair that hit my face each time that she bent over to kiss it. It poked my eyeballs. That's what bothered me the most. She always tipped well. I so badly wanted to tell her that first week that she had been my first woman, but I just couldn't bring myself to tell her something so personal.

She was not much older than me and that terrified me more than anything. I don't know why. It wasn't a big secret that the women of all ages who strolled in there wanted their pick of the young ones.

But why did someone who was so young need a man like me?

At first, she came in almost every day. That was for about a month, and it was always to fuck. Nothing else. Gary, the Mister, told her in confidence that I didn't mind fucking her when she was menstruating. He told her a lie, she bought it, and mounted me anyway.

I could smell the peach shampoo in her hair as she rode me. The blood trickled out of her and into my inner thighs; sticky, but slick.

I vomited that day and for three days after. The smell of her blood never left my nostrils.

He put the pen down beside the journal on the table and let the tears fall softly down his cheeks.

He could still smell her blood as though she had been on top of him just moments ago.

Breathe.

One.

He yanked open the top drawer.

James wouldn't be back for three days this time.

He was out protesting again.

Two.

One of these days, Darrin knew, James would get arrested.

He may not come home.

He was free to poke himself until his arm went blue.

He remembered something he wanted to write and quickly scribbled it down before he forgot:

Five years ago today. Five years have passed and yet I still remember her and all of this. When will it end?

Then came the vein.

Then came the needle.

Then came the bliss.

CHAPTER 35

Darrin awoke to the sound of the tea pot whistling on the stove.

He furrowed his brows in contemplation of when he had managed to do that.

He examined his surroundings.

He had slept at his desk, with the needle laying dangerously close to his right eyelid.

Her coarse hairs poking at his eyeball as she bounced.

He held his head in his hands.

He hadn't bothered to write legibly while high. For that, he paid the price by having to squint through the chicken scratch.

I got used to her smell, the way her body felt, and how she liked it. Other clients frequently left unsatisfied because I didn't want to know how to please them. She was my regular, after all, so I learned about her body more than anyone else's.

Gary often beat me and used me to punish me for bringing in so little. He pounded me to repay him for the room he had so graciously given me. Until he threw me out because I had become a liability. He told me I was way too old, way too used up for any woman.

I remember coming to her, that horrible woman who used me, and asking, begging, her to protect me, but she didn't, did she? It was one of our last times together and she just let me down.

Why had I been so damn naïve? She didn't care enough to protect me. She never fucking cared —

That's where he had trailed off.

He picked up his journal, furious that he had thought about *her* during what should have been his moments of pure bliss.

He scratched through the whole page, blacking out all the lines he had written.

He began at the top of a new page that was not stained with the ink of the previous page.

She was my best paying customer. For two years, I was indebted to her for tipping well enough for me to afford my room and board. Gary still pounded me, but it wasn't nearly as bad on the days when she paid to talk to me.

Some of the other boys who worked with me were treated much worse. H——was picked up at fourteen. He was working for himself at first, but after Gary gave him a room to call home, he had to work twice as hard and please twice as many women. He was barely seventeen when me and T—— found him hung in his room, dangling from the ceiling fan. He had been popular with the women too. They liked that he finished himself and them off at the same time.

'What a shame!' was the only thing that Gary had said.

Many of the other boys were jealous that Althea was my first and still came around.

Althea always ran her soft fingers over my shaved skin. She was so gentle with me when she just paid to talk to me. Even though I lay in front of her completely naked, she just talked and touched me in the most kind ways. She even massaged my hair as we talked. She let me talk. She made me feel so special. Like I meant something. Like I wasn't just some boy in a house on Fredricton. She even coerced me into dreaming about my future.

I really believed that she cared about me and saw me and knew me, but she betrayed me and H—— and T—— and all the other boys who knew her. She could have helped me escape. Find a different job. Something, anything, but she did nothing. She just paid Gary. I told her in confidence that he would pound me every now and again and she didn't do anything about it. She just said that she didn't mind sharing. She said she couldn't get involved.

I hated her. I loved her. I cared about her and I just wanted her to leave me alone. She came back, first almost everyday, then once a week, then never. I called her in a frenzy that one morning in June 2069 because I needed money. No one else wanted me, only her, and Gary wanted me out because I had made only twenty bucks getting an old woman off once.

Desperately, I had snuck into Gary's file with all the clients' numbers. She had been more than willing to pick up and listen, but she did nothing. She just said that she was sorry that I was having a hard time, but that I should lose her number as quickly as I had gotten ahold of it. She couldn't help me anymore. She couldn't be seen on Fredricton. She had a job now, a partner, and a reputation to keep up.

I had fumed and ran the four miles that stood between the house and her apartment. I had knocked loudly on the door. She never opened it. I could hear her and she never opened the door. She betrayed me. She used me. She fucking used me for her own pleasure and when I needed her, she didn't repay my kindness.

I was a child when she had me. I was only seventeen! I had no idea what the fuck I was doing. Did she know that?

I should just forget about her now. She's just a woman in my past who means nothing to me now. I should count my blessings that James found me when he did, and took me in. —

CHAPTER 36

Magda had decided to take a breather and go away for the weekend.

Natalia welcomed the decision with grace.

She had managed to convince Magda that having a *son* be the Hayworth legacy would be disastrous. Magda had finally nodded in understanding.

Natalia loved the solitude that came with Magda's departure. She basked in Magda's upkeep of their house.

She would have the fridge stocked with pre-cooked meals that were perfectly portioned for the three dinners.

The front entrance smelled faintly like vinegar, but more strongly of lavender. Different essential oils were used in different parts of the house to ensure the aromas lingered in a concentrated area.

Natalia could always count on the upstairs bedrooms smelling like roses.

Rarely lilies.

The lilies were for special occasions: anniversaries, birthdays, and sometimes when Magda wanted more than just their nightly routine.

All the bathrooms smelled like grapefruit.

The scents never fused.

The beds were always made in each bedroom, each morning, without fail.

Even though Althea didn't live with them anymore, by her own volition for the first time since she was conceived, her room was always kept spotless, just in case.

If there was dust, it was cleaned by the time Natalia got home. If there was nothing in the fridge in the morning, it was full by the time that Natalia got back from the office.

Natalia looked around the living room and smiled.

She took a breath in.

Peace.

Magda made this house into a *home* and for that, Natalia was grateful every day that she was with her.

That's why when she sat down on their recently reupholstered, grey, mid-century couch to drink her mid-afternoon wine on that beautiful spring day, she was shaken out of her bliss by a notification from Olivia.

Natalia hadn't thought that Olivia would have found anything amiss with Althea so quickly.

Perhaps it wasn't about Althea.

The message read: 'Found something. Meet at Deja's.'

She frowned, highlighting the two ever-deepening lines on her forehead.

She wasn't about to dignify that vague message with a response just yet.

Make her sweat.

She smiled to herself.

Bing.

Another distraction.

This time, it was a welcome one.

Her mysterious, intellectual opponent had written another piece.

The title caught her eye: ON WOMEN HAVE THE PRIVILEGE TO BE OPPRESSORS AND OTHER BULLSHIT

She had never wanted to click on anything so fast.

She skimmed through the article from the BBC attached at the top of the blog post.

It read:

This week, the UK decided to ban any protests that insinuate women are capable of being oppressors.

The Liverpool police force, made up of courageous women, took to the streets to protect the public from the merely fifty men, holding signs, demonstrating against what *they* claim is an affront to their freedom of speech and civil liberties.

Some signs read "we are not just our sperm" and "men have been raped too".

Fallon DeRosy, the chief of police, said that the new law in the UK disallows men from claiming 'Status as a Victim', as that is now a claim reserved *only* for women.

Frank, aged 38, standing outside the courthouse with the "men have been raped too" sign, said: "Women believe that they have the right to deny us the ability to be victims of crimes such as rape because of what our ancestors did, but they are all dead now. We do *not* condone rape, and we believe that rape can be committed by *both* sexes."

The police force and others made it a point to pepper spray all the men when they refused to disperse by 5 P.M. GMT.

"Protesting is our democratic right! We are just peacefully holding up signs!" John, aged 19, said before being pepper sprayed and falling dramatically to the ground.

Women yelled in their faces "you are not victims!", "you are the rapists!" and "go clean our toilets!".

A lack of victimhood status means that men who have been allegedly sexually assaulted cannot *legally* claim that they *were* in fact victims of assault.

"Unlike in the US, where Rape Courts are already a part of the justice system, in the UK, men were *still* considered to be innocent until proven guilty. No longer granting men Status as a Victim will go a long way in certifying that women who have been abused and wrongfully accused will get better justice," DeRosy pointed out.

DeRosy further stated in her press release that the UK is excited to bring in Rape Courts, as they have seen the success rates of abusive males' incarceration increase 2000% over the past decade in the US.

"This was a necessity in the UK. So few women lie about being raped that it makes no sense to think they are being dishonest until their rapists are proven to be guilty. We were falling behind, and now we have the tools to allow women to come forward with their allegations and have them be believed and trusted *right* from the get-go," DeRosy said, smiling.

Goddess save the Brits!

Upon reaching the end of the article, Natalia was satisfied.

She went back to the blog post.

When she reread the title, she chuckled.

ON WOMEN HAVE THE PRIVILEGE TO BE OPPRESSORS AND OTHER BULLSHIT

After having read the above thoroughly, all I can say to my fellow MRAs in the UK who are reading this is to change the signs to make them more politically admissible, but keep fighting.

You are *not* alone. You can see the damage that the *Believe Survivors Act of 2028* and the *Victimhood Status Act of 2029* have caused for us in the US.

Women have had these absurd "rights" for the last ten years here and things have gone from bad to worse.

No they haven't, you little shit...

It started back in 2020, when women would accuse men of rape without a *shred* of evidence and would be believed by *hoards* of women (and men) around the world. They called it the *trial by media*. These men would lose their jobs, their reputation, and in some extreme cases even custody of their kids. In essence, they were "cancelled".

Now we have *courts* to back up their delusional idea that we are guilty until proven innocent. They can just *accuse,* and men get arrested, charged, and put into jail. In most cases, for life.

As they should be! As they fucking bloody well should be!

Until next time, for liberty, equality, and the brotherhood,

Yours,
DA

For fuck's sake.

Hopefully, whatever Olivia found was about Draven Alec and not Althea.

That little fucker.

If only she could get his hands on him, she was sure she could teach him a thing or two about the realities of women who had been raped.

He had been brought up in a time of *privilege* when women were doing all the heavy lifting.

All that he had to do was *shut up* and be a pretty little plaything.

What a shame it was that he had chosen to be a spokesperson for psychotic men instead of trying to aim for something a little more tangible like a modelling contract or being a pretty little pet to some rich woman.

Natalia threw her phone on the couch as she got up.

Men like him shouldn't have the freedom to say whatever the hell they wanted.

Some men should just be silenced. *Permanently.*

She paced around the living room, pausing only twice to look out of the window at the sunset.

The desire for revenge bubbling in her mind had all the blood from her head shooting straight down between her legs.

She felt the urge to rub out an itch.

Magda would understand.

Natalia had more needs than Magda did anyway.

She quickly grabbed her wine glass and sped upstairs to find the most powerful vibrator in her drawer.

It was going to be a long night.

CHAPTER 37

Olivia parked outside Deja's as she had done many times before.

Even though a lot of transactions with her clients were cash-only, she had occasionally surrendered to accepting pre-paid VISA cards.

Cash was hard to come by.

It was only used by those who *didn't* want their expenses questioned.

With cash, there was no trace.

With cash, you didn't have to give a thirty percent cut to the government.

That meant less money for the men who were on welfare.

That was the benefit for her.

Fuckers.

As much as she supported the current regime, the Trump-Kushners were still assholes who loved stealing a cut of her hard-earned money and handing it to people who could have just worked for their own damn selves.

She was in favour of free handouts for women as much as the next woman, but that didn't mean that they needed to come via forced charity.

She would have been willing to pay for women through her own volition. As long as they took all the men off of welfare.

Deja's was the only place in town that still took cash.

No questions asked.

It was also the only place in town that still employed men under the radar.

She felt comfortable in the sleaziness of it all.

She felt comfortable with the hard-working men.

When she saw Natalia's face through the window, as she walked towards the door of Deja's, she wondered if Natalia would actually want a little boy to inherit the family fortunes.

She was bracing herself for a possible outburst.

At least that would have been overshadowed by all the commotion that the delinquents at Deja's usually stir up.

Hence, the choice of location.

A simple arm raise gestured her towards Natalia's table.

Olivia kept her brows furrowed in place.

Her anti-wrinkle cream seller still needed to make a buck.

Natalia already had a scowl on her face and a cup of black sludge in a muddied, cracked mug.

"Your future daughter-in-law has a son. The papers are being put through as we speak," Olivia announced.

There was no time to waste.

Natalia raised her eyebrows.

"I was expecting news about Althea. *Not* Felicity."

What was *that* reaction?

Surprise?

Disgust?

That Olivia wasn't able to pinpoint the emotions running through her client's mind unnerved her.

"But that's the *least* of your worries," Olivia said.

Natalia took a sip from the dirty coffee mug in front of her.

She expected that for dirt cheap, the day old coffee would come with dirt in it.

"Hmm?" Natalia prompted.

Olivia beckoned over to the man arguing with a woman about how to make an espresso-latte.

Morons.

"Black. Thanks," Olivia said curtly.

Now that's something that Rodger didn't need fifteen directions to make.

"Coming up, Liv!"

He smiled at her lustfully.

"Not sucking your dick tonight, Rodge. Not for seventy-five cents. Maybe tomorrow for that espresso-latte that I like, once you learn how to make it," she quipped.

She smiled, displaying her silver canine tooth.

Natalia kept a straight face despite her intense desire to hurl insults in Olivia's direction.

She was thoroughly disgusted by her lewdness.

Since they would be interrupted again, Olivia just stared past Natalia onto the street until her coffee showed up.

Natalia cleared her throat once Rodger brought over Olivia's own cup of black sludge.

"Thanks, boy. Now fetch me Andy, will you? And make sure he wears those tight blue shorts," Olivia jested, shoving a dollar down the front pocket of his pants.

"Anything for you, Liv," Rodger said, swinging his hips a little more than usual while walking back to his place behind the counter.

Olivia chuckled at the stern look on Natalia's face.

"Come on, Nat, have some *fun*. These boys are just *playing*," she said, patting Natalia on the shoulder.

"I just want the info that I paid a hefty sum for. I could do without all this extra baggage." Natalia waved her finger in a circle, motioning to the interiors of the cafe.

Olivia read impatience all over Natalia's face.

"No better place in town to get coffee, though. Am I right, boys?" Olivia asked the question loud enough for the men to hear.

They hooted and hollered in response.

Natalia rolled her eyes and shifted in her seat, almost ready to get up.

Olivia sat back in her chair while Natalia moved closed to her face.

"You want to keep my business? Next time we meet at a reasonable place in town, alright?"

"Alright, alright. But what I also wanted to tell you was that Felicity named the little boy Aibek, and filed the papers with your good friend Val," Olivia said matter-of-factly, before pouring in a diabetes-inducing serving of sugar into her coffee.

"Val?" Natalia asked.

Natalia became uncomfortable in her own seat.

How could she?!

"Yeah. So if you have any hesitations about this thing, you can basically stop it."

"Does Al know?" Natalia asked.

She was hopeful about the possibility of her daughter's innocence.

"Doesn't seem like it."

Natalia sighed deeply.

Olivia paused to stir the coffee around.

"Felicity seems to be waiting on Al's signature."

No fucking way was Felicity going to make that happen.

No. Fucking. Way.

Natalia wasn't used to being caught off guard by a situation like this.

She had enough power to stop this thing in its tracks.

She was more confused that she hadn't seen this coming from that conversation, at that lunch, on the day that Felicity had asked for the Chatthum ring.

'I'd love a son and daughter equally,' Felicity had said.

"As I said, you can stop this thing, if you want," Olivia said.

Natalia stared past her, shakily bringing the coffee cup to her lips.

After a few sips had calmed her rattled nerves, she changed the subject.

"What about our standing order?" Natalia asked.

"Haven't found anything yet on DA."

Natalia cleared her throat and gulped down the rest of the black sludge, almost gagging when the residual beans hit the back of her throat.

Natalia couldn't stay in this dingy, backwards, male-infused environment anymore.

She quickly got up and pushed back her chair.

She had been holding onto the empty mug so tightly that her hand had lost all feeling.

She let it go and left it at the table.

When she went to grab her purse off the floor, she couldn't move her hand the way she wanted.

Can't control a damn thing anymore!

"Damn it!"

Fucking Felicity.

Fucking Draven Alec.

Fucking fuck fuck fuck.

Olivia got up and grabbed Natalia's purse for her.

Natalia yanked it from her with the hand that would cooperate.

"Fine. When you have more, you know how to get in touch. Until then, check under your ass ten minutes after I've left," Natalia said.

Olivia had felt the crunch of the envelope as soon as she had sat down, but she just nodded in understanding.

Any semblance of composure that Natalia thought she had maintained had been replaced by the anger she felt at the situation.

"You got it. Anything on DA, I'll let you know," Olivia said, as she watched Natalia's face wince in a dark pleasure.

Natalia nodded in reply and went straight for her car.

Her legs shook with rage until she reached her car door. She tried getting her car keys from her purse.

She saw her hand tremble as severely as if she had Parkinson's. She placed both hands on the window, breathing in and out and trying to stop herself from shaking all over.

A part of her was relieved that Althea hadn't been up to anything moronic.

She had had a history with that in her late teens and early twenties.

Another part of her wondered if Olivia hadn't been fishing hard enough for what else could have been swept under the rug.

She supposed the information about the potential grandson was worth the three grand Olivia had just sat her warm ass on.

*Grand*son! *Despicable!*

She glanced back into the cafe and saw that Olivia had gone back to joking with the boys. Andy had made his way into the seating area and began belly dancing for all of them.

Fucking freaks.

She wondered if Aibek would become one of them?

Aibek. Despicable!

Olivia was probably going to unroll a few twenties and blow them on this hell-hole.

Natalia sighed. Nothing she could do about it now.

Fucking Liv.

She fumbled with her car keys with the hand that she finally had under control.

But first, she had to make a call: to stop this thing or not?

She got into her car.

Gripped the wheel so hard that her knuckles turned blue.

She liked Felicity. She had always thought that Felicity was a good influence on Althea.

Felicity kept Althea from going back to her old habits of frequenting bars and those horrendous houses on Fredricton. She had helped her settle into a comfortable life that Natalia and Magda had approved of. So far.

Couldn't she just look past the gender of this child?

No! NO NO NO!

He was a boy. A fucking *boy*.

She could have picked a beautiful, brainy, brilliant girl.

She had picked a boy instead.

The timeline fit.

Felicity had already adopted *this* boy before asking for the ring.

Althea had never been too fond of kids. She was like Natalia in that way. So when Felicity had first shown up on Althea's radar, Natalia had counselled her that this was the right match. Especially if Althea ever wanted a family of her own.

Althea had promised that Felicity had made her realize that the Hayworth legacy was important, and that she was starting to take her future more seriously.

Then, when Natalia had helped her get that job at the university, Althea had seemed stable enough to request an apartment closer to a subway station, and inevitably Natalia and Magda had agreed to pay for it.

 "Kids want their privacy," Natalia had said to Magda at the time, to console her sense of empty nest.

Maybe this kid *could* really help solidify Althea's future, but there was always the possibility that he could drive her away, make her have more of those outrageous ideas about equality between the sexes.

Almost like how the pressure of having Althea almost drove Natalia herself away, until she finally decided to accept her role as matriarch.

Fucking Felicity.

A million thoughts still churning in her brain and no clear decision in sight, Natalia drove on autopilot all the way home.

CHAPTER 38

Telling Althea about Aibek should have gone better than that.

Felicity was struggling to understand Althea's cold detachment towards the whole affair.

She saw Aibek. She looked into his face. She hugged him like a mother would.

And then she left.

At least that's how Felicity remembered it.

Her mind refused to engage in any other perceptions of what Althea might have thought of Aibek.

The more she thought, the more she came to the conclusion that this was the *only* way telling Althea about Aibek could have gone.

Felicity felt nauseous with the fear that Althea was going to bolt.

She was going to *leave*, and Felicity would have no way of keeping her around.

On her own, Felicity could provide for some of his financial needs, but she worried for his and her own emotional ones.

She needed her crutch.

She needed Althea, by her side, fighting for Aibek, and fighting for his future.

She wondered if she had crossed a line by adopting a boy.

It wasn't unheard of, but certainly unorthodox.

It was definitely discouraged.

Perhaps Althea was just trying to convince Natalia to accept Aibek.

What if Natalia convinced her to abandon me?

Given how their conversation had gone, Felicity wasn't convinced Althea would give up her life to support a *son*.

Last Tuesday, Althea came over unannounced. That's when Felicity knew she had to come clean. The boy was too young to have an excuse for his presence here.

He couldn't have been a cleaner. Definitely not a playmate, not that she was even looking for one, and too young to be a cook or a handyman.

Then there was the pesky little issue of him calling her 'mommy'.

Althea had opened the door to the boy screaming at the TV.

"Mommy, the giant panda is talking! Look mommy, *look*!" Aibek screeched in Felicity's direction.

"*Mommy?*" Althea said, looking at him and dropping her purse on the ground in the front hallway.

Aibek ran towards Felicity and hid behind her, peaking around her hip to get a glimpse at the woman by the door.

"Who is that, mommy?" he asked Felicity, unfazed by the gravity of the situation, but still cautious of the stranger.

Who knows what he had seen in his short life?

A question Felicity had asked herself the day she had picked him up by the docks, and a question that kept repeating in her mind ever since.

"Aibek, this is my…umm…"

She hesitated to put a label on it.

Were they soon-to-be life partners? *Would* they be, after Althea saw what Felicity had done?

Althea had sprung into crisis aversion mode.

"I'm your mommy's very dear friend. My name is Althea, but you can call me *Al*."

Althea shook her brunette hair to give it new life.

Damn.

She was beautiful.

"Maybe not *Al*," Felicity said, trying to regain a bit of control over the situation.

"Maybe you could call me *Auntie* Al, then?"

Althea looked at her and smiled.

A controlled, almost pained, smile.

Felicity knew she had gone and messed everything up, but there was a sliver of hope that Althea would forgive her if she just knew *why*.

This was *not* her forte.

The being a 'mommy' bit, *that* was her forte.

"Hey, Aibek, right?" Althea said, walking towards him and opening her arms to embrace him.

Aibek looked up at Felicity.

"Mommy?"

"Well, go on then, hug Auntie Al," Felicity said, nudging him towards Althea.

He ran right to her.

He craved affection from almost everyone.

It was terrifyingly adorable.

What if one day he happened to hug the wrong person?

Felicity let Althea hug him while she shakily placed two cookies on a small plate.

"Aibek, take these cookies and keep watching Panda," she said, handing him the plate.

He pulled away from Althea and ran towards his mom.

Kids.

They had so much energy. It made Felicity feel young and vibrant again.

She wondered if this was just the distraction that she and Althea had been missing.

It was about time for a little kiddo that ran around.

It was about time to forget about the complacency that had settled into their relationship and focus their attention on a brand new addition.

She was convinced that this was the right move to make.

"Aibek, mommy and Auntie Al are going to go to the bedroom to talk, okay?"

"Okay, mommy," he said, his mouth half full with a chocolate chip cookie.

There were crumbs all over the floor, but Felicity cared little about those. Her mind was preoccupied with how quietly Althea had been following her to the bedroom.

She sat on the bed.

Althea closed the bedroom door softly.

Felicity was grateful for that gesture of kindness.

She looked at Althea earnestly, in a feeble attempt to convey her apology.

"I know you have questions."

"*Questions*?" Althea asked, glaring at her.

"I know I should have talked to you about this sooner."

Felicity folded her arms under her breasts.

Althea looked around the room, lit in the tricolour of the afternoon sun.

"I don't know, *Fess*. When did *this* happen?"
Althea nodded towards the closed door.

Felicity couldn't think straight.

The emotions that had made her shake were now rising up to her chest and into her mouth, making her teeth chatter.

She rubbed her arms up and down, trying to cling to a sense of comfort, only to feel goosebumps instead.

She blew air out in an attempt to regain some semblance of equality in this conversation.

"I can explain."

"You can ex-plain. *Ex-plain.*"

Althea emphasized the 'ex'.

"There's a bloody little *boy* calling you 'mommy', living quite comfortably in your apartment and you can *explain.*"

"Alright! I can tell you what happened, or you can just *stand* there mocking me and — "

"I'm not *mocking* you. This is me showing you my goddessdamned shock!"

Felicity bunched up her hair into a knot and defeatedly put her palms out in front of her.

"Unexpected, but a *good* kind of unexpected, right? I mean, neither one of us was too fond of the idea of child-bearing. He even looks a little like me, doesn't he? Well, he *definitely* looks like his grandma, my Ma. She died, and I don't know, he's just *her*, you know? And…I don't know what to tell you, Al. He was just standing there, knee busted open, a gaping wound, just standing there. He was picking at it, you know, and I just couldn't help myself. He was headed for Fangsel and he was in line and I don't know, he was just so young, you know? The whole time, I just kept thinking to myself, *why was he here*? He was too small to be here, in this line up. Then I saw his knee and knew that his leg would be amputated, without a doubt. I hoped you would understand…"

She looked at Althea hopefully.

"When did this happen?" Althea asked curtly, looking at the ground.

"When?"

"Yeah, Fess, stop playing dumb. *When*? When did *this* get here?"

Althea seemed aggravated at Felicity's desire to bide time.

"Almost…four months ago."

"*Four months*?!"

"Yes! Okay, *yes*! I got him four whole months ago."

"*Goddess*! You've had a fucking *kid*, for *four fucking months*? Were you just keeping him hidden from me this whole time? Were you *never* going to tell me?"

"Yes, Al, I was *never* going to tell you. That's *exactly* why I have been asking you to come over for weeks!"

"So, *what*? You've been *lying* to me, *hiding* things from me for *four* months and now what? I just have to *accept* that once we're life partners, I have that *child* from day one? He, they, all of them, out there, are never going to believe he's yours! Look at him! He's darker than you, darker than me. They'll all know as soon as they see us all together. They're going to ask why you didn't get *rid* of him. They're going to have *questions*! *Goddessdamnit!*"

"Are *they* going to be the ones asking questions, or are *you* right now?"

"I am."

"Well, I gave you an explanation. It clearly doesn't seem to be…enough."

"It's *not* enough! It's not enough because I now have to contend with being a goddessdamned mother the day we become life-partners. What the hell do you not understand about that?"

"You know what, Al? I'm getting fucking tired of all the bullshit you're laying on me."

Althea laughed callously.

"Me? *I'm* the one laying the bullshit on *you*?"

"You've been hot and cold for *months*. You're literally never even around. You never call when you say you'll call. You barely ever keep our dates anymore. You slipped that ring on my finger and mine on yours and that was it. You're always off doing *goddess* knows what with who the *hell* even knows, and *I* wanted a kid," Felicity said, pointing at her chest.

"So, what? You don't remember the champagne dinners celebrating our goddessdamned engagement? *Twice*, by the way! That's some selective memory you have, Fess. Goddess, Fess! I'm not the one that's been hiding a fucking BOY!"

Althea's face contorted to display disgust as she clapped mockingly.

She saw the desperation in Felicity's eyes and she *knew* that it was going to be impossible to talk Felicity out of this insane decision.

Althea dreaded the answer to the question that she knew she had to ask.

"So, what is *he* to *you*, right now?"

"My son. Just *my* son. Although, I told Val that you'd sign the papers too. That made it easier. So did us going to WEB and putting these rings on. But we need to become life partners already. He needs stability, Al…"

"Jesus, that explains Val's weirdness around me after the ball," Althea whispered to herself.

Felicity was so lost in thought, she didn't even notice Althea thinking out loud.

She looked hopefully into Althea's face.

"You'll sign them, right?"

"Fucking fuck, Fess! Fuck!"

Felicity cringed at the overtly masculine swear word.

Althea had paced around the room for a good minute.

When she was done pacing, she had leaned against the closed door and begun to run her hands through her hair.

"Fuck. FUCK! I guess if I'm going to become life partners with you, it's not like I have a choice, right?"

Felicity and Althea stood in the silence that rang still in the room for what seemed like years.

Felicity had broken the silence by clearing her throat.

"Will you…?"

Althea looked straight through her and with a straight face had said, "*You* will call Ma, tell her about *this*. She will warm Mom up. *I* will be doing *none* of that."

She recalled feeling fear crawl up the back of her throat.

What if she had messed it all up?

"It can't hurt to get to know him."

Felicity could do all but grin at her future life partner.

So, Althea did. She played with him and watched movies with him for a couple of hours.

She even taught him some literature and basic math, as he would be nearly seven come September and could finally be put into school. Segregated, of course, with all the other boys.

This is what Felicity had wanted.

This is what she had hoped for and yet now, a week later, Althea was back to ignoring Felicity's phone calls.

Their communication had been reduced to texts.

Then, after Saturday evening, there was just nothing.

Felicity decided she would call Magda after all. Maybe she would be sympathetic.

CHAPTER 39

How in the actual hell had I missed this?

The morning after the library's gala, when Felicity had sped home, I hadn't thought anything of it.

In fact, I had been *grateful* when I had heard nary a peep from her for the next few days until we met for dinner.

That's when we had celebrated our engagement.

Again.

With another hundred dollar glass of champagne.

The clinginess was exhausting.

I simply couldn't eschew my desire to delve deeper into Michael's world.

I remember saying yes and slipping the Chatthum ring on her finger and her small white gold band around mine.

I figured that I would work Michael out of my system by the time that we actually got married.

I had hoped that she would back off after that, and give me some time and space to talk to my moms about the details of the wedding.

By the time Moms had congratulated us on our engagement, we had gone out to two more dinners, with two more glasses of hundred-dollar champagne, and it had blossomed out of spring and into the dreaded heat of the summer.

Mom didn't seem as happy as I thought she would have been.

I was finally settling down with a woman, and she had had a fake smile plastered on her face the entire time.

Realistically, Moms said that I *could* marry her within the next few months, but that I should wait for at least a year to get the best venue.

I agreed with them, but more because I had bought myself another three hundred and sixty five days to get over Michael.

So when Felicity finally told me that she had plucked Aibek out of a line-up headed to Fangsel for a life of hard labour, my mind refused to grasp the reality of the situation.

I had to drastically shorten my 'Get-Michael-Out-Of-Your-System' plan and play the Mom role now?

Oh my fucking Goddess!

A *Mom*.

'Mom' was not a word I ever thought I would have associated with myself.

All the paperwork held my name as the second guardian.

All this time she had been a mother.

 All I had to do was sign.

That little dotted line.

Easy.

Peasy.

Lemon squeeze-y.

A few inked black squiggles and I could join her in taking care of this *child*.

This *boy.*

I felt cornered.

How would moms react?

Shit.

I had shoved the papers into my purse, smiled broadly at *that boy*, and taken off on the subway to spend my PMS week with Michael.

CHAPTER 40

I slipped into Michael's bathtub while he was out buying us ingredients for dinner.

I rested my head on the tiles at the back of the tub, looking at my ring.

How did we get here?

It was last June when this all began.

I had walked around believing that people were either rightly opinionated or just plain wrong.

That's it.

It was as black and white as that.

Any moral ambiguity confused our ability to make hard decisions.

Society had a pretty good baseline for that, by encouraging women to live lawfully.

Simple.

Just follow the rules and you'll be fine.

No one could have forced me to see another way.

I suppose I came to the realization that I had been so blatantly wrong when I was confronted with my own lustful desires at around this time last year.

I stumbled upon Michael at an Issues Facing the Modern Man conference, unsurprisingly panelled by only women, on just as blistering of a hot day as today, last year, at the university. I wasn't paying attention to the attendees, except for when they would introduce themselves to me.

The conference consisted of prominent policy makers, budgeteers, and the like, all of whom had brushed shoulders with Mom at some point in her career. I, obviously, had to shake hands with all of them and pretend like I gave a shit about their existences.

What had been unusual was that the conference's attendees included the public.

Even men.

Albeit the men, as usual, had to wait their turn to speak.

Exactly two men had gotten the chance to ask questions to the female panelists.

The first man was most concerned with what would be done about rising incidents of females abusing their male tradeship partners.

"Would the universities and Department of Mental Health consider increasing funding to provide men with the necessary resources to tackle loneliness after a tradeship?"

Overwhelmingly, the panelists assured the young man that while he may have *thought* that depression amongst men was on the rise, it simply *wasn't*. And even if it was, there were still sufficient resources to satisfy the needs of men at the moment.

According to one of the panelists, men who were in official tradeships had the unique opportunity to get state-funded physical and mental health care for all of their needs, including physical examinations and mental health check-ups once a year as well as three supervised visits to a psychologist. In addition to that, sixty-eight percent of men in the country, who were not behind bars and didn't have labour jobs, were sponsored by the state's *Stay Home Save Lives Act* of 2062.

They didn't even have to work! The man was told. What more could men *possibly* need these days?

This amazing, all-inclusive act came from the taxpayers' desire to ensure that women in the work force could have emotionally and physically stable tradeships.

We had all democratically agreed to this under the Clinton presidency in 2062.

Apparently.

At some point.

I don't remember being consulted. I also don't remember being given a choice to *repeal* this law that gave taxpayers' money to jobless men.

According to the panelists, these programs *were* sufficient and would *have* to suffice, as budget cuts had been made to state-funded tradeship programs.

There were simply *not enough* women going into official tradeships with men anymore. Someone like Michael, who had unofficially entered a tradeship with me, wouldn't get any physical or mental health care. What on earth was he supposed to do?

How *did* he get health care?

Why hadn't I bothered to ask?

I now wondered why the man at the conference hadn't pushed the panelists on the needs of the other thirty-two percent of men.

I suppose he would have gotten booted out.

Then, there was the man with dark hair who was told he had precisely thirty seconds to make his point, as they were running out of time.

He asked them point-blank: "Will men *ever* have the opportunity to sit where you are and discuss the issues plaguing us?"

He was as mesmerizing as they come.

His voice sounded like a smooth piece of jazz.

The murmurs around him barely made a difference in his posture.

I didn't know I liked men like him until I laid eyes on him.

He was poised, composed, and well-spoken.

And his hair, so neatly curled up against his strong jaw.

Damn.

I felt it first in my crotch. The aching desire to have him.

That was the start of me making decisions in the greys.

It wasn't a *new* feeling, but it was a feeling that I hadn't known I could feel for men.

Especially not men like him, who boldly questioned the status quo.

> *"I'm sorry, Mr. what was your name again?"*

> *"Michael Nolan."*

"Mr. Nolan, yes, sorry, but time's run out."

As he walked back, proud and tall, we locked eyes just once, and ever since then I couldn't stop the smile beaming on my face from ear to ear.

An early century romance.

Before the Revolution of '27. Before Alberton's infamous divorce from her husband and marriage to a woman, which changed absolutely everything for womankind.

Well, that's how I *hoped* we would have met.

With our eyes meeting.

Then he would smile.

Then I would smile shyly in response.

But, of course, none of that was true.

In my world, he was the darkness to be avoided like the bubonic plague.

He was an *abomination*.

He should be sent to get himself psychologically altered with estrogen.

But that would have been a shame.

I knew his kind of man. I knew he was the type to support men like Draven Alec. A man my Mom absolutely hated, and so I went after him. I hunted him down. Searched his name in the registry of walk-in guests at the conference.

I stalked him for months and eventually he drop-kicked me and pinned me to the ground outside his house and asked me why I had been following him.

Then, we went out for coffee.

That was more than six months ago now.

Now I was in his bathtub.

Without him.

If you asked him, he would probably tell the story differently.

I suppose you could say that I had wanted a sort of simple, all-consuming, brain-numbing Nicholas Sparks kind of love story.

I had snuck a Nicholas Sparks book into my room from Granny's trunk when I was five. Read it and re-read it until the copy fell apart.

Granny had said it was a *classic*.

She had said that that was the kind of love story that she and grandpa had had before the world had changed.

Ma and Mom had met on the internet. Then, the world had gone and changed again.

My generation wouldn't know *romance* if it smacked them in the face.

No one just *fell* in love. It was all calculated. Calculated by the WEB.

In time, as I slowly started to reach the age where my frontal lobe had fully developed, at about twenty-five, I had been put into the online dating pool and matched with someone.

Well, *several* someones.

The first set of matches would all be women.

Then, if I *really* rejected every single available woman, I would get my pick of men.

But that wasn't a big lot either. Supposedly, this eliminated a lot of the time wasted on the selection process.

It made falling in love easier because the WEB already wanted what *you* wanted: more of the ideal lovers — two women — less of the heterosexual couplings.

I did that with Felicity.

I would have stopped there. Ventured down the calculated path, but some male poet in a dusty copy in Granny's trunk once said something about a path not taken.

Some man named Frigid or Frost.

Someone as cold as that.

I forget what it is now, but it's stuck with me.

Michael was a path not taken.

CHAPTER 41

It wasn't that Sigma enjoyed the thrill of the catch.

What she enjoyed more than anything was maintaining her hundred percent catch rate.

This was the absolute last throat that she had to slit today before she could go about her day job.

The Cavaliers had found this man wandering the streets like an utter *loon*.

After yet another protest against late night curfews outside City Hall, a lot more of *them* had come out onto the streets, demonstrating against good quality justice reforms.

These fucking male supremacists.

He had the crazed look of a child that had never been reprimanded for being an asshole to women.

Hence, he couldn't be fixed.

Once they hit a certain age, that was it. There was no prison in the world that would provide enough rehabilitation.

Her team had stalked him for days until he finally committed the heinous act: masturbating on the street while staring at some women just living their lives in their apartment in a two floor walk up.

Toxic masculinity.

Unfixable.

He was unfixable.

So he had to be *killed*.

Sigma knew the drill. But this guy had *really* gotten under her skin.

Even when she confronted him and asked if he wanted to lose his balls or his life, he didn't fear losing his balls.

Scaring him wasn't enough. A stern talking to wasn't enough.

He had laughed in her face and told her to take whatever she wanted, but said that this was *natural.*

His public masturbation to women was *natural.*

Well, *fuck him.*

She slit his throat. She didn't even use him one last time like she normally would have.

His blood spilling all over the sidewalk gave her the satisfaction that nothing else in life could.

CHAPTER 42

Once the water in the bath had run cold, I got out of the bathtub.

It was the first time Michael had ever left me alone in his apartment.

It was the first time he had trusted me for long enough to leave me in his apartment while he went out for groceries.

Two and a half miles of distance between us at this very moment.

I was *ecstatic*.

As with every other person I had ever slept with, I decided that I had to take a closer look around.

My curiousity led me into his closet.

I convinced myself that it was innocent enough. All I wanted was a t-shirt anyway.

As I sifted through his shirts, I noticed a well-established pattern in the way that he put them away.

Every third one was dark grey, while the two that came before were white or black or navy blue. All of them were the same deep v-necks that, as I remembered fondly, showed off the muscular lines of his pecs.

I pulled out the black one with the red logo and slipped it on, letting my towel fall to the ground.

I wasn't one to snoop, but when given the opportunity, how could I not?

I wish I hadn't.

Hindsight is twenty-twenty.

I pushed aside the mild adrenaline rush in my brain from the excitement of doing something I shouldn't have been.

I was surprised at how similar this felt to the first few times I had met with Michael.

Behind a coat that I had never seen him in, I found a little nook at the very far left of his closet.

I felt a surge of fear race from my gut straight into my throat.

Stay calm.

I tried to pull the coat off the hanger, but it seemed to be glued to it.

I didn't want to leave any traces of my snooping.

I felt my way into the nook with my fingertips.

It didn't feel as smooth as a wall.

It felt like plastic.

A cover that held an object.

Damn it! Why was there no light?

I tried to feel my way into an opening.

Come on. Come on.

Just like that, with a little pull, the opening gave way and out came an old phone.

The screen was as big as my face.

I turned it on.

30% battery remaining.

That was all that flashed on it.

I wasn't about to give up.

Damn it!

Fingerprint technology?

Seriously, Michael?

Why the hell did he need a phone so secretive?

What did he have to hide?

I stared at the screen for a long time.

I had figured he wasn't *just* a one-woman man, but these feelings of jealousy that began to surface were unexpected.

What had I done?

It felt like I had shattered the illusion of a perfect escape.

Damn it!

Damn!

Damn!

I was convinced that this would be the end of our tradeship.

It was more that I didn't want to get into a pesky trap of having to explain why I may have given Felicity crabs or herpes.

I pulled my damp hair back with my fingers, letting the tears fall off my face onto the floor.

What if he had been with other women? Other men?

Why hadn't I felt the need to ask him any of these questions before this?

Why, Michael? WHY?

I screamed internally, wanting to throw the phone against the wall by the bed.

I stared at the phone through glossed eyes.

Fuck Felicity. Fuck that stupid child. Fuck you Michael.

A tiny box beamed onto the screen: 'Congratulations, Draven Alec! You have reached 1000 comments on your recent video, 'M…'

Wait, what in goddess' green earth?

I tapped on the screen.

'Congratulations, Draven Alec! You have reached 1000 comments on your recent video, "Men and War in the 21st Century".'

A million thoughts rushed through my mind.

He wasn't...

He couldn't be.

There was no way.

What the hell would Moms think?

What am *I* thinking?

I felt the fear that Michael would inevitably feel if he came face to face with Mom.

The absolute terror *I* would feel if Mom found out about me cavorting with a political nemesis.

Her version of our reality, the reality of this world, was so jarringly antithetical to Draven's.

What the *hell* was he doing playing with fire?

I wiped away the tears that had fallen down my face in shock.

It all began to make sense.

He wanted me to go to all those MRA meetings for a *reason*.

He wanted me to agree with him for a *reason*.

Shit.

I had been *played*.

I put the phone into the coat pocket.

I got up slowly.

I wanted him to *panic*.

I *wanted* him to suspect something was amiss.

I grinned.

Nothing had to change.

I had his balls in the palm of my hand.

I knew his secret.

Oh Michael, what have you gone and done?

CHAPTER 43

For almost a week, Michael and Althea spent every waking moment together.

Except one day.

Michael felt compelled to sneak out to an internet cafe to publish an important piece.

His identity as Draven Alec had been one of the only secrets that he had kept from Althea.

The only one.

He had even told her about his nightmares on Wednesday night, after they had had intensely passionate sex.

He had had the same needle nightmare when she was asleep in his arms.

He woke up sweating, clawing away at her hand instead of his balls.

He almost drew blood before she shook him awake.

"*What the hell, Michael?!*"

"*Oh, Al, oh no…*"

He had jerked out of bed in a panicked frenzy and rushed to the bathroom to get her a moistened towel.

He had dabbed the little dots of blood lining her hand.

"*I'm so sorry. I just…I have these dreams sometimes.*"

He had mustered up the courage to tell her the rest.

She held him close.

He felt like she could understand his internal struggle.

"You don't have to tell me if you don't want to, but I'm here to listen," she said into his shoulder.

He then started to feel a sharp pain in his flaccid penis.

He pulled away from her and began to sob.

That imaginary pain hadn't made him cry like that since he'd been a teen.

Through sobs, he told her about how he had started having these dreams after the time they had put a cotton swab into his dick for his first ever STI exam.

It had scarred him.

He told her with his head hung in shame.

It wasn't a story he was *proud* to share.

It wasn't something he wanted to tell a woman.

He had to be *stronger* than that.

He liked her comfort.

He told her all the things they did to him when he was barely thirteen.

She began to cry.

She pulled him deeper into the bed and cradled his head in her breasts.

He had never felt so comforted before.

He started to understand the appeal of feminine companionship.

This was the reason why men were so willing to fall on the sword. He would have *died* just to have another taste of this. He would have sacrificed his whole life just to have that moment of comfort again.

It was difficult being strong.

It was difficult being *weak*.

It was difficult pretending that he didn't need a woman.

It was difficult accepting that he *did* need a woman.

It had been soul-crushing. Until she held him there as he cried softly into her warm, delicate, mango-smelling skin.

That's why on Friday, he had published the piece on men in wars.

It felt cathartic.

Men had emotional needs too.

Emotional needs that he now understood only *women* could fulfill.

CHAPTER 44

As soon as Michael left the apartment, I got on my laptop.

I had a hunch.

Today was the last full day I would be spending with him until my PMS days ran out for the month.

Five days.

They gave you five days to recuperate.

Five days of freedom from work.

If you wanted it.

Every woman I knew took that time off only to spend it shopping, relaxing, getting massages, or frequenting Fredricton.

The men at Fredricton didn't care.

They would do the deed with anyone who gave them a buck.

Five days of fifty percent off of wines and chocolates at any grocery store if you flashed your PMS card.

Five days of indulgence in my escape.

While I hadn't had my period on Monday, I had had enough of Felicity's bullshit over the weekend.

I had had to deal with that *child.*

I felt my throat go dry with the reminder of that knowledge.

After I had found the phone I simply *had* to know more.

So, here I was, sitting on his dark grey arm chair, hitting *refresh* every two seconds.

I *had* to know if this is what he had taken off to do.

Refresh.

What if it was as bad as I had suspected?

What if he really *was* Draven Alec?

Refresh.

Nothing.

Maybe I was just being paranoid. Maybe he just re-uploaded Draven Alec's videos before they were taken down.

The call for internet censorship had been louder than ever during these past few years.

But with barely enough women to fill the demanding roles of cyber security, and the lack of women going into computer science fields, the demand did not have the supply to match.

I walked over to his kitchen and decided to make myself some coffee.

These past few nights had kept us up and active.

He had one of those voice-activated coffee machines that you could order around.

I bellowed, "Cafe au lait!"

"One cafe au lait. Please make your selection: almond, soy or hemp milk?"

"Almond."

Least amount of calories.

I looked at myself in the mirror wondering why I needed to watch my weight, but at twenty-eight, I could never be too careful, I supposed.

I tied my hair up into a messy bun and adjusted my glasses while my coffee was being prepped.

By the time I got back to the chair, there was a new post by Draven Alec and my suspicions had been confirmed.

Moms always told me that a woman's intuition was the strongest asset that she had.

If my intuition was so strong, I wondered why Felicity hadn't yet gathered that I was with a man. And better yet, that I never wanted to have a child.

I clicked on the title with avid curiousity.

The crisp black webpage with white writing struck a chord with me.

Draven Alec loved monochrome.

Just as Michael did.

Not a spelling error in sight.

Clean, calculated, cold writing that resembled the way that Michael wrote in the many, many texts he had written to me.

I read with a twisted curiousity.

MEN AND SUICIDE - A SCATHING EXPOSÉ

The Daily Guardian published an interesting piece of propaganda this morning, beseeching all of us to consider the horrible statistics on female suicide.

Supposedly, of all the 79 287 suicides last year in the USA, 18 156 were females. The headline boomed: "Female rates of suicide higher than last year", with the sub-heading: "more funding requested for female mental health organizations".

But these headlines ignore the *core* of the issue: the people most *severely* disadvantaged by this statistic are (still) *males*. This statistic indicates that men are three times more likely than women to commit suicide.

It is *outrageous* that the media will not address this disparity, and instead sweep it under the rug to rebrand women as the victims time and time again.

Men are *still* struggling to find their purpose. To make matters worse, they are being disenfranchised even *more* by the present day cock-block being put on them in almost *every* white collar job imaginable.

Most CEOs are now women. The few men who *have* managed to remain CEOs live in constant fear of being pushed out. If they try to get ahead, they are now met with glass ceilings.

Men still work the majority of the hard, manual labour jobs like construction, sanitation, and worst of all, slaughterhouse work. We are being forced to do the jobs that women have *never* wanted to do, but which form the *backbone* of our society.

Without *us* building roads and houses, women wouldn't be able to live their cushy lives and drive around in their fancy cars on freshly tarred roads. Without *us* doing the dirty work of keeping their cities clean, they wouldn't be able to walk around in their shiny shoes and pretty clothes (or *unflattering* clothes, in some cases).

Imagine living in a world *without men?* It just *wouldn't* be a pleasant place, because we are *still* picking up your fucking slack when it comes to the physical, demeaning hard labour.

"Equal pay for equal work" they said to us fifty years ago, but only if it benefits women in white collar jobs — not *men* making sure that the grimy foundation of this country keeps running as smoothly as possible.

We're *killing* ourselves, picking up *their* trash, fixing *their* roads, building *their* homes, slaughtering and harvesting *their* food, while they get to sit in air-conditioned offices and look *down* on us for being dirty and filthy.

Men *have* purpose.

We do the dirty work. We always have. But now, we're paid and valued less and less for doing it.

Let's *not* kill ourselves over this. Let's lift each other up and find our purpose again. Let's ensure that we can become equal again —

Draven Alec had posted about male suicide rates being on the rise.

A topic that Michael had discussed just a brief forty hours ago with me.

He was writing about things that we had discussed.

He had been thinking of what to write in his popular men's rights blog while I was sleeping beside him, giving him my body, letting him feel a woman's touch.

My touch.

I felt *violated.*

I wasn't sure if this was the appropriate feeling in the moment, but I felt violated nonetheless.

I wasn't sure how to shake off the feeling of stumbling upon a secret and finally having it confirmed.

I was furious, sad, frustrated, and felt betrayed.

Mostly because he simply hadn't been honest with me.

I wondered if he hadn't been honest with me because he didn't trust me with his secret.

Was he afraid that *I, me* of all people, would actually rat him out to the authorities?

Or worse yet, *judge* him?

He would have called this misplaced disjunction in my head a false dichotomy.

What the hell else could the reason be?

I hated his logic.

I hated that he couldn't just *tell* me what he had been hiding.

He had divulged more vulnerable secrets this week.

He had told me why he had plucked the hairs on his balls until they were hairless.

Why couldn't he tell me about *this?*

Did he think that I would tell on him?

To whom?

Mom?

I almost *wanted* to tell her now.

Out of spite.

Fuck you, Michael. Fuck you.

I slammed the screen down.

I didn't need to read about how men had it *so* bad that they were offing themselves left, right, and centre.

I wanted to know his reasons for hiding things from me.

I wanted to know, but more than that I wanted him to *want* to tell me.

I didn't want to confront him.

Not yet.

Not yet.

Not until he found the phone.

Or had he already found it?

I gulped fear down my throat and rushed to the bedroom to check if he had taken the phone with him.

He had.

Shit.

Shit. Shit. Shit.

He knew. He *had* to know something was amiss.

I had been the only one in his apartment.

But I had plausible deniability.

I had been in the bath tub.

I had placed myself back into the bath tub when he had come back from the grocery store.

Shit.

He *knew* something was up.

I pulled the guardian papers for Aibek out of my purse.

Sign here.

Sign there.

Done.

If I couldn't control Michael, I could at least control my future with Fess.

CHAPTER 45

There was a long pause in their conversation.

"It would be foolish for you to just *confront* her with this suspicion. You don't know how she'll react."

"Where am I supposed to store this pain?"

"The same place I'm storing what I feel. She and her mom are cut from the same cloth. They will keep secrets from us for as *long* as we are married to them."

"I…"

"Just keep the boy safe. I suspect she's going to try to get out of her responsibilities, but she'll come to her senses. Her mother did. It was hard at first, but she eventually settled into it."

Magda heard Aibek mimic the voices on the television.

She had a deeper appreciation for Felicity's decision to adopt the child once she had learnt of his condition.

She loved him despite never having seen him.

"Thank you, Ma. This conversation put a lot into perspective for me."

"Things will work out for the best. If shit hits the fan, I'll give you the number to my personal private investigator. Althea isn't as sneaky as she thinks she is."

"Love you."

"Love you too."

CHAPTER 46

It was time.

It made sense. I knew their secrets, so I figured it was time to let spill all of mine. It only made sense. I could decide what to do about each of them once they both knew about each other.

I began my morning by sending a message to Michael that I was concerned that after the wedding I wouldn't be able to keep up with both him *and* Fess.

I said that I wanted to meet to discuss the future of my involvement with the MRAs. I kept it short.

I then sent a message to Felicity that I would be in the neighbourhood and that we needed to talk.

Those four ominous words that could have alerted her to something being amiss had she not been so distracted by Aibek's playtime.

See, I had always wanted to be upfront with Felicity.

I had never intended to keep me and Michael a secret for as long as I had.

She always knew I had a wandering eye.

She knew I needed *more*.

I knew I needed more, and yet…

I had kept pretending that she could satisfy my every need.

The thrill of Michael and I being my secret just got *so* into my head.

I'm really *not* a terrible person.

Right?

Felicity would understand my tradeship, if I would just explain to her *why* I was doing it.

Since she sprung Aibek on me, not too long ago, I had a right, didn't I?

I had a *right* to spring this on her.

I felt spiteful towards her.

That's where I was mentally, when I confessed.

She had made a quick lunch for us because she had to go back to work at the gallery.

She had just taken the first bite of her salad when all my conviction held my breath hostage in my chest.

I put my fork down.

All the movements after that moment felt deliberate.

Calculatedly slow.

I remained focused on her quick pace.

She didn't have time to process anything right now.

Do it.

Do it *now*.

I cleared my throat and put my hand on hers.

"Fess, I need to tell you something," I said, looking at her.

"Yeah?"

I pulled my hand away and touched my index finger to my lip.

"Um, I just…I need you to pay attention to what I am about to say."

She put her fork down.

I could see her scanning my face for emotion.

I didn't know if I was just lacking any in that moment, or if I was *actually* able to conceal my fear well.

I didn't know what compelled her to jump to the conclusion that she did, but her mind had already raced to where I knew it inevitably would.

"You're leaving me. You're leaving me alone with Aibek, aren't you?"

I hung my head down in contemplation for a long while.

When I looked back up at her, she had her brows furrowed together, her mouth in a twisted frown ready to let the tears spill.

"No, Fess, I'm *not* leaving you. But I *do* need to talk to you about something."

Why was this so goddessdamned hard?

It wasn't supposed to be like this.

Not between us.

There was a time when I told her every minute, boring, ridiculous detail of my life.

There was a time when we actually laughed when holding hands and kissing.

There was a time when I didn't feel like I was being torn between this life with her and my intellectual curiousity with him.

I swear, there *was* once such a time and I swear if I could have it any other way, I would stay committed to this life with her.

Months ago, that changed for Fess.

She hid Aibek.

Months ago, that changed for me.

I hid Michael.

Goddess!

"Actually, I need to tell you about someone. I have to tell you about Michael."

"Who's that?"

"He is…"

She was looking right at me. Her gaze made me uncomfortable, so I looked away.

Right in this moment, I should have felt spiteful and vindicated that I had held out on keeping a secret longer than she had.

She had a boy, I had a guy. Both well-kept secrets for the past few months.

I should have spit out what Michael and I were, and yet I felt like I could *burst* with the guilt that was consuming me.

"Michael and I have been involved in a tradeship for a while."

She didn't look surprised.

"I always knew there was somebody else. I even talked to Ma about it," she said, picking up her fork again.

"You *did*?"

I was shocked.

"Yeah, I talked to her last night. I told her about Aibek. If I had it my way, she would have known about Aibek before you did," she said between bites.

I looked at her, astounded by her nonchalance.

My own goddessdamned *mother*!

"So, you *felt* that something was amiss, but never just came out and *asked* me, even though we were going to become life-partners?"

She didn't say anything and just shrugged me off.

What the *hell* was going on here?

My future wife and my Ma were snipping about me behind my back.

Was she emotionally cheating on me with my own mother?

I shook my head, trying to rid my mind of the wild theories it was conjuring.

"*What the hell*, Fess?"

I pushed my seat back and frustratingly yelled into nothingness.

Her non-reaction to my outburst angered me even more.

The cling-clang of that *damn* fork against that *damn* plate pushed me over the edge.

I shot straight up and walked right up to her.

I saw her eyes look right at my stomach.

I pulled her face up to mine so that our eyes would meet.

I saw a glimmer of mischief in hers.

"I am *not* going to leave you for him, but I want my freedom to do what I want until the wedding."

She blinked in response, not giving away a single emotion.

I bent down until my face was squarely on top of hers.

I could feel molecules of precipitation from my nostrils hit her lips.

I looked into her eyes, digging my thumb and index finger into the sides of her face.

She didn't wince.

Her jaw felt soft in my hand.

I could snap her neck if I wanted to.

I could.

It confirmed in my mind that I held the upper hand.

She knew that.

If I refused to become life partners with her, her whole carefully crafted plan with the boy and me would collapse.

Her parents were counting on me taking over.

My parents were counting on me taking over.

Guardianship was serious business.

Michael.

The thought of him brought me back to seeing insolence in her eyes.

I pushed her jaw violently to the right.

She quickly recovered from that, only to return to forking the last few spoonfuls of salad into her mouth.

Goddess!

That sound alone was enough for me to want to slap her across the face.

I quietly went back to my seat opposite her.

This was *not* the woman that I had expected to speak to today.

She had curated this secret life away from me that I had had *no* idea about.

Seems like Ma was convinced that *I* was the malicious one.

I would have to deal with that.

How?

How could I deal with a defiantly passive mother?

Goddess!

I made myself eat.

I shoved the vegetables into my mouth and pretended to be satisfied after eating them.

The knot in my stomach only worsened.

I suddenly felt like Cooper in Interstellar.

Rage.

Rage, rage against the dying of the light.

CHAPTER 47

At least I had managed to maintain control over Fess.

I got on the subway as soon as I could, after hearing back from Michael that I could come to Fernando's to get ready.

There was no reprieve from this insane heat wave that we were having, and the subway was packed.

I was wearing what I deemed to be perfectly acceptable, given the heat: shorts and a tee.

It *would* have been appropriate, too, until Michael saw me in it after I got off at Walhberg's Station.

I was led back to Fernando's, where I could change into a baggier shirt that hid my womanly figure and a pair of jogger pants that didn't reveal an inch of my skin.

Then came the mask. Two holes cut out for the eyes, a hole for the mouth and nose, and the logo.

The eve of my confessing to Felicity that I was an uncommitted woman, I was partaking in a protest.

What was the protest even *for*?

I didn't care.

I just wanted to scream.

What I wanted to do more than anything was to confess to Michael that I was *done*.

I couldn't be with him.

I couldn't be a part of this and be celebrating my love for Felicity in less than eight months.

I couldn't.

I could.

I should.

Stay.

Shit.

I walked to the biggest train station in the city in a disguise that made me look like a man.

I recognized Mae Tolbert on the steps to the station. One of the most prominent news anchors in all of Connecticut.

We were ridiculed, leered at, and shoved with batons by women who didn't know that I was a woman.

"What do we want?"

"Equality!"

"When do we want it?"

"NOW!"

"Men are forced to be drafted into the army! We are USED and ABUSED by women for our physical differences under the guise of reparations! We want equality! One man for one woman in the army!"

I saw a masked man screaming into the speakerphone.

"One man for one woman!"

We echoed the chant.

"Equality!"

Through all the shoving, pushing, poking, and prodding, I was able to hear most of his speech.

"Seven thousand, one hundred, and ninety nine men have died defending this country! Only forty six women have been killed in direct combat. We protect this country with our bodies. We sacrifice our bodies and our lives to protect a country that doesn't even give us equal pay for equal work."

All the stats had checked out when I had researched it on my own.

They were just screaming facts.

Nothing wrong with that.

A man's life and a woman's life sacrificed equally for our country made sense to me.

This was something that I could stand for.

I stood taller, prouder, and manlier than I ever had.

I saw the way that women passers-by glared at us.

We were *nothing*.

We were *less* than nothing.

We were like *animals* to them. To be gawked at like monkeys in chains.

We could be whacked with batons or pepper sprayed or beaten or maimed and no one would bat an eye.

I would be considered a *traitor*.

I knew what I was risking.

I didn't care.

"Men and women are equal! We are the same! We all bleed red!"

I screamed at the top of my lungs.

Hearing a woman's voice seemed to create a ruckus and before I knew it, the man with the microphone was being pinned to the ground by two officers.

"You can't say sexist speech like that in our country!"

"We have a right to protest! We are a part of this country too!"

"We are a part of this country too!" Other voices echoed the sentiment.

Some voices chimed in, gaining popularity: "Men like you don't belong here!"

Then what kind of men do belong here?

I wondered if I was the kind of woman who didn't belong here.

I wondered when it had become justified for some group of people to decide who belongs in this country and who doesn't.

If they had the wrong opinion.

If they had a dick.

The women with the batons began charging at us.

Suddenly it was all limbs and tear gas, and I was being pulled towards an opening away from the crowd by a hand I recognized.

"Come on, come on! Let's go! We gotta get the hell out of here!"

CHAPTER 48

Natalia walked over to the kitchen sink and threw her mug into it.

It inevitably shattered into a dozen pieces.

Here we go again.

Magda winced visibly while shifting uncomfortably on the couch.

"What now, my love?" Magda asked.

"Have you seen what those assholes have written about inclusive programs in companies?"

Natalia pointed in the direction of her laptop.

Her finger was twitching with the amount of caffeine she had had first thing in the morning.

"Which assholes, love?" Magda asked with exasperation.

"Draven! Draven the asshole, that's who!"

"Nat, come on…"

"Don't you *dare* tell me not to read these things. You *should* be reading these things! Look at how significantly they affect *everything* for us!"

"I know. I heard there was a protest outside of Central Station, for the fourth day in a row. What have they been saying?"

"We should eliminate *all* inclusivity laws. As if we can just *erase* what men have done to our mothers."

"It's unbelievable that men like Draven are still arguing against this progress."

"Exactly! They want *equality*, they say, but they don't even know what equality *is*!"

"These boys have *so* much to learn. They are just childish, young and naive…"

"They know what they are doing! They aren't *that* young! They deserve to be locked the *hell* up! We need more police in this damn country. More jails. More than just *one* where they try to stuff in *all* the miscreants."

"They are just stuck in their teenage phase. Come on now, give them a break."

Natalia yanked Magda up by her arm so harshly that it felt as though it would come out of her shoulder.

"You stay at home and work, Mags. I have to face the doings of the public *every damn day*."

"You're hurting me…"

"No, I *would* be hurting you if I disagreed with you and constantly told you that you were overreacting to all the crazy *shit* happening in the world."

"Nat, stop it. Okay? I'm sorry."

Natalia put Magda's arm behind her back, digging her nails into Magda's forearm.

Magda winced.

Natalia looked square into Magda's eyes.

"You don't know *anything*. You got that? You don't *know* anything."

Natalia threw her phone onto the coffee table.

With her free hand, Natalia spread Magda's legs wide apart, pulling down her underwear as far down as she needed to be able to put two fingers deep inside Magda.

"This is how much I *own* you."

She scratched inside of Magda's delicate vagina with her two sharp nails.

Magda cried out in pain and closed her legs together, pushing Natalia's fingers out of her with her free hand.

"Stop it! *Stop* that!"

Natalia wiped her fingers on Magda's shirt.

"I have a ton of work. I won't be back till late tonight. Don't bother staying up."

Natalia grabbed her phone and her purse before walking out the door.

Magda melted into the couch in shock.

Tears fell down her face and she couldn't stop until she was screaming at the walls.

CHAPTER 49

Magda curled up into the fetal position on the couch.

What the hell just happened?

The walls had absorbed all her screaming and yelling to their capacity.

No matter what kind of day it had been, other than the consistencies of grocery shopping, picking up the dry cleaning, and returning library books, Magda's day always included the timely and inevitable yelling match with the walls.

She always won.

That's what she liked about these walls that she had so carefully designed with high-end art that had once hung at the MoMA.

Especially since Althea had left home, Natalia's rage had grown even more bitter with each passing day.

When Althea *was* at home, Natalia had stuck to yelling.

Magda *liked* being told what to do.

She *liked* being given objectives for her day.

But the moment Natalia left, and Magda was left alone with her thoughts, she resented Natalia for her unhinged brutality that came along with the orders.

That's when she yelled at the walls until her lungs gave out.

The way Natalia spoke to her was as though she was a *child.*

A spoilt child, as Magda saw herself, who needed to be told 'no' more often than 'yes'.

She loved the idea of immersing herself in hours and hours of online shopping to be able to find the absolute perfect outfit.

Then, of course, came the accessories.

With the burden of trying to find the accessories came the intense desire to search for a distraction.

The distractions were hidden in websites dedicated to interior design.

Bed, Bath and Beyond, Ikea, and DownFind were the places she *craved* to go, but settled instead for their alluring websites from the comfort of her home.

Her impatience began *after* the fact, when she had to *wait*.

Wait for the delivery notification.

Wait for the "In Transit" status update.

Wait for the "Out for Delivery" message.

Once that happened, there was still more waiting.

She *loved* the wait.

Waiting for the delivery truck.

Waiting till the strong women dropped off her carefully selected possessions.

Waiting till she could open all the boxes and give all her new possessions a home in her neat and tidy place.

The 'shop, wait, put away' system made her forget about her familial and marital deficiencies.

Without this system, she would think about her empty nest too much.

Without this system, she wouldn't have had a way to deal with Natalia's manhandling.

She could be a better wife to Natalia with her system.

She was a submissive wife to Natalia with her system.

Less moody, less obsessed with the cleanliness of the place, and less dramatic about the trivialities of everyday annoyances.

Natalia liked Magda's system.

She gave her an account of her own, with an allowance, and Magda never overspent by even a penny.

It worked.

Until today.

Today, she found no joy in the websites that she loved to frequent.

Today, the walls would be insulted again and again until she cried herself to sleep on the couch.

She decided that it was time for her to get a *new* hobby.

CHAPTER 50

Darrin was cautiously aware of the lateness of the hour.

James hadn't returned home yet.

He looked around his apartment, noticing all the cracks and edges.

He wondered what would finally drive him over the edge long enough to write anything again.

He had lost his inspiration.

Breathe.

One.

Two.

He was resolved not to do it.

He knew that James would be home any minute.

If he found him like that again, he would have a fit.

Breathe.

One.

Two.

When his neck started to cramp, he looked straight ahead and out of the window again.

The dissatisfaction with his lack of creativity left him slumped on his desk chair.

Don't do it.

But the needle was right there.

Hidden in plain sight.

It had the vial sitting right next to it.

He rolled up his sleeve.

It wasn't as though James *hadn't* seen him spiral before.

This would be just one of *many* times.

Even if James came back before he sobered up, Darrin presumed that he could convince him that it was a one off.

A one off that had become far too common a habit for the past year and a half.

It would help him fight the mundane.

He yanked the top drawer open.

The rubber band, the finding of the vein, and the needle were all such intensely familiar experiences.

The opening of the drawer led to the inevitable grabbing of the syringe.

Get the vial next.

Just get it, then think.

His right hand shook as he pulled the syringe back.

The liquid filled the plastic vessel.

His heart rate accelerated to match the sound of the rain drops beating against the windows.

When had it begun to rain?

He steadied his hand, seeing the dotted line on his arm from the countless times he had done this before.

Breathe.

One.

Two.

When the needle almost grazed his skin, he retreated his hand back towards the table.

No!

He shouldn't.

He put the full syringe on the table, fully committed to breaking the needle in half so that he would not give in to his baser instincts.

He ran his fingertips through his dark hair.

He curled some strands around his index finger.

What's the harm?

Creativity.

A sudden burst of inspiration.

He stared at the vein that bulged and throbbed under the pressure from the elastic band tightened around his bicep.

Bulging and throbbing in sheer anticipation.

He grabbed the syringe, pushed out a bit of liquid before piercing it into his skin.

The liquid gushed through his vein.

If only for a moment, if only for this *one* moment, he had become *au present*, as the syringe drained into his arm.

He pulled out the needle and pressed his skin with a Kleenex.

Where had the Kleenex come from?

He released the elastic band around his bicep, slumping back into the office chair, staring at the ceiling in a newfound amusement.

The colours in the patched ceiling blended together as he began to dream of the stained glass windows at a museum he had seen in Virginia two summers ago.

While he remained in this state for hours, James lay in a holding cell, drenched in sweat, begging for his one phone call.

The one phone call that could have made the difference between getting the hell out of that place or being trapped for another forty hours with rats and men alike gnawing at his body and shitting in front of him.

He should have called Michael.

He called Darrin instead.

His husband, who he believed would have rushed over to help.

He chose wrong.

CHAPTER 51

He was working as fast as he could to patch me up.

It wasn't the bruised lip that hurt or even the elbow that was probably going to be out of commission for a week; it was the fact that I was going to hurt him by telling him what I should have told him *months* ago.

He looked at my bruises the way that Ma looked at them when I was younger.

He tenderly touched them all one by one as he put rubbing alcohol or bandages on them.

I found myself enamoured by this maternal gesture coming from a man like him.

I thought these were reserved only for the *Mas* of the world.

"We have to work twice as hard in this place that wants to keep us down just to get an *ounce* of freedom. I've gone through this before."

He tilted his head to look at me.

I winced as he dabbed the rubbing alcohol on my elbow.

"I don't know how we are supposed to go on living like we are equals."

"You and me, both."

He dabbed the rubbing alcohol onto my bruised lip.

"Do you want to tell me why you wanted to see me today?"

"I have a son. I mean, I *will* have a son."

He nodded his head in understanding, almost to himself, moving onto dealing with my bruised knee.

"I didn't even know…"

"Yeah. Her name is Felicity. I call her Fess. We're engaged."

"When's the wedding?"

I blinked back tears.

"In a few months. She wants it to be as quick as possible."

He paused mid-swab, contemplating.

"What are you thinking? Can you just *emote* for me? More than this? Right now, Michael, please!"

He looked at my ring finger.

"The ring. I should have figured; I didn't. That's on me, isn't it?"

I put both my hands on his shoulders.

Leaning on him.

I wondered if he thought I was consoling him.

"I didn't want to hide this from you. It just sort of happened. She knows about you though."

He shrugged my hands off of his shoulders.

"You can't come around here anymore. I shouldn't tell you any more."

"You mean you shouldn't tell me that you are Draven Alec?"

"What?"

The look of bewilderment on his face said it all.

"It was a hunch, but I figured as much."

"How..." he said, clearing his throat before continuing, "Okay, you know."

I could tell he was trying to play it off as though it didn't bother him.

"The cell phone, in my jacket, was that...?"

"Yes."

"Fuck. I thought it had been some woman I had seen walking around here."

I stood up to move closer to him.

I snuggled up and into his chest.

"It doesn't change anything between us," I said

I was trying to convince myself that nothing had to change, now that all the secrets had spilled out into the rooms of my lovers.

He pushed me away.

"How doesn't this change absolutely *everything* between us?"

CHAPTER 52

Michael looked at me with crazed eyes.

I could tell I had messed up.

Bad.

He asked me with some uncertainty creeping into his voice, "are you completely insane?"

"I could be," I blurted out.

I wanted to say, *"...but I'm just trying to play by the rules. Just like you."*

Instead, I just watched him shut his eyes and place his thumb and index finger on his eye lids.

"This wasn't real life, this was a *fantasy*. You and me, we were a *fantasy*," he said softly, under his breath.

"But this *is* real! What I feel for you *is* real, Michael!" I exclaimed, almost screeching.

I couldn't lose *this*.

Him.

I couldn't lose *him*.

"I don't want to stop talking to you. Not now. Not when I have so much I need to know from you. I *need* you."

"No, no you don't."

"Stop it. Stop that! Stop thinking that I don't need you. I *do*. I need you to show me, teach me things that I have been sheltered from my whole goddessdamned life!"

I tried to reach for him.

I wished I could turn back the clock to before Fess' name had left my lips.

"No, just stop it!"

He pushed my hands away.

The urgency inside me insisted I say anything to keep him.

"I didn't claim to *love* you, Michael."

He looked at me incredulously.

"I'm not fucking lying, Michael."

I grabbed his forearm in a desperate attempt to keep him close.

I dug my nails into his skin, softly trying to assert the limited control I thought I had over him.

He slowly sat down on the side of the bed.

I saw the weight of the conversation make his shoulders droop.

This wasn't how this was supposed to go.

He was supposed to not care.

He no longer had that confident tallness that I had come to adore.

"I could read between the lines Al, and it doesn't sound like infatuation to me," he said with his head in his hands.

"Then what *does* it sound like to you?" I almost screamed in exasperation.

He swiftly got up.

He walked away from me.

Trying to keep at least a six foot distance between us.

Like he was disgusted with my mere *presence* in his vicinity.

"It sounds to me like you care a little too much about a guy that your mommies hate, just to piss them off. It sounds like you fucking *played* me. And like you still *want* to play me. What was your *plan*, huh? Get with me? Get with the MRAs? Find out all our secrets?"

He turned around to look at me.

I don't know what he was expecting from me.

I began to blubber with incoherent rage.

"What are you talking about?"

"Oh of course not Al, you will tell yourself that *now*. You can tell yourself that you're *not* playing me, but you *are*. You have no *choice* but to play me."

"Are you just trying to *hurt* me now? Trying to push me away? I am *not* going! I am *not* leaving. I'm right here. I want to fight your fight with you."

"No. No you don't. Fuck! We've been playing *each other*, this *entire time*. You're trying to find a hint of Noah in me, and I've been trying to find a hint of Allie in you. There, I said it. We've been trying to travel back in time to a place that isn't our reality."

"But isn't that what Draven *stands for*? Trying to reengage women in chivalry?"

I regretted asking that almost instantly, but that didn't stop me from making even more verbal blunders.

"Doesn't he try to make women understand that there is more to the sexes than just wanting to beat men into submission for their ancestors' mistakes? Trying to help them realize the beauty in the old?"

"NO! You have it all wrong Al. Draven stands for *equality*. Draven stands for learning to understand that there are fundamental differences between the sexes and that we can use them to our fucking *advantage*. The world would be better off if we hadn't forced women into power positions when what they *really* wanted to do was be homemakers the whole time."

His demeanour made it clear that he wasn't viewing me as someone he could talk to, but rather just talk *at*.

He looked at me like I was an insect that he was able to squash with the weight of his words.

"Are you, Michael, the man who is all about *equality*, trying to claim that women were not influenced by men to feel like they *should* be homemakers? That they were not told that they couldn't adequately take care of themselves without a *strong* man? We don't *need* you!"

His face contorted with annoyance.

He sighed audibly in frustration.

"You just *said* you needed me. Now you're saying you *don't* need us. You make no sense."

"And you *do*? You are so full of *shit*. You talk about equality but what you *actually* want is some meek little woman who won't question your heteronormative patriarchal regression into the middle of the last fucking century, when women were *still* not given the fundamental *choice* to be in positions of power. Some women were *still* not given the *choice*. They were still influenced by their husbands, mothers, and fathers to be fucking *playthings* for men. Some of them were still *forced* into the domesticity that you crave so desperately."

"That! *That* is precisely the insane fearmongering that the Alberton regime used. In the twenties, women *could* choose what they wanted to be, *here*, in this country. *Today* they are *forced* into positions of power because of stupid laws that keep men from pursuing their desire to…"

I felt Mom's rage burning through my bones and blocking my ears from hearing any more of what he was saying.

"Are you trying to say we don't *DESERVE* this power, Michael? We don't *deserve* to be in power for *ONCE* since forever?"

He came up to me and dragged me to his book shelf where I met Mill, Rousseau, Wittgenstein, and Russell eye to eye.

"Maybe you should read *more*. Educate your feminized, one-track mind," he said, nodding his head at it.

"You know I've read some of these already."

"Seemingly not enough!"

"Stop patronizing me."

I glared at the side of his face.

"Maybe you should start from the top and end at the bottom. Maybe you need to stop judging all men through your *mothers'* fucking eyes."

"And maybe *you* need to stop spending so much time with your deviant MRA friends and understand that women have more rights now than ever before, and we *deserve* it."

"Then I guess we're at a stand still and I can't fucking deal with you anymore."

I shook myself free of his grasp.

He took a step away from me.

"You were hurting me, and not in the way I like."

"I think you should leave. Go back to your moms, to your wife-to-be, and to your *son*." He pointed towards the door.

"Okay, I'll do just that."

I didn't want to give him the satisfaction of seeing me cry.

I walked away from him to get my purse off the ground.

I stormed off towards the door, tears streaming down my face.

I turned around to see him staring intensely at the ground.

"You know, you could have *thanked* me for keeping your secret. You could have *thanked* me for not going to my Moms and exposing your shitty *side hobby*. You could have done *so* much more than just talk *down* to me like I'm just another one of the many women who look down on you and your kind. I was trying to *understand*. You should have been *grateful* for me. We could have taken the world on, side by side, with no one stopping us. You could have had me on your *team*, Michael, and now what? You're all alone again daring to fight a fight that you don't even stand a *chance* of winning. You could have had *me*."

He said nothing.

He didn't even look at me.

The ground was more interesting, it seemed.

What the hell?

"I thought that you would treat me like your intellectual equal, but you *can't*, can you?" I asked rhetorically.

"We're in different positions, Al. You have all these choices that you can make freely, and I am bound to a life of misery if I come out as a strong, heterosexual man who says *fuck* this system," he said, exasperated.

I walked back towards him.

Without an ounce of hesitation I kissed his cheek.

I cupped his cheek in my hands and smoothed the spot I had just kissed.

He whispered into my ear, "I hope you do right by your son. I hope you teach him to be a man."

I felt rage intermingle with pity in my throat.

There was *so* much I could have said.

"Goodbye, Michael."

CHAPTER 53

"I tried calling you, Darrin! I tried and *what* were you doing? High out of your *damn* mind!"

"Babe, I know. I know, and I'm sorry."

"Don't be sorry, be *better*! I thought you got rid of all that *shit*."

Darrin ran his fingers through his hair.

Breathe.

One.

Two.

He wasn't used to being yelled at by James. He was used to the disappointment, the slick interventions to get him into rehab, and the emotional pleas to stop.

He wasn't used to this *anger*.

He had crossed a line this time.

James had needed him, and he hadn't been sober.

"I should have been present. I know I should have been there for you when you called, but I just was so completely…"

James sighed.

The anger was about to fizzle into disappointment.

He knew how to deal with the disappointment.

"The things that they did to me, in there…You can't even *imagine*. It was forty-eight hours of pure *hell*. Michael got me out on a *warning*, because he told the cops that I would clean the streets every day for the next two months! Two *damn* months, Darrin!"

Darrin put his arms around him to pull him close.

"I'm here now, babe. I'm *so* sorry. I'm so *incredibly* sorry,"

Darrin softly whispered 'I'm sorry' over and over into James' ear.

James ran his fingers through Darrin's hair and massaged his scalp.

The fingers, James' touch, and the pressing of their bodies together felt so comforting that Darrin forgot for a moment that he had slipped up.

When James finally pulled away, Darrin knew that he had run out of time to engage in excuses, much less bask in the warmth of his husband.

"I'll get help. I *promise* you, I'll get help," Darrin said, not meaning a word of it.

James burst into tears.

"I can't handle you leaving me for so long again."

"I *won't* leave. I don't *want* to leave. I want to find a way to *stay* and get help."

Darrin held James' hands up to his chest.

This had become a conversation far too intense for either one of them to fully grasp.

Too much had happened.

Darrin was forgetting to breathe in deeply.

Breathe.

One.

James chastised him through sobs.

"I *want* you to get help, Darrin, I *mean* it. I can't *deal* with this on top of my own shit right now."

Breathe.

One.

Two.

"I…I don't want to fight. But what happened to you in jail, isn't my fault. It's yours."

Darrin regretted his words as soon as they came out of his mouth.

James pulled back and paced to the back of the room near the window, wiping away hot tears from his face.

"I'm trying to do this for *us.* I don't know why you can't *see* that."

"I *have* been understanding, on all the long days and nights that you have left me alone to go be with *those* people. I *have* been understanding and seeing and listening, but I can't keep on letting you believe that I am the *only* one at fault here."

"I don't want to fight."

"This isn't a fight."

"It sure seems like it's about to blow up into one."

"Can't you just take a break?"

"Men in that place, in those damned houses on Fredriction, in Fangsel, they don't get a *break.* For crying out loud! I'm trying to get men like *you* out of there!"

"I think you maybe just need to start taking more estrogen."

James sighed and walked to the bathroom.

"I should have known better than to get into this," he muttered under his breath.

Darrin ran his fingers through his hair in quick successions of two.

One.

Two.

A calming method that seemed to have worked for so long now irritated him instead.

He made it a point to inhale every time he wanted to exhale.

He made it a point to scratch his wrist every time he wanted to run his fingers through his hair.

Cognitive behavioural therapy had taught him that.

Replace one behaviour with another compulsive one.

He longingly looked at the top drawer of the desk.

What he wouldn't give to have one more shot at the needle.

Just a little flow of that liquid into his veins.

More than James' contentedness with him, more than anything else in the *entire* world, he wanted his needle.

In this space.

With his journal.

Without a single sound or man interrupting his thoughts.

All for himself.

He wanted to be *selfish*.

He knew James resented him for that.

He resented *himself* for that.

CHAPTER 54

It had been a week since Natalia had touched Magda in any capacity.

Not a kiss, not a slight touch of a hand on hers, *nothing*.

The bed felt empty despite having two bodies occupying it.

Magda didn't sleep a wink, but didn't dare to toss and turn either.

Natalia had left this morning in a huff.

One ping of a text.

That's all it took for Magda to be left alone again.

In the silence of this place she called home.

Once in a while, she would get up, walk over to the window, and look outside.

She nervously ate her sandwich, while breadcrumbs fell onto her clothes, the couch, and the floor.

She would make sure it was spotless by the time Natalia returned home that night.

Even if they weren't talking, she didn't dare recoil from her duties.

She had ordered a gold-plated bedside lamp that was supposed to be delivered by 8 P.M. that night.

It was 7 P.M.

She refreshed the webpage to check the updated delivery time.

Your delivery is guaranteed by 7:03 P.M.

She had denied herself any lunch, just in case the delivery van arrived while she had been preparing her meal.

Hence, the sandwich for dinner.

She didn't want to miss a *minute* of the excitement as the van stopped at the curbed, the delivery woman buzzed her, and she signed for the package.

It was the only female interaction that she got all day, and she *craved* it.

The pleasantries were always such a delight.

Refresh!

Your delivery is guaranteed by 7:18 P.M.

She nibbled on the last bit of the sandwich.

Refresh!

Your delivery is guaranteed by 7:39 P.M.

The minutes seemed to go by slower and slower.

When the clock struck 7:50 P.M., she refreshed the page one last time.

Your delivery could not be made today. Please contact our customer service if your delivery does not arrive by 8 P.M. tomorrow.

She dejectedly walked to the kitchen and put her plate on the counter.

She had hoped for some company.

She pulled out a glass from the cabinet above the sink.

As she was about to turn on the tap, she noticed a spider crawling on the faucet.

"Hey, little guy."

She watched his speedy little legs working fast to get away from her finger as she placed it on the faucet near him.

He ran down the faucet and into the empty sink.

On an impulse, Magda turned on the faucet but quickly put her glass under the running water.

Stray drops of water fell into the sink until one fell squarely onto the spider's head.

"Oh dear, oh dear!"

She watched as he struggled under the weight of the liquid.

She thought of putting her finger near his legs again.

She withdrew her hand instead.

She gulped down the entire glass of water, keeping her eyes focused on the insect.

The spider had managed to shake himself off and crawl towards the edge of the sink.

Magda quickly stopped drinking, just to pour the rest of the water into the sink.

She was giving him a reason to *live*.

A *challenge*.

He floated on top of the pool of water that had formed in the sink.

The pool just *narrowly* avoided the drain.

It stood still in one corner of the sink.

Then the spider's leg began twitching uncontrollably.

The faucet still dripped water ever so slowly, but did not add any more water to the still little pool.

The spider quickly flipped over onto his legs and began his upward climb onto the counter.

Magda watched.

Why was he enjoying the struggle?

The second he got to the top of the sink and onto the counter, she slammed the glass on its body until the glass broke in her hands.

The spider squirmed for a few seconds before it lay still.

With one half of its body attached to the bottom of the glass and the other smeared on the counter top, Magda began washing her plate.

She had more to clean now than before he had shown up on her sink.

But, more than ever, she wished that she could have his company again.

CHAPTER 55

In the anonymous cloak of nightfall, Olivia belted her burgundy jacket close as she shuffled through an insane crowd that had gathered around Union Station.

Even more protests.

She had already seen nine men and a woman get arrested over the past few days on TV.

She sat down next to Natalia without a word, slightly smiling and showing her silver tooth.

"Do you have the money?"

How else could she have begun this conversation?

"Yes."

Natalia slipped the huge manila folder towards her.

"This is subtle."

"Well, I'm not paying you to be subtle. I'm paying you for information."

"Then why the fuck are we whispering?"

She looked at Natalia's face for a reaction.

Natalia offered none and cleared her throat instead.

Natalia knew that she was the best person for the job when she had hired her. Their relationship had been the same for years: Natalia texted, Olivia found something, she texted back, they met at one of two places, Deja's or here, and this time Natalia had picked *here*.

"Cut the crap, Olivia."

"Do you want what I have or not?"

"Yes."

"Al is having an *affair*."

"An *affair*? This isn't the last century, Liv, for crying out loud. She isn't married."

"You know what I mean."

"Okay, with whom?"

She whispered a name.

"Come again…"

"Draven Alec."

"You are fucking kidding me. You are *fucking* kidding me. *Goddessdamnit*!"

"Calm the hell down, Natalia. People are *staring*."

Natalia rubbed her temples.

The vein in her forehead pulsed wildly.

"What's his *actual* name?"

"Michael Nolan. Quiet guy. Lives on welfare mostly. Hasn't held down a job in over six years. He has a wall full of books by male authors. It's not like he was trying super hard to hide, either. He goes to an internet cafe, has an old phone, and times the publishing of his blogs."

She showed Natalia pictures of them on her phone.

Natalia shifted uncomfortably in her chair, feeling the rage burn deep inside the pits of her stomach. She rounded her palms into fists, digging her nails into the tender flesh.

*That piece of shit. How **dare** he touch **my** daughter.*

"How much more to get a goddessdamned address?"

"Four Ks."

"Get me that damned address."

She looked deep into Olivia's eyes for signs of deceit. She found a staid look of sympathy instead.

"I don't need your pity," Natalia said.

She kissed Olivia on her lips. Just for good measure. A polyamorous relationship, even an *affair*, would be much easier to explain than what she was *actually* doing here.

Natalia pushed her chair back.

Across the street, Magda watched her wife through the window of the coffee shop.

I knew it.

Just as silently as she had followed Natalia to the shop, she slinked back home.

CHAPTER 56

Why had I gotten involved with such a *brute* man?

I threw myself on my bed and wasted absolutely no time in screaming into my pillow.

"*Draven, fucking, Alec!*"

No one heard me.

Why would anyone have heard me anyway?

Closed windows, no air, no room to breathe.

Breathing?

Who needed that?

Jesus.

Maybe Mom was right.

I had become a *floozy*.

An *air-head*.

I should just dye my hair blonde and go with it.

I knew who he was.

I had known for a while and I hadn't cared.

Now, all of a sudden, since *he* knew that I knew, it *mattered*.

Why?

The way he condescended to me, as though I didn't know reality...

The thought of him patronizing me made me scream into my pillow again.

He had the *nerve* to talk to me as though I were *beneath* him.

Somehow my lack of knowledge of *all* the things he knew made me *less than*.

Men like him just *mansplain* and *mansplain* until they get into your brain like little ear worms that won't stop until they've eaten your *entire* brain from the inside out.

Well, *fuck him.*

I should just pay more attention to Felicity and Aibek.

At the very least she gives me a reason to live.

Felicity.

She is *so* beautiful.

Now, with that little boy, no less.

She *knows* what she wants.

She wants *me* and wants to be a *mom* to Aibek.

She doesn't talk back to me, doesn't patronize, doesn't belittle me.

She's not Michael or Draven or whoever the fuck.

She is *herself.*

Her *own* goddamn person.

A person that I *want* and *need.*

She doesn't need to hide herself from me.

She may have hidden that boy, but she's never hidden herself from me.

She *loves* me.

Loves me.

Isn't even afraid to say that.

But, Michael.

He pushed me to see the other side.

He made me *think* in ways that I never have before.

Challenged me.

He didn't accept my bullshit at face value.

He didn't love me out of *compatibility*.

He needed my *whole* being, out of a lustful devolution into a nostalgia for the past.

I have become *that* girl now.

I have become the girl that my Moms warned I would become if I didn't find a suitable match and get married.

Goddessdammit.

I didn't want them to be right.

Why did they *always* get to be right?

Why did they *always* get to tell me how badly I had messed up?

How could they just *know* what was right?

They were only human too.

How on earth could they know?

Somehow they knew.

Somehow, about Michael, they were right.

My head hurt, knowing that the future was crystal clear.

Although I had asked her for my freedom, in this moment, I would gladly run into her open arms.

I would have to settle down with Felicity.

Actually settle down with her and that *boy.*

Shit.

CHAPTER 57

Work had pulled her away from her marital and familial obligations.

Natalia was pissed at herself for not acting on the information that Olivia had given her about the *child.*

Now there was this.

Natalia hadn't been convinced that her daughter was so immersed in the world of men's bullshit until she had seen all the pictures of Althea with Michael.

On that damned woman's damned phone.

She hadn't paused to consider the possibility that it could have been even *worse* than what she had been anticipating.

"Draven Alec."

The second that those words slipped Olivia's mouth, she had sunk deeper into herself.

That fucking worm.

Natalia's strength was maintaining composure in difficult situations.

Then, in private, she could have a proper meltdown.

She shoved past people rapidly trying to get home, as there was a curfew set due to the men's rights protest in the city.

Even though she hadn't boxed in years, she wanted to grab her gloves and hit every person that walked past her.

Especially the men.

She couldn't bare the sight of a testosterone-filled creature walking past her without a bruise.

All her carefully laid plans were coming undone.

All her hopes and dreams for that *spoilt* girl.

The "excuse me"s and "ugh"s were drowned out by the struggles of her rational mind to maintain composure over her emotional one.

She felt heat burn through her whole body.

The fever crept up from deep inside her stomach into her neck.

Frustrated, her head about to explode, she fumbled for her keys in her purse.

When she got inside, she dropped her bag on the floor.

"Mags! *Mags*!" she screamed.

Where the hell was this woman?

"Mags *goddessdamnit*!"

She raced upstairs.

The emptiness, along with the smell of lilacs, hit her nostrils the second she got into their bedroom.

Her stomach churned.

She gagged.

How had I missed this?

For months, she had suspected *something* had been amiss with Althea.

She had hidden enough.

She raced downstairs trying to get away from the smell, the emotions, and the thoughts that kept circling in her head.

The kitchen smelled like citrus.

She inhaled deeply.

She began opening and closing the cupboard doors with loud thuds.

She wouldn't get away with this.

Adrenaline coursed through every vein in her body.

She began to see dark spots in places where stark white plates existed.

She shook her head a few times before staring at the same spot again.

She rushed to open the top drawer.

Four knives.

In pristine condition.

Polished and sharpened by Magda.

Goddessdamnit!

She couldn't.

If she killed her own offspring, she would be considered unstable and therefore unable to hold her position as the Ministress of Female Health and Well-Being.

Shit!

She pulled out the biggest knife.

She pulled the tissue box close to her and stabbed it twenty times in quick succession.

Next!

She pulled out every plate from the drying rack and smashed it onto the floor.

Next!

She pulled off her socks and carefully walked on the broken plates until the bottoms of her feet bled out onto the kitchen floor.

Every cut made her cry out in pain a little louder than before.

That's how she had known how to cope.

That's how she was told to get to the grief stage as quickly as possible.

She found a more effective way to get to the finish line.

She walked on the broken plates.

Anger to sadness. Anger to sadness...

CHAPTER 58

Magda saw the lights creeping through the living room window covered with the pale peach curtain she had picked out a few years ago.

She knew she had to ask her wife about the woman she had seen at the cafe.

Solemnly, she braced herself for the impending confrontation.

This time, she was resolved to stand her ground.

When she opened the front door, she noticed Natalia's purse on the floor.

"Natalia?"

"Love! Darling! Beautiful baby," Natalia cooed, looking up at her.

She saw Natalia polishing the floors of the kitchen. A sight she had never seen in their thirty two years of marriage.

"What are you doing?"

"Oh, I had a bottle of wine crack and spill everywhere."

Natalia gestured towards the kitchen floor.

She put the handle of the wet jet against the wall and stared at the ground.

Magda felt her pulse quicken with anticipation as hot blood rushed through her veins.

She had to ask her *now*.

She had no choice.

She *had* to know.

Natalia's odd behaviour could await further scrutiny.

Magda firmly placed a hand on Natalia's, pulling her towards the couch.

"We need to talk."

Natalia pulled her wife close and kissed her deep.

Magda could smell coffee on Natalia's breath.

Lies.

There was no *wine* involved in this cleaning process.

Magda wanted to demystify her wife as quickly as she had become a stranger to her.

As they sat down on the couch, face to face, Magda braced herself for Natalia's outburst.

"Nat, where were you?"

From the corner of her eye, Magda saw the boots that still covered Natalia's feet.

She compartmentalized the odd observation into the 'things to ask later' part of her brain.

Magda kept her focus on Natalia's face.

Natalia felt woozy from the blood loss, but she held onto Magda's hands for dear life.

She knew she had to come clean before she fainted or worse.

"I had hired someone to look into Al. I was meeting that woman."

The insides of Natalia's boots were soaking in blood.

"Don't lie to me, Nat. I saw you. You were...*intimate* with her."

"You *followed* me?!"

Natalia felt herself slipping in and out of the conversation, blinking rapidly while trying to keep her focus on Magda, unable to fully articulate her ire.

"Yes, I followed you," Magda sighed. "I was worried that something was going on."

"How long? How long have you been following me?"

"Just today."

Natalia felt her eyes dart wildly.

Magda's face scrunched up until she frowned.

"Please, don't cry. Don't cry, baby."

Her blood-soaked socks would have given her away had she not put on her rain boots.

Why hadn't Magda asked about the rain boots?

Natalia suddenly became fixated on the notion that Magda no longer cared about her enough to question her strange choice in attire.

That's all she could think about until Magda began to sob uncontrollably.

"I'm sorry I questioned your loyalty."

She sobbed into Natalia's shoulders as Natalia held her close.

This was the woman she knew and loved.

This was the woman that Natalia had married.

She hugged her back, but mostly for her own stability.

Once a few minutes had passed and Magda's sobs had turned into sniffles, Natalia pulled herself away.

"Mags, listen to me: Al has been spending time with that *loon* who writes those evil things online."

The blood-soaked socks would have to wait.

The bandages were ill-equipped to create the blood clots necessary to slow the bleeding.

Magda sniffled.

"Are you able to focus, Mags?"

Natalia blinked rapidly as Magda's face began to blur in front of her.

Magda nodded through sobs.

She no longer felt the courage she had when storming into the house with the intention of berating Natalia about her cheating.

Her daughter was *not* who she thought she was.

That scared her into silence even more than Natalia's snooping.

"W-what about Felicity?" Magda asked, suddenly incredulous at the notion that her daughter wasn't committed.

"What *about* Felicity? She probably doesn't even *know*! The poor girl has been overwhelmed with a *child*."

"I knew about the child."

"You...you *knew*?"

"Felicity called me. She said she needed my help and that I could talk to you better than she or Althea could."

"Goddess damn it! Every time, every *damn* time, there's something new! I can't get *through* to you people!"

Natalia got up off the couch suddenly.

She had to *do* something.

She realized that her feet were cramping up.

"Agh!"

She grabbed her feet and yanked them out of her boots.

The rush of blood from her head to her toes left her feeling unbalanced.

She tipped over and fell to the floor in agonizing pain.

Magda gasped as blood began to ooze out of Natalia's feet onto the perfectly clean floor.

The sight overwhelmed her sensitive stomach.

She collapsed onto her knees next to her wife and clutched her stomach in an attempt to stop herself from retching.

"Call the doc..."

Natalia fell unconscious.

Magda shook her for what felt like hours.

"Natalia! Natalia! Wake up! Wake up! Oh my goddess!"

Magda felt adrenaline take over her brain.

She rushed over to her purse and dialled her wife's office straight away.

"That's the quickest way to get medics to our door, Mags," she remembered Natalia had said when she first started working as the Ministress of Female Health and Well-Being.

Within two minutes there were women rushing to her wife's side and treating her injuries.

Magda struggled to find composure through all the buzzing activity around her.

Through the chaos, she managed to leave an incoherent message on Althea's answering machine.

A few hours later, Natalia woke up from her forced sedation.

She was confronted with the harsh reality that her daughter had merely sent her some flowers.

Not a visit.

Not even a *phone call* to her Ma.

Just flowers.

CHAPTER 59

Sigma was given a choice: either hang him on a tree for everyone to see, or cut off his balls.

The recent protests around the country had stirred up in Sigma an even more *intense* desire for blood.

She knew *exactly* what she was going to pick.

It wasn't that difficult for Sigma to know which punishment fit which crime.

By some bizarre luck, or just a heinously miraculous turn of events, one of the two CFOs of PepsiCo, charged with domestic violence against his daughter, had managed to settle out of court.

Supposedly the fucker had had the *nerve* to grab his daughter's hair and shove her head towards her mother.

He claimed it was to get her to apologize for being disrespectful to her mother.

The story had made headlines for weeks, until there was nary a peep from anyone.

That's when Sigma's antenna went up.

The man was a multi-*billionaire*.

He was *hated* by the women in power and had thus kept a low profile until that point.

Weeks of buzz around him and then *nothing* for a few days made her nervous for the women in his life.

She recalled the events leading up to the Larding murder-suicide that happened in the early sixties. She knew that silence by the media only meant one of two things: either they were told to shut up because the bastard was going to be taken to court to have his life stripped from him in Fangsel, or something terrible had befallen both him and any women with whom he was closely associated.

With the Lardings, the fucker had decided to slip sleeping pills into everybody's food.

A lethal dose.

Coward.

Men.

The sons of bastards always had to take out both themselves *and* the women who had refused to evolve and leave the men of their lives behind.

Sigma understood that sometimes it was the promise of inherited money that lured the women to stay.

She couldn't imagine herself being *that* naive.

Then, all of a sudden, a breaking news bulletin yesterday showed Mr. CFO of PepsiCo signing away his estate and half of his net worth to his daughter.

Too little, too late.

He was one of the few fuckers still lingering around after having made billions back in the twenties and thirties.

Through whispers in the wind and some digging by the Cavaliers, she had gotten hold of his whereabouts. They put him squarely between two blocks of where she currently was.

She was promised a wondrous sum of cold hard cash by someone if he was made to pay a hefty physical price for the bruises he had left on his daughter's neck.

That poor woman.

When she saw him from the corner of her eye, she was finishing up her coffee in her to-go cup at the intersection of St. Flounder's and Percy.

He was getting out of his car.

It was dead at this time of evening in this neighbourhood.

No one would be a witness.

She nodded towards the fair-haired women waiting across the street.

Before he could close the driver's side door, he had been tackled to the ground by three sets of muscular arms and gagged with a chloroform rag.

When he woke up, he was in his hotel room with the end of a broomstick shoved into his rear, looking up at the ceiling.

His screams were barely audible through the gag when he saw that his testicles had been cooked sunny-side up and served to him on a two-hundred dollar china plate for breakfast on his night table.

CHAPTER 60

As much as I wanted to be there for my Mom, I couldn't.

Not in this state.

One look at my face would tell her that I was wallowing in self-pity.

She would ask a *million* questions and I would have to lie.

Again.

Lying is what had gotten me into this mess.

As pathetic as it was, I missed the man who had told me that I wasn't good enough to be his intellectual equal.

I missed his voice.

I missed the way he smelled.

I missed that I could escape the monotony of the life I had with Felicity, my moms, and work.

Since it was dark, hot, and humid, I missed him even more.

Nights were the worst.

I reached for the book he had given me a few weeks ago.

"It's written by a gay man, so you can probably read it in public without any odd glares."

The Picture of Dorian Gray.

Although my eyes glanced over at the words, I couldn't stop thinking about that horrible fight we had had.

"Maybe you should read more."

I threw the book against the wall. As it slammed against it in a loud thud, out fell a bookmark that he had given me.

I remembered the quote on it like the back of my hand.

A man can be himself only so long as he is alone; and if he does not love solitude, he will not love freedom; for it is only when he is alone that he is really free.

Schopenhauer.

I scrambled into my purse to look for my phone. He had downloaded his favourite melody onto it.

His favourite melody.

I put my earphones in and pressed play.

I heard the needle brush against the record as the melody began.

I tucked my phone into my bra, freeing my hands to let them move in tune.

I looked around in frantic fear at my empty apartment.

Searching for any eavesdroppers.

I was overwhelmed with guilt at enjoying a piece of Michael again.

Bach's cello prelude began to envelop my mind.

I walked to my bookshelf where I had stashed all the books by all the female authors that I had been told were the absolute best ones to read.

This man's beautiful composition made me feel like I was climbing out of a well; being drawn out like a bucket of water against my will, unable to resist.

It felt like a *crime* to never hear his most melancholy compositions.

It was a crime to listen to him as I was.

He was not an artist suitable for consumption by womankind.

If someone knew, saw me, like this, they would lock me up, put me on pills, shock me until I reignited my passion for the Bingens of the world.

The intermezzo amplified my paranoia.

I wanted to hide, so I bent forward all the way until I could hug my legs and wrap my arms around them while staring at the floor.

I would rather be in *Fangsel* than never listen to this most *marvellous* piece of history.

I bent towards my toes and mimicked putting on a pair of dancing shoes.

My heart swelled with a deepening understanding of what I had missed out on, as I rose to the first position with my arms.

I let tears fall down my face as I closed my eyes and nodded my head side to side in harmony.

I pliered, sautered, and elancered all over my apartment.

I felt like Nina in Black Swan.

Just as the courante began to embrace my mind in its complex notation, I began to feel an overwhelming sense of courage to rip up *every* piece of Virginia Woolf I owned.

I darted back to my book shelf.

I began to rip through a Room of One's Own.

I didn't need her freedom anymore.

But here, in Bach's melody, I felt *freedom*.

Free to enjoy a man's work.

CHAPTER 61

Natalia's feet healed faster than she expected.

Less than week after her catwalk on the broken plates, the bottoms of her feet showed signs of scabbing.

As long as she didn't itch at the scabs, the doctor said that she would be walking without pain in no time.

Natalia shuffled uncomfortably in the hospital bed, trying to find the perfect position to rest.

She grew more irritated with each passing second at both her incapacitation and her daughter's freedom from repercussions.

While her anger had seemingly made her recovery accelerate, the sedatives had made it hard for her to *act* on her desire for revenge.

She had managed to read the one text from Olivia that assured her that reprieve from the distress was imminent.

She had an address.

She daydreamed about the way in which she would inflict pain on *that* man.

She imagined choking him until he was unconscious.

She pictured him being hung off the side of Fangsel.

She wanted to yank his balls until the skin stretched to its limits.

She imagined *paying* someone to do that to him.

She knew women.

Who knew women.

Who would get the job done.

She blinked hard, trying to regain focus.

The intravenous sedatives had kicked in again.

It had been five days of pure hell.

She needed to make that man *suffer*.

For all those horrendous things he wrote.

For touching her only daughter.

For being a *man*.

She recalled with sudden fury that Althea hadn't come to see her in the hospital. The recollection felt like a knife plunging straight into her heart.

She held on to that rage when she turned to face her wife.

"Mags. *Mags*, are you awake?"

She didn't realize how weak she sounded.

Rage.

"Yes, sweetheart, what do you need?"

Rage.

"I need to get out of this place."

"You're being discharged in less than a day!"

Rage.

Magda wanted to push her back on the bed. The caretaker in her *knew* that this is what she *should* be doing, but the glint in Natalia's eyes made her think twice.

"You're on sedatives, Nat. Be sensible. We can leave tomorrow."

Magda brushed her face with the back of her hand.

The maternal gesture wasn't met with kindness in return.

Natalia slapped it away and grabbed her forearm instead.

"I *said*, I want to fucking *leave.*"

Natalia blinked rapidly, trying to fight off the incoming medicated comatose.

Magda didn't move.

Her arm was bruised with fingerprints.

Slowly, Natalia's hand loosened its grip as she blacked out.

The next morning, Magda was ordered to get into the car and *drive*.

Natalia stayed in the passenger seat, drinking coffee, wide-eyed.

Magda didn't dare ask her where.

Natalia simply sipped her coffee, nursed the wounds on her feet, and barked out directions.

Magda did as she was ordered to do.

Obedient.

CHAPTER 62

When Sigma saw what little effort Martina had put into her appearance before coming to The Queen on King Street, she *knew* it was her payday.

That was the thing with these shady types in law enforcement. They always wanted to hide their *true* natures under the humility that the uniform represented.

Their outfits had to scream 'Look at me, I make a government salary!'

As such, they couldn't been seen parading around in Stella McCartneys.

Sigma knew that there was an underbelly of officers with offshore accounts that they could tap into to send their precious kids to precious universities so that they could become just as *precious* as their mamas wanted them to be.

Skinny jeans, a hoodie, and no makeup on Martina meant that she had told her equally law-abiding wife and kids that mama had to make a quick little pit stop to the Quickie Mart just before dinner to get a couple of beers and maybe some candy for the little ones.

Sigma kept her composure, but deep inside, she was *exhilarated* by the thought of another list.

She got a *high* off of just *knowing* that there were more that she was sanctioned to take down.

No authority in this city would touch a hair on her head as long as she had Martina's approval.

She had it. For *all* of them. The Pepsi CFO, the masturbator, and the many others, she and the Cavaliers had singlehandedly taken care of with zero hesitation.

When Martina's heels finally made it to underneath her table, Sigma stood up with her back purposely facing the wall behind the table.

Sigma kissed her on the mouth as though they were lovers while Martina stuck her hands into Sigma's jeans.

Martina slipped the cash into one of Sigma's back pockets along with another list.

When they finally pulled away, Martina cleared her throat.

"Thank you."

Sigma wiped her mouth with the back of her hand covered in a long sleeve pullover.

"I can't stay long."

Martina settled for the vodka soda that had somehow appeared at their table.

The lounge area was playing some nondescript heavy metal, which didn't leave much room for voices to hold conversation.

For the next ten minutes, they looked at each other in silence, nursing their drinks until finally Martina drank the last drop.

Sigma recalled the first time that Martina had found the Cavaliers.

Martina hadn't been introduced to Sigma until one of the Cavaliers had been given a stern warning by Martina to stay in their lane.

The poor girl, Amber, had just been doing what Sigma had told her to do.

"Cut off Mr. Goethrie's balls and feed them to his equally heinous son while he watches."

Martina hadn't felt compelled to take the Goethries' case seriously until she had met Sigma.

Once she heard the backstory of *why* Sigma had ordered Amber to do what she did, Martina was thrust into a world of suspicion about the justice system.

She spent her free time reading about too many cases where men got away. They had inherited money from their bastard dads who had secretly left them handsome sums in offshore accounts instead of leaving money to their daughters.

Sometimes it was the *women*, who had clearly *never* been wronged by *any* man, making sure that deplorable men were able to pay their way into maintaining a sickening lifestyle.

It was when she found out how many accused rapists got away with the crimes they had committed that she had become disillusioned with the system. Three years for touching a woman without her permission, at a club, while purporting to do great work for a woman's empowerment charity overseas was something that Martina *couldn't* tolerate as the law.

Day after day, as Amber was being held in contempt of the law, Martina received pictures and videos of the victims of men who had gotten away with their improper conduct.

These men didn't *deserve* to live with their family jewels intact if they violated women. They didn't *deserve* to have the opportunity to have their genes passed down from generation to generation while they made women feel unsafe.

It was only after she had seen pictures of the girl who had been raped by a man thirty years older than her that Martina had come to the sickening conclusion that the Cavaliers were necessary.

She had made herself retch until her intestines threatened to come out.

The man was only getting a slap on the wrist and a fine to donate half of his monthly salary to the girl's mothers.

First offence.

The judge had been a man.

This was when a few of them were still around.

That's when she had dropped the charges on Amber. She had slipped Sigma and Amber some cash to get that man off the streets.

Martina's colleagues questioned her decision, but didn't push too far.

Sigma had a *reputation*.

They had *all* heard about her.

The woman with the buzz cut and that knife.

In hushed tones, she was told by the authorities in charge that she had made the right move.

Martina had been a fresh-faced graduate of the Police Academy when the Goethries' case had fallen on her desk. Now, at forty-nine, with twenty-six years of experience in this unfair system, Martina was convinced that Sigma and her band of mischiefs were actually Sigma and her band of *necessities*.

They needed to put the law in its *place*.

The legal loopholes and sleazy lawyers who took cases like the Goethries' to this day made her stomach churn.

At the time, Sigma was making a name for herself too.

Twenty-six years ago, she believed that the police brought about justice.

Twenty-six years ago, Martina believed that the system would change for the better with time; and while there *had* been strides in favour of women, it was *never* going to be enough.

So, Martina became Chief of Police at the young age of thirty-five.

For that, she owed Sigma a great deal. Sigma got her the dirt on all her fellow officers to keep them blackmailed out of running for Chief.

Sigma made it clear, however, that the only thing she wanted were names, addresses, and most importantly, the *freedom* to deal with the bastards in *any* way that she wanted.

She had gotten the green light from Martina.

For that, she owed Martina a great deal.

It had helped her maintain her sanity. Given her *purpose*.

Martina slid the glass towards Sigma.

> "Next week, then?"

> "Yeah."

Martina went home that night. She peacefully made love to the woman of her dreams. She kissed her two perfect daughters.

Sigma read the four names. Four more bastards who would go down by the end of the week. Four less aggressors, potential rapists, potential molesters, and definitely four less *men* on the streets.

One of the four was a name that Sigma had heard right out of Martina's mouth.

Martina slept well that night, knowing that her father would no longer breathe the same air by the end of next week.

CHAPTER 63

Felicity hadn't brought up Michael again.

Thank goddess for that.

Instead she focused on the wedding, now that the guardianship papers had been signed.

I sent them to her in a drunk frenzy, cementing my future.

She demanded a champagne fountain.

I wanted a simple ceremony with a champagne toast.

I gave in to her demands.

It was going to cost my moms an arm and a foot, but I gave in to her demands.

Every two hours, I had another message waiting for me.

> "Remember that the Finks can't sit next to the Partriets."
> "We should probably just go over the guest list the next time you're over."
> "Aibek misses you, he just wanted to say hi."

Of course, that led to a minute of Aibek saying the usual pleasantries and telling me about his day.

Goddess!

The *clinginess*.

I felt nauseous.

Moms.

Hadn't heard from them.

About the flowers. About Mom. About anything.

No messages from Michael.

Goddess damn it!

None.

More than a week of deafening silence from him.

I had to do *something*.

Anything.

Work was draining me.

Life was overwhelming.

Waking up felt like a chore.

I had to go back.

I had to see him again.

Even if for one last time. I had to see his face.

I had to let him know that he had been more than just a tradeship.

But my body resisted the calling of my heart.

Follow your head.

So, I stayed put.

CHAPTER 64

Sigma had begun writing the names in her book only when she believed that there was no reason for their deaths.

She only wrote the names of those she believed were *innocent*.

Despite the rumours surrounding Martina's father, she put his name into her book.

She had to find out more before she could do the deed.

She had waited for Martina to put her father's name onto a list for over five years.

When it hadn't come as quickly as Sigma had anticipated, she had begun to suspect that he was either dead, or had been threatened to stay the hell away or be thrown into Fangsel.

Martina had pull. She didn't *need* Sigma to eliminate him.

Then, there it was.

Right there on that list of names: Jorge Flores.

Sigma didn't always *need* a reason to deal with the men on the lists, but she had to seek the right punishment for the right crime.

She needed to find a *way* to deal with Flores.

That was the problem.

That's why he was in the book.

When she found out his condition, she was perplexed at what punishment would be justified.

The man was breathing through a ventilator, holding on to the last few strands of his life.

Why now?

It was only when she heard back from her connection in the Juvenile Records Department of the Bureau of Justice that she realized what had happened.

Martina had had a *love-child* with her father.

A love-child whose records had been hidden to this day. Sigma couldn't even find out about the child.

This wasn't about her dad.

This was about the love-child.

Some little kid that had been dumped at the WEB, carrying Martina's DNA, and inevitably adopted into some family that Martina hadn't been able to find.

Sigma was perplexed that Martina hadn't gone the route of hiring someone to look into this kid's whereabouts.

She didn't dare question Martina about it.

Sigma understood what punishment fit the crime now.

It didn't matter to her that the man was on his death bed. Torture was worse than death. For every year that this child had been alive, a little slice by Sigma's knife would suffice.

Then, of course, the pulling of the cord.

It's what was expected for this kind of crime.

She crossed his name off in the book, leaving just one name standing alone.

At the top of the second page, scribbled in ineligible writing with a bloody thumb print partially covering the last name was: Holland Norman and the year 2067.

Long dead, but never forgotten.

CHAPTER 65

Martina saw Sigma waiting by the pool tables, so she waved.

Sigma waved back and smiled with all her teeth showing.

It wasn't like Martina to wave.

It wasn't like Sigma to smile.

Martina raced over in a semi-skip towards Sigma with two vodka sodas in her hands.

"We're celebrating," Martina said.

"That was the plan."

"Do you want to rack up the balls? I'll get us some fries or something."

Sigma watched as Martina's behind bounced a little more than usual all the way back to the bartender.

Grease and alcohol seemed like the combination from hell, but it seemed to work for their celebratory needs.

Sigma wished that whatever fat she ate would go directly to her breasts, of which she had none.

The flat chest and the buzz cut, however, had come in handy in her line of work.

She could blend in with men if she really needed to, and no one was the wiser.

Martina skipped back over just as Sigma had taken off one more cue stick.

"Are all of them gone?" Martina asked, smiling.

Sigma pulled Martina close so that their hips were touching.

Martina felt her heart drop into her stomach.

She put a stray piece of hair back into the long braid that Martina was sporting while looking deep into her eyes.

"He was on his death bed. Why *now*?"

Martina pulled back, struggling out of Sigma's arm around the small of her waist.

She positioned the white cue ball from where she wanted to break the nine.

"You did it, right?" she asked.

Sigma picked up the vodka soda on the pool table.

One long sip and the entire drink had disappeared.

"You say. I do. Remember?"

Martina searched Sigma's face for any signs of deceit, but she found none.

"Good," Martina said, as she sent the nine balls fleeing in all directions.

"Do you have another job for me?"

Martina picked up her vodka soda and sipped seductively while looking at Sigma.

"Your turn," she said.

"So, *do* you?"

"Win this game and I will give you the best job I ever could."

So Sigma did.

So Martina pulled out a fat envelope from inside her hoodie and pushed it into Sigma's hands.

Between the stacks of hundreds, there was a little piece of paper.

On it, there was just one name: Draven Alec.

CHAPTER 66

He looked around him.

He couldn't shirk the feeling that someone was watching.

Someone was always watching, of course, but this time the threat felt *closer*.

He had seen the same face numerous times in odd places.

The same face.

Again.

Here.

The alley behind the coffee shop where he would meet Althea, the bedroom window in his two storey apartment complex, the car across the street. Someone was always there.

Someone was always *watching*.

This same, plain-faced woman.

No expression.

Always.

There.

Had she gone and told people?

God fucking damn it!

All his interactions with the people he wanted to know about his secret alias were private, in hushed tones, behind closed doors, away from any cameras. He had let his guard down with Althea. He shouldn't have trusted her. Not like this.

He knew that with the internet, his public profile as Draven Alec, the man behind the resurgence of the MRAs, wouldn't be hidden for too long.

Especially with the ongoing protests now happening across the country.

He saw her, right there, in the corner of his eye.

Talking.

There was nothing wrong with talking on the phone.

Or being herself.

He could have asked why she was following him, and risk looking paranoid.

Once he knew the truth about the woman, he would no longer be able to invent stories to keep himself from losing his mind over Althea.

He climbed up the stairs to his apartment.

The door was open.

Slightly ajar.

He didn't remember leaving it that way.

His first thought was that the plain-faced woman had ransacked the place.

His mind instantly fled to the place where his hard drive and disposable phone were hidden.

He tentatively opened the door.

His head pounded.

He felt like he should pound it against the wall for being so completely *foolish*.

He rushed over to his centre table and ran his hand under it.

The little pamphlets he had stuck to the bottom of it were still there.

He looked around his living room.

Nothing had been tampered with as far as he could tell.

A cold shiver ran down his spine when he heard a sigh in his bedroom.

His heart beat faster.

He couldn't stop himself from going in.

He felt like a rat.

He *was* a rat.

A rat in the sewers that they wanted to catch and kill but kept missing because he had been too smart for the traps.

That was when he heard the shower.

The *drip, drip, drip* onto the floor of the bathtub.

How had he not heard that sound before?

In a panic, his heart pounding in his ears, he raced towards the shower.

Al.

It *had* to be Althea.

"Hello, Draven."

He stopped in his tracks and looked at the woman who had just stepped out of his bedroom.

He should have been more paranoid.

It could have saved him.

CHAPTER 67

It was the mere sight of her that sent shock waves down his spine.

She stood tall and proud in a hospital gown, holding her phone in one hand.

"G…get out."

"I will, but I need to make sure of a few things first."

"What?"

He stood frozen in place, watching her face contort into a disgusting smirk.

He would wonder for years to come why he didn't *run* in that moment.

"Are you and Althea in a tradeship?"

"Sh-shouldn't you be asking your own daughter that?"

He gulped hard when he saw the gleam in her eye.

"Don't try to play smart, *Michael*. Or should I just call you Draven?"

She inched closer to him and put her perfectly manicured nails against his freshly shaven face.

Her sudden movements made him almost soil his pants.

She waved her phone in his face. It was opened up to his latest blog post.

Althea must have told her.

How many other people knew?

Fuck.

"Oh, you have *no* idea how much this little *hobby* of yours has pissed me the *hell* off."

"Is that why you're here?"

She dug her nails deeper into his cheeks as she tossed her phone onto his couch.

He winced as she drew blood.

"No you goddessdamned *imbecile*. I'm here because you're *using* my daughter."

He felt her spit the words into his face and eyes.

He blinked hard and clenched his jaw as he felt blood drip down the side of his face and onto his neck.

His knees shook and his teeth clenched hard with fear, but he remained standing.

"It was consensual. But you still haven't answered my question; what do *you* want?"

She pushed his head back into the wall until he heard his skull crush against it.

"What do *I* want? I want *you* to stop using *our* daughter. Stick to using *men*."

He felt the blood rush into his brain and engulf his eyes in blackness.

All the adrenaline that he had been holding onto fell from his pounding head into the deep pits of his bowel and didn't stop until it felt like he had ants crawling up his legs.

The next few minutes seemed like a blur.

First he felt her flip him around.

Then he felt a jolt of electricity rush from his lower back into his legs, until they buckled and he fell to his knees.

He felt himself be dragged by the shoulders.

He felt the cold floor against his back.

When did my shirt come off?

That was when he felt two other hands on his legs, positioning him in some way away from the wall.

Two unrecognizable hands.

Four hands, touching him.

He believed that he was struggling against the hands that bound him to the floor.

He thought that he was struggling to get himself free.

When he opened his mouth to let out a scream, he realized that something was being crammed down his throat.

His mouth felt as dry as an hour after he had eaten that spicy Thai soup that one time.

He touched his tongue to the roof of his mouth, trying to moisten it again.

His tongue had expanded inside his mouth with thorny, prickly little ridges all over.

Before he knew it, there was another tongue inside his mouth trying to suck whatever saliva was left.

It sucked and sucked until every millilitre of saliva right up until his tonsils was *gone*.

He tried to swallow a piece of phlegm caught in his throat.

He groaned.

He was slapped.

His eyes shot open and he noticed colours that shaped out another human aside from Natalia.

His head pounded with a dull ache.

He struggled against the other woman's grip.

"Hold him down better, Mags!"

Finally! His body was listening to his brain.

Mags?

Who the fuck was that?

What the fuck was happening?

Slap!

Shock jerked him to full consciousness as he gasped for air.

He choked and coughed.

"Leave! No!"

Slap!

He felt blood gush into the back of his throat.

He had a full frontal view of who was straddling him.

"Shut up!"

He felt her hands around his throat, driving the salty, sickly taste of blood all around his mouth.

He blinked hard, trying to retain consciousness.

"Mags, *Mags*, you want a turn after I'm done?"

He couldn't hear the rest.

He felt warmth crawling up his shoulders and shooting straight into his arms.

"Ow!" He screeched.

He heard laughter.

His arms felt like they were being tickled.

He laughed.

"You like that, huh?"

He saw his arms grab hold of something that felt like flesh.

"Yes, just like that," he heard.

Her voice felt smooth, going into his ears reaching his heart.

He groaned in defeated ecstasy.

Why me?

He thought he heard himself cry, but he laughed instead.

"Yeah, I know you like that, you sick bastard!"

"Water…" he said meekly.

He stuck his tongue out and it was only met with the same mouth that had sucked it dry.

Water.

"Water…*please.*"

Slap!

He felt the right side of his face pushed into the ground.

One of his ears against the floor and the other being crushed by the weight of an arm.

He heard muffled moans through the gaps and water draining through the pipes through his floor.

It felt like he was being pulled down into the ground beneath the hardwood flooring, beyond the cement in the basement, and well into the dirt.

The weight on his body increased as he felt his nipples being pulled and pinched.

"Ow, OW!"

"Shut the *hell* up!"

He felt a hand cover his mouth as he slipped into a dream.

His eyes fluttered as they began to see the lucid images that his mind was conjuring.

He saw a house in the middle of the road.

The roof, worn down by the weather. The brick walls cracked, and paint matted against the brick barely holding onto its colour.

He felt himself *become* the ground, sinking deeper and deeper until his eyes stood still for a moment, beginning to recognize the place.

He was back at his parents' home as a young boy.

He ran down the road and straight into the house.

Everything was as it had been for *years*.

The same entry way, the same coats, the same table and chairs in the kitchen.

"Mom! Dad!"

He scurried into the kitchen.

"Mom! Dad! I'm home! Look! Look, it's me! It's Michael! I'm home! I'm home!"

His mom didn't stop yelling.

She kept yelling at his dad to make sure that Michael was showered and clean.

This would be the day that they would find out if Michael was worth keeping around.

He saw himself being told by his father to get out of bed as quickly as possible.

He saw himself willingly walk into a cocoon.

He burrowed himself into it, basking in its comfort and warmth.

He slept until he felt a push and a tug between his legs.

His wing was trapped in the tight confines of the cocoon that they had made for him.

He struggled until he felt a tear in his right wing.

He could feel the fear overtake his body.

He focused on what he had left — his six legs still intact, and one wing.

His drive to survive emboldened him to try even harder than ever before to push out with his strong, newly developed legs.

He kicked through the remaining shell as the bright light blinded him.

He ignored the pain that came with the bruised wing and pushed as hard as he could until he flew out into the light.

It was only when he left the comfort of his cocoon that he discovered the two eyes that had been peering at his struggle the entire time.

He had been made for the entertainment of some mad scientist.

Murmurs penetrated his dream only long enough for him to realize that the mad scientist wasn't real.

He still felt relief as he flew towards a jar with a sliced orange in it.

The scientist could have him, as long as he could suck on that delicious orange.

Parched.

Slap!

"You're no fun when you're asleep. You bastard! Wake the hell up," he heard.

Slap!

He licked his lips with his dry tongue.

"I just came anyway, you fucking piece of shit," the voice said.

He felt his head being jerked from side to side.

"Mom?" he asked aloud.

Snickers.

"Mommmmm?" he asked even louder.

Snickers.

"Everyone wants their mommy when they're helpless, don't they? Eh, Mags?"

He kept his eyes shut.

"Nat. Nat! You're bleeding! You're bleeding again!"

"Mags, stop being such a goddessdamned *nurse*. Come here, come on, help me up. You should try him out."

He felt some pressure release on some part of his body, but he couldn't quite pinpoint where.

"If you shove a bottle up there, he gets harder," she urged.

That same voice.

He felt something rammed into his ass.

Four hands tugged and pulled on his body.

He just wanted to slip back into the land of the mad scientist.

Fly around, carefree, and suck on the slice of orange.

So he kept his eyes closed.

CHAPTER 68

He gagged as the smell of her skin hit his nose.

He felt her body lay heavy on his weakened chest.

"Get —" he heaved.

His eyes glazed over as he felt himself slip into darkness.

Am I going to die?

"The bastard wants to say something. What's that?"

The voice cackled.

His wrists had gone numb where they had been pinned to the ground.

How did I get here?

The blood rushed to the tips of his hands, but the strength in them had disappeared.

The shower water was still dripping into the bath tub.

"— Off."

He saw Natalia's face upside down, above his, glaring into his eyeballs.

She slapped him.

"Don't you dare talk to my wife like that, you bastard!"

He felt the woman on his chest get off of him slowly.

He saw her thighs slick with sweat, as she pushed herself off the ground and reached for her underwear.

He turned his face away, closing his eyes tightly.

Slap!

He was being pushed up into a seated position, with his head being cradled by Natalia's strong hands towards Magda's bare body.

"*Get off*" wouldn't be his last words.

He was alive.

Lucky him.

He blinked rapidly, trying to shake off the rush of blood to his head.

He saw a pale woman with deep blonde hair putting on her jeans.

She turned to look at him with a blank stare.

Natalia held his head straight towards Magda.

"Look at her. Isn't she just *beautiful*?"

She laughed.

It wasn't sinister.

It was a genuine, hearty laugh.

As though she had just heard the funniest joke in her life.

She let him go and watched his head fall to the ground with a giant *thud*.

She chuckled.

"Mags, I think we wrecked him."

"Mhmm," was all Magda could muster up.

What have I done?

CHAPTER 69

When Magda got home, she ran to the bathroom.

She had hurled in a bag all the way home.

The smell of Natalia's blood, the taste of his, and the smell of bleach as they cleaned his place while he lay there motionless, had made her sick to her stomach.

Natalia had just sat in the driver's seat beside her without offering any comfort.

What have I done?

Natalia hummed her favourite tunes all the way home.

Now that Magda had made it to the bathroom, she tore the clothes off her body and tossed them into the bathroom trash.

She heard Natalia turn on the Swift album they had played at their wedding.

Magda turned the tap on as hot as it would go.

She drowned out the sound of the cheery music.

She settled herself into the bathtub.

The water was scalding hot.

She didn't want to feel her skin.

The heat stung, but she didn't care.

She poured the body wash over her exfoliator sponge and began to scrub her face.

She scrubbed her lips extra hard.

She remembered Natalia sitting on Michael's chest and her head being pushed towards his crotch.

Scrub.

Her lips were raw.

Yet she kept scrubbing.

She could still taste his anxious sweat inside her mouth.

Mingling in with the taste of his blood.

She scooped up the bottle of mouthwash off the bathroom vanity and poured it into her mouth.

She gargled and scrubbed her neck, her back, and her chest.

She saw small drops of blood on the exfoliator and yet, she kept scrubbing.

She wanted all traces of him *gone*.

She scrubbed all over her legs, her arms, and her torso.

Natalia sang the love song that made Magda nauseously nostalgic for a time before Michael, before Althea, before *any* of this had happened.

She stifled the feeling of throwing up in the bathtub.

She looked at the sponge, longingly, wishing she could put it deep inside of her and scrub her insides clean.

She bent over and hurled a concoction of mouthwash and hydrochloric acid into the garbage can sitting next to the tub.

She quickly recovered and picked up the mouthwash again.

Her body had gone numb from the heat of the water.

She sat in the bathtub, gargling, and closed her eyes.

His skin, his limp legs, Natalia on top of him…

NO! *NO!*

She spat out the concoction spinning in her mouth into the bathtub, letting it mix in with the soapy water.

She picked up her razor.

She looked at her left wrist.

She saw the vein.

The skin quivered as it beat along with the Swift song playing downstairs.

Thump. Thump. Thump. Thump.

She drew the razor tantalizingly close to the vein.

Thump. Thump.

She looked at it closely.

How easy would it be to just…?

She rested the razor on the side of the tub, gripping the bathtub hard and trying to regain some vestige of sanity.

She reached for the shaving cream, deciding to shave off every hair on her body except her head.

She carefully moved the razor against the skin of her legs and arms.

Thump. Thump.

She saw the vein again.

Reconsidering.

She spread her legs apart, feeling the soapy water against her pubic hair.

She put the razor between her legs and pushed it in.

CHAPTER 70

Last time I was in here, I was told to leave. Sort of.

The reverberations of that conversation haunted me the minute I walked in through his front door.

The air inside the apartment smelled stale.

I just wanted to make things right.

The clock struck eleven.

So close to midnight.

Where could he have gone?

If only I hadn't ignored all the muddy footprints on the floor, I would have had a clue as to what had happened barely a few hours ago.

I had fought the urge to see him.

I had told myself that a few more hours of Michael-less sleep would help me gather my thoughts.

When a short nap, boxing, spin class, and crying hadn't worked, I decided to swallow my pride and write him a letter.

I sat quietly on the one accent chair near his window, holding the pillow close to my chest.

Tick, tick, tick.

I had brought him that pillow from my place.

> *"I just want you to have a little piece of me. Something to hold, whenever you want to."*

"I love it."

We had cuddled in bed after that.

My eyes wandered around the room.

The corners were mostly bare.

With nothing to gaze at, I looked outside of the windows and tucked a foot under my rear.

Tick, tick, tick.

The streets were silent except for a plastic bag floating on the ground.

Across the street from Michael's apartment, through a window, I saw an old woman giving a young girl a glass of milk.

Tick, tick, tick.

I remembered when I gave up drinking milk.

11:10.

It started with Ma taking me to her Pa and Ma's dairy farm. I had always wondered what happened in there.

I was such a curious child. Ma and Mom really should have driven the curiousity out of me.

We drove in on a fairly normal Sunday afternoon in the summer.

I smelt the manure even before I set foot on the farm, but my excitement kept me from caring.

Ma gave her Ma and Pa a hug. More her Ma than her Pa. I remember that.

There were strong bulls out back near the mother cows. All behind metal bars. A few of the bulls were strapped down by some ropes and had a rod shocking them right where their tails were. There were buckets of something being collected.

I would later find out that this was the method used to forcibly extract semen from the unwilling bulls. Once they ran dry, they would be worked in a farm.

Then, everything goes blank in my mind regarding the next twenty minutes. I suppose we were just walking until we got into the calf crates. A few were marked with bright red X's. It should have been clear what was going to happen to them. I *should* have known, but being a bright-eyed, curious little eight year old girl, I kept watching.

"These are the boys, Al. They are useless for us," Ma said firmly.

Without hesitation she pulled the ones marked with the X's out of the crates and lined them up.

They were going to face a firing squad of one woman.

"This makes their moms stronger. They get to live with their baby girls, but the baby boys have to go."

One down. Shot squarely between the eye.

His eyes were so beautiful. He wasn't even terrified.

I remember being so shocked that I couldn't speak. I just kept watching.

Then the second. Then the third.

"This is the most painless way. I'll teach you one day."

Thankfully, she never got that chance as her Ma and Pa died and she sold the farm.

The smell of blood and manure finally hit me hard.

The moms would moo loudly in the background. *Boom, moo, bang, moo, bang, moo, moo, bang, bang.*

Relentless.

I wanted to puke as the boys' blood and brains splattered on the grass, but my body didn't respond and my eyes stayed wide open. Mom would have been so disappointed in me if she knew I had thrown up.

There were six boys.

I named the last one Bruno. I don't know why I named him. His brown patchy skin with the white tail reminded me of a dog I saw in a kids' book once. Also named Bruno.

I saw him look into my eyes with a look of blissful innocence, chewing a piece of cud. His ears flapped with the dry wind.

I just didn't know what else to do except stand there stupefied as I watched Ma shoot him squarely between the eyes.

His only fault was being born a boy.

Tick, tick, tick.

11:20.

I saw the girl and the old woman laugh while drinking their milk.

Seems like Michael isn't coming back tonight.

I left a letter on his centre table before walking out the door.

CHAPTER 71

He ripped through the envelope and read it once.

None of her words could erase what had unfolded over the last thirty six hours.

When had she come here?

He read it again.

Did she hear him? Them?

He read it again.

Dear Michael,

I truly am sorry for what transpired between us. I don't want to end things that way. I have cruelly ended things before with men when I was young and naïve, but I don't want to be that way with you.

I want you to know that I don't change my mind about the way that I feel about you. I don't think I am in love or just being with you because I want to infuriate my moms. You have just given me something that I was missing in my life. Some excitement, something different, and I am grateful to you for that.

I have known for some time now that you're Draven Alec, but I never used it against you or used it to blackmail you into staying with me. I need you to know that that's not the type of person that I am.

Please, just call me and we can talk things through. I want you in my life, for however long you can be there. I don't need you to be there for me forever, I need you now.

Yours, Al.

He read it one last time.

He almost wanted to call her, but what would he say?

"Hello, Al, your moms broke into my apartment and...*raped me.*"

He paced around the room, slowly ripping hair out of his skull.

Counting it one strand at a time.

He picked up the letter again and smelled it.

Searching.

Searching for her in the paper that held these words.

He shredded the letter into a million pieces, threw it into the sink, and let her words drown.

CHAPTER 72

Everything in the room kept spinning out of control.

The remains of the letter had finally vanished into the darkness, under the pressure of the water in his kitchen sink.

He replayed the sound of the door slamming shut as those two horrendous women left him alone in his apartment again.

He remembered trying to move his frozen limbs.

It had taken him what felt like a few hours to peel himself off the floor and clothe himself again.

The smell of bleach hit his nose with such strong intensity that he dizzily fell to the ground.

How did I get here?

He had kept asking himself.

Until the drug wore off, he walked around his apartment confused and numb to the events that had unfolded.

He had marched to the bar where they had had their MRA meetings, curled up into a ball, and slept there until last night.

Greeted by the letter, written by the daughter of the two women who had raped him.

He knew he should panic, act, storm like an out of control, terrified bull all over the room, burning every last trace of himself.

Burn it and start all over somewhere else.

He should run.

Just don't move.

He put his head in his hands, folding his knees into his chest, and he rocked himself back and forth.

"If you just put it in like this, he gets hard."

Tick, tick, tick.

The thoughts kept flooding in.

"Just hold down his arms. He isn't strong, Mags!"

"The more you hesitate, the more I want it. Bad."

He felt her drool in his hair as though it was yesterday.

As though he hadn't showered a dozen times since it had happened.

He felt her hot saliva all over his mouth and recalled his desperation for water.

"So you're hard for me, huh? Fucking good."

Her groping hands fondling every inch of his being.

He rocked himself back and forth again, shaking his head from side to side, trying to shake the memory of her.

He clenched his knees hard to stop himself from itching his inner thighs raw until the memory went away.

He imagined the scalpel threatening to carve into his vas deferens.

Slap!

He closed his eyes tighter.

A woman like her would *never* be punished for what she had done to him.

She might just flip this all on *him*.

He chuckled.

A terrified, throaty chuckle.

What if...?

No.

He couldn't go there. This wasn't the time.

He raised his fingertips to his eyes and pressed them in, trying to stop the stress headache coming on.

Act now, emote later.

But the mind had a funny way of racing.

Speeding through all the thoughts that it shouldn't bring to consciousness.

He tried to comfort himself by hugging himself harder, burying his head deeper between his legs until the soft scent of urine combined with the smell of body wash in his nostrils.

He could really use a pill to put him back to sleep.

He dejectedly got up, knowing that his mind would not cease unless he *made* it stop racing.

He walked into the shower with the full intent to drown himself.

He pulled off his boxers, standing naked in front of the mirror, letting soft tears fall down his face.

No one would miss him.

He turned on the tap, letting the water fall onto his back.

He didn't care if it was hot or cold.

He turned off the tap, dried himself, and then walked into the shower again to take another one.

As the water fell from the crown of his legs into the drain, he felt his body become unburdened by the emotions he had been holding in.

He cried out in agony, tasting his salty tears mingling with the water.

How did I get here?

   "Look at her."

No!

He got out of the shower, drying himself, leaving the water on.

He tied the towel around his waist.

He rubbed his eyes until they were red.

He danced around the room like a madman playing all the music that had been banned for the last half of the century.

He laughed.

He watched Ricky Gervais talk about humanity.

He cried.

He wept and wept until his entire pillow was covered in slobber and tears.

In the morning, when he heard the sirens outside his window, he *knew* it was the beginning of the end.

CHAPTER 73

I was sick of being alone.

It had been a couple of days since I had been to Michael's and left my heartfelt apology letter.

No New Messages.

I decided I had to make amends with *someone.*

Anyone.

I had to see my Mom.

I figured she could forgive me more easily face to face.

Without a second thought, I marched to Moms' and sat in the kitchen chair with her back facing me.

She said she would make us tea.

I felt her disappointment cloud the room.

Tick, tick, tick.

These stupid goddessdamned clocks.

"Mom? Mom."

"Yes?"

"I'm just so sick of pretending like I am this strong, independent, go-getter woman. I am *not* one, Mom. I am vulnerable and weak. I want to show emotions and wear my heart on my sleeve…"

I contemplated saying the rest.

"…for *men*."

I could see her head snap backwards towards me, defying all biological restraints as to how swiftly a human head could move.

"And I, Althea, am sick of *you* pretending like you are some low class *hooker* from the time that your grandparents fought hard as *hell* against, working to satisfy the needs of baseless, immoral, classless men like Draven Alec."

"How did you…"

"I went to his place actually. It's cute. I now understand why you kept saying you wanted to live in an apartment with huge windows."

I tried to rack my brain for any moment that I had given myself away.

"What does this mean?"

"What do you mean?"

"I mean, what does this mean, for *us*?"

I felt blood crawling up my neck, into my cheeks, making them bright red.

"Well, you and I are going to be *fine*. We have *always* been fine. No matter *who* you love."

I scanned her face for signs that she was being honest.

"Do you *mean* that?"

She looked me in the eye.

"Well, considering he *is* Draven Alec, you are off as *scot-free* as you could be."

She looked away.

I felt a hot flush of panic shoot right up from my spine, into my shoulders, up my neck, and turn my face red. The one bead of sweat that had been growing on my temple finally fell down the side of my face.

"Mom."

I couldn't quite place the emotion that I had seen in her eyes.

"*Mom*, look at me."

"Hmm…"

"What did you *do*, mom?"

"You will thank me later."

"Why…"

I felt a lump in my throat.

"Val's going to take care of the rest. You remember her?"

"Val?"

"Valentina. You know, the one who…"

"Yes, I know her. But, why, Mom, *why*?"

"She's the best one for the job."

She had a twisted smile plastered on her face.

I recalled watching The Dark Knight with Michael and recognized the Joker's look of madness all over my mother's face.

Has she gone mad? Truly and completely mad?

"*What did you do*?" I screeched at her.

"*Me*? I did absolutely *nothing*."

She looked at her feet, still smiling.

What was she thinking? What was she feeling?

Women were supposed to have high emotional intelligence. And yet here I was, with an emotional intelligence of *zero*, my head blanking every two seconds and my stomach in a knot knowing that everything was being pieced together.

I had been played. Hard.

"Fuck!"

"Mind your tongue!"

"Mom, *Mom*, square with me. Tell me what you did? What is happening to Michael? Where is he?"

I was desperate, searching for answers in her face, but she just smiled.

She could have lied.

She could have shielded me from the horrible truth.

"He's in Fangsel."

"*What?*"

"He. Is. In. Fangsel."

I blinked at her emotionlessly.

"Or will be anyway, soon."

CHAPTER 74

When they had come to get him, he was plucking away at the minimal hair on his balls.

He had just woken up from yet another one of his recurring nightmares.

This time, instead of a scalpel, a long dull knitting needle was being pushed through the opening of his penis.

Deeper.

Pushed deep enough until he could feel a little dull stab all the way in his anus.

Poke.

When he had woken up, he was trying to pull out the needle, grabbing and pulling at the air.

It didn't exist.

He had rushed into the bathroom to make sure there really *wasn't* a needle sticking out.

He had grabbed his crotch and squeezed until it was numb.

His new coping mechanism.

Then the plucking had begun.

It was soon after that they had barged in.

The police women had pulled him off the floor of his apartment.

He hadn't hesitated when they put handcuffs on him.

He saw their tasers and remembered the shock he had felt on his spine when Natalia had...

Relax, Michael, relax.

He knew that he would have eventually been arrested.

He had avoided getting caught in the protests for so long.

His luck had run out.

He knew that Natalia would have made herself the victim.

> "You understand, Mr. Nolan, that you are being arrested on the charges of possession and distribution of sexist materials?"

He had stayed silent.

Wait…What?

He nodded.

> "I need you to say it out loud for me, Mr. Nolan."

> "Yes, I do."

> "You have the right to remain silent and refuse to answer any questions."

> "I understand."

> "Anything you say may be used against you in a court of law. You have the right to consult an attorney before speaking to the police and to have an attorney present during questioning now or in the future."

> "I understand."

> "You will be given an attorney if you cannot arrange for one yourself."

He had already made the arrangements.

> "I want you to call Ms. Georgina Baer."

The guards looked at each other.

That was a name they had heard often.

> "We will in due time."

They pushed him out of his door.

He deeply inhaled his apartment's stale air, one last time.

He tried to remember everything.

The smell of the body wash lingering in the apartment.

The smell of the day old toast.

The smell of *her* on that letter he had drowned.

Breathe in.

CHAPTER 75

Two days after Michael had been arrested, Natalia knew what she had to do.

Valentina sat back in her chair.

She looked contemplatively at Natalia's furrowed brows.

A woman she trusted, knew well, and had brushed shoulders with on many occasions, had just told her that she had gotten a man arrested on charges of reading, writing, and promoting sexist material and perpetuating hate against women.

Valentina had nodded in approval, insisting that she would do everything in her power to make those charges stick and put him in Fangsel.

But in the past few minutes, Natalia had been trying to convince Valentina to convince the chief of police to also charge him with *rape*.

A crime whose punishment would be forced labour in prison for life, with the potential to be a living organ donor.

Such a punishment did not fit the crimes he had been detained for, awaiting trial.

"I am just trying to understand here…"

"I am telling you to take on this case as a personal favour for me and Magda."

"Okay, I understand, but…"

"Althea claims this man *raped* her. Isn't that enough?"

"Yes, it is, but that's *not* what he was initially charged with."

Valentina hesitated.

She couldn't believe that someone like Althea would end up in this position.

A woman with such good breeding, born to such an amazing pair of mothers, would *never* get involved with a man like Michael Nolan.

"*But* nothing! It's that simple. You know that the second he walks into that courthouse, Magda, Althea, and I *have* to get *our* justice."

"Is there any other proof that I should be looking for that he *did* in fact rape her?"

"Yes. They were having an affair for almost a year, Val, she…she was having an affair with a *man*, a *men's rights activist* for almost twelve bloody months and Magda and I…we didn't even know!"

"Holy shit. Do you mean to say that she was having an affair with *Draven Alec*?"

"He called himself Michael, but Draven it was."

"What the hell? How do you know that?"

"I had a PI look into him. Look, it doesn't matter how I know, I *know*. He's a *menace*. He's a piece of shit *bastard* who needs to be a *permanent* fixture at Fangsel, you understand? I can't have him *ever* coming out of there."

"Does anybody else know? Magda? Althea?"

"Althea knows. She came to me last night, looking to confess about Michael, and we have her back at home now."

"For the best. She should see a therapist. I know someone…"

"Yeah, Mags will take care of all that. But can you do this? Can you stick this on him? Look for Althea's DNA at that bastard's place. It's all there. Right there. Magda and I will testify, do anything to put that *man* away for what he did to my daughter."

"Of course. Any proof of their correspondence on the record that you can give me?"

"Lots. I just need to get into her phone."

"But that might only be enough to prove that she was in a consensual trade-ship…"

"Just because ninety-nine percent of the time it was consensual, that doesn't mean it was still consensual that last *one* percent of the time."

"You're right, I can argue that."

Natalia slammed her hands on the desk and swiftly got up.

"I shouldn't have to tell you how to do *your* job! I shouldn't have to give *you* ideas! You should just be doing it based on *fact*. And the *fact* is that Althea claims that Draven Alec *raped* her. Therefore, in the court of law, that is *true*."

"Nat, I *know*. I get it. Just sit and here, take this."

Valentina slid over a shot of whiskey, maintaining her composure despite the outburst.

"I don't drink."

"You should. Especially today."

"I should... I...thank you."

Natalia gulped her shot, feeling the warmth of the liquid trickle down the back of her throat.

"We will get Draven to Fangsel and keep him there *permanently*."

They both smiled.

Natalia eased into the chair, feeling the whiskey warm her brain.

Draven Alec would lose his head or his manhood.

To her they were one and the same.

CHAPTER 76

Michael looked outside of the greying window. The bus had jerked him awake.

He had been in a holding cell for what felt like two days, but it may have been shorter or longer. He couldn't tell.

The clock tower looked as sturdy as it had looked the day they had hung the entire Harrell family off its side.

He itched his eyebrow.

The salt had concentrated around his eyebrow from the sweat drying on his face.

He had been hauled off on an air conditioned bus early this morning.

There were blank spaces in his brain where chronological events should have led him to how he got on the bus.

How did I get here?

He saw three women wearing their police jackets, carrying their batons in their hands and tasers in their holsters.

They had the police women take testosterone to make them brutish and large. All of the police that he had encountered in his life had had some amount of facial hair, very broad shoulders, and deeper voices. These women in this bus were no different.

He fixated on one of them in particular. She had broad, muscular shoulders, blonde hair slicked back with gel, and a light moustache growing.

"What the hell are you staring at?"

She whacked him across the head with her baton and snickered as she sat down again.

The others laughed along with her. Deep, throaty laughs as the side of his head bled a little.

How many days have passed?

"I'm sorry."

"Yeah, you better be, you bastard!"

His eyes wandered back out the greying window.

He saw two bodies hanging off the side of the clock tower.

He could pretend *not* to know where he was headed, but he knew where he was.

His shoulders drooped forwards with the knowledge of what was waiting for him.

Fear crept into his throat and created a lump so huge that swallowing it was not an option.

He had heard the stories.

Now he would have to face all the same things that many men before him had.

He felt blood rush to his face.

He rotated his wrists in his handcuffs, pulling them apart and putting them back together again.

He began to shake his legs, mimicking a jogger.

He felt the bus jerk on a speed bump as the driver pulled into a gate with two cruel-looking female guards awaiting his arrival.

CHAPTER 77

A dark-skinned, straight-haired woman pushed him towards a room.

She didn't say a word to him, even though she kept a scowl plastered on her face the entire way there.

In the hour that it took to get from his holding cell to the main gate of Fangsel, he had seen more news reporters wanting to shove a microphone in his direction than he had seen in the thirty years he had been on this planet.

Reporters driving behind his bus as they escorted him to Fangsel.

He felt an odd sense of pride swell up deep within him.

When they reached the room, the guard took the shackles off his arms and legs.

"Take off your clothes."

"All of them?"

"Yes, all of them."

As if the ransacking of his place, the destruction of his life's work, and his heavily publicized arrest were not enough humiliation.

He felt a slight breeze circle around his feet.

Elsewhere, in the dark underground room of the abandoned bar, James gathered with the MRAs in their usual meeting spot.

Michael had a thumb stuck into his asshole.

At the abandoned bar, James turned on the TV.

Michael was told to get down on his hands and knees.

The reporter said, "In an unexpected turn of events today, the identity of Draven Alec was leaked to the press as *Michael Nolan*, who was arrested on charges of spreading hate speech against women in Draven Alec's blog. It is currently unclear whether Nolan was the *only* man behind the nefarious blog, or whether he employed other henchmen. More on this breaking news story at six with Katie Cunningham."

He screamed in pain while the woman in the grey uniform branded the back of his shoulder with his prisoner number.

He was injected with something immediately after.

The men murmured and gasped in surprise around the screen.

He crawled on his hands and knees like a dog on a lead until he was swiftly kicked in the rear and forced to scramble upright.

   "Get up!"

He wondered if he would ever see what his unique alphanumeric code was.

The men wondered what would happen to him.

He suddenly felt completely calm.

They scrambled to find out what had happened to his blog.

The guard scrambled to put the handcuffs back on him once he stood alert.

James put his arms around himself and rubbed his hands up and down in an attempt to comfort himself when he saw the blog had vanished.

Michael was as exposed as he had ever been. Yet he stood proud and tall, with his shoulders back and head held high.

By now, his name would be on everyone's lips.

Followed by: *what a bastard, my hero,* or *shit, I knew that guy.*

The final shove of his naked body into the cell, which was a freezing cold room with one toilet, no bed, and a clock ticking high up on the ceiling, made Michael fall to his knees in defeat.

They won.

Those women *won.*

He would spend seven miserable days in this four by ten cell, unable to wipe his own ass.

His hands bound in front.

He wouldn't be able to plug his nose to avoid smelling himself.

He got used to the smell on what felt like the fourth day.

His grumbling stomach became his consolation.

The water from the sink helped fend off temporary pangs of hunger.

He heard no one.

No guards.

No women.

No men.

He tried to ignore the clock, but he never could.

Tick, tick, tick.

On and on it went.

When he was released to shower on the eighth day, he tried to shove the shower head into his ear just to drown out any sound.

It was too big a hunk of metal.

Permanent ear damage would have been better than having to hear that incessant ticking any longer.

CHAPTER 78

Mom urged me to take the sleeping pill.

Again.

She coaxed me into it, but I don't think I even *had* to be convinced.

I knocked it back without a second thought.

I was out like a light for a good thirty-six hours.

Then they both came into my room with that goddessdamned therapist, and I screamed until they left.

Rape.

What had happened?

I wondered the exact same thing.

I had to say he *raped* me.

What was happening?

Rape.

How did they find out about us?

Oh, wasn't it obvious!

I had been foolish!

I had been stalked.

For days.

Followed like a criminal for days.

Seen through glass windows, tailed in the subway, and treated like a cheat.

Stalked all the way to Michael's apartment.

Stalked all the way back to my apartment.

Stalked to Felicity's.

I felt as though all the perfectly curated lies to get away from the peering eyes of my moms and Felicity had been for naught.

Valentina was involved.

Felicity was involved.

Somehow, and I had no idea how, I was the *only* one left with nary a clue as to how they had all conspired against me and Michael.

They wanted him *gone*.

Here he was…*gone*.

Gone all the way to Fangsel.

Goddess only knows what the hell was happening to him in there.

Thinking about it now, after the therapist had given me my hormone stabilizers, made me feel absolutely nothing.

Water.

I reached for the glass that had the aspirin dissolved in it from hours ago when either Mom or Ma had come in to see my sleeping body.

I gulped it down in one go.

I sputtered on the volume of water.

I felt the water rush up my nose, burning my nostrils on its way out.

I tried to breathe in deeply to catch my breath.

When my breathing had returned back to normal, I looked around my childhood room with an increased desperation to do something.

The adrenaline rushing through my body after having almost *choked* to death made me irritable.

I hadn't looked at myself since I got here.

That realization led me to the bathroom.

I purposely avoided looking in the mirror when I went in.

I needed to ease myself into it.

After a shower, the *one* shower I let myself take for the first time this week, the steam clouded the entire bathroom and the mirror.

I saw a blurred version of myself in the mirror as I wrapped the towel around my body.

I turned away from the mirror as quickly as I possibly could.

Any vision of myself would mean I had to *face* what I had done.

I would have to face *myself*.

"What is Michael being charged with, Mom? What did you do?"

*"Rape. He **raped** you, Althea."*

"No. No, Mom, he didn't! How can you say that?"

"You're telling me you willingly walked into that man's apartment all this time? What the hell is wrong with you?!"

*"Yes, I **willingly** walked in! So what?!"*

*"So what?! So **what**?! That man is an evil, sexist, misogynistic monster! He **is** Draven Alec! Or did you forget about that?"*

She had come straight up to me and glared into my eyes.

I had sat down, with fear buckling my legs under me.

"You're going to say what I tell you to say. You understand, Althea? You got that? If not, I won't hesitate to throw you in that place along with him."

"Yes, Mom."

Rape.

That's what I had to say he did to me.

Ever since that conversation, I had hid in my old room like a little melodramatic piece of shit.

Ma was in the other room.

She never came out.

I didn't ask why.

Now would be the right time to go to her.

Ask her what she knew.

With such conviction in my mind, I fell to the floor of the bathroom and wept until I laughed.

I laughed at the absurdity of the situation.

I laughed at how quiet the entire house had been this entire time.

I laughed and laughed until I cried again.

I pulled myself off the floor and into bed to stare at the wall clock in my room until night time.

Tick, tick, tick.

It was so quiet I could hear myself breathe.

I dared not go outside my room again.

CHAPTER 79

Was there *finally* going to be a new man in here?

Azazel had been so bored for months that she had taken up playing cards with herself.

Someone *exciting* needed to come around.

The toilet felt hollow under her ass.

It was useless trying to push anything out.

She had been on a water fast since finding out that she had gained over ten pounds from just being in here.

Shitty food.

She got up from the toilet seat and wiped whatever bit of piss was left over.

When she was decent, she beckoned to the guard outside her cell.

The brunette guard nodded.

"Rosie, get me Norma."

Two minutes later, Norma was at her cell door.

"Yeah?"

"Introduce me."

Women and men weren't separated in the prison anymore. Once the procedure was done on a man, he was safe to integrate into the regular prison.

"He isn't clean yet."

"Then introduce me at night."

"Done."

Azazel walked over to her cot.

She brushed a few strands of grey hair off of her face.

She smiled to herself.

She could hardly contain her excitement.

CHAPTER 80

Michael had jolted upright, gasping for breath, as he tried to recover from a series of repetitive nightmares that he had been having for the past few nights in his cell.

He looked around at his new residence.

No more handcuffs.

He was free to wipe his ass when he wanted.

Across his cell, a large man with a beer gut slept on the floor, snoring through his mouth.

Freud would have probably called his new nightmares "a longing for the warmth of the womb", or maybe just a longing to get *out* of the fucking womb.

They always began with his body being flung from the side of a helicopter.

He would frantically try to grasp onto the rope that bound his legs, doing all sorts of anti-gravitational backbends.

Useless.

Eventually, the tips of the hairs on his head would graze the ocean waters in the middle of the night.

Then, he would be dropped.

The ropes would be cut or released.

Never the same way.

Always a different person doing the cutting.

First night, it had been his mother.

The second, Althea.

The third, James.

Sometimes the person above would make deliberate eye contact as they were cutting the rope. Other times, they would become faceless as they dropped him into the dark abyss of the ocean.

As he fell into the deep darkness that was the middle of the ocean, he could feel himself clasp his hands together in a namaste as he braced for the water.

The first night he couldn't *move.*

There was just the sound of a huge *plop.*

The displacement of water.

Then, his whole body being submerged.

He would swim and swim until he couldn't swim anymore.

He would swim frantically trying to get out, until he ran out of breath.

He would swim harder when he saw all the different sea creatures baring their teeth and speeding at him to get a taste of his fresh meat.

Somehow, they would *narrowly* swim past him and towards each other instead.

Eating, feeding, gnawing at every bone they could find until all the prey had dissolved into a red, sickly liquid that covered his entire body.

That's when he would freeze, breathless, diving deeper underwater, so paralyzed by shock that he could fight no longer.

Only when he was beginning to drown in a pool of his own drool, a sensation so eerily similar to drowning in a bathtub, would he jerk awake.

His eyes would struggle to adjust to the dim lighting in his cell.

He would gasp for air, breathing in quick, short bursts until his breath steadied.

He would attempt a cough when he could barely get enough fresh air into his lungs.

One.

Cough.

Two.

Cough.

It was useless.

The second he closed his eyes, he was back in the darkness.

He would wake up in the middle of that ocean in the cover of night, drowning —
and yet somehow, still alive.

Althea!

CHAPTER 81

Darrin had decided that a change of venue is what he needed to write and think.

He wanted space from the insanity that had become his domestic life with James.

It was a continuous barrage of emotional breakdowns after James' clean-ups with the city, and questions about when Darrin would *finally* get help.

Even though it was well past five in the evening in the dark of winter, he left to go out to the nearest cafe.

He told James he was going to get help.

HAA - Heroin Addicts Anonymous.

He searched for hours, but all the programs were closed off to men.

He sat at a table for two overlooking the street, and pulled out his journal.

His plan was to publish his testimony *somewhere*. *Anywhere* that would accept it.

Even if it meant staying anonymous.

As long as someone could benefit from what he had to say, he cared little if he got credit for these words.

He slowly scratched out the names of the women.

This wasn't about exposing Althea or any *one* woman in particular. He just wanted to expose the abuse that happened behind the closed doors of these bars and houses.

The hustle and bustle outside reminded him that it was, in fact, the holidays.

People out shopping for nonsensical knickknacks that didn't satisfy anyone's need for *community*.

He remembered that he still had to get *James* a knickknack.

This year it had to be *bigger*.

He had screwed up.

He had *been* a screw-up.

He hadn't been sober when James had needed him, but he couldn't dwell on that now.

He began writing:

December 6, 2075 —

I feel like a fraud. I have been depressed. Depressed because I'm bored. Bored because I can't find work. No one will hire me. Not even for petty labour. I am too small, too weak, too something. That's the problem these days.

He paused and looked outside the window.

He looked up and saw a pair of heads on the second floor watching something on T.V.

It looked like a movie.

He resumed:

I want to have what women have. I want to have a life, a goal, a career so that I can actually wake up every morning without having to apologize for my existence.

I feel like a burden on James. I need something to do. I've let my brain go numb from the boredom so many times that I just want to get high to escape it.

I want to escape, but where can I go?

I see these beautiful places to travel, but James and I can't afford it. How can we if only one of us is working, and even then only part time? We can barely afford our studio as it is.

I wish my mothers had kept me and raised me and fought for me. Why did they dump me onto the street and force me to fend for myself? In a world that doesn't fucking want me?

Why didn't they want me? What about me made them so disgusted that they couldn't bear to live with me anymore?

I could always try to go back to that life, become what Gary was, a house Mister, but then I would just be bestowing the same fate on other young boys.

Do I want that?

But having money would mean that I would have the freedom to go to these places that I want to see with James. I wouldn't be a burden anymore.

I have always loved numbers, maybe I could be good at it.

He looked up at the couple on the second floor and let his eyes wander to their T.V. screen.

His eyes widened at the news report that they were watching.

Her.

He saw her face.

He got up and moved closer to the window, pressing his face against it.

Passersby looked at him strangely, but he didn't notice.

He squinted to try to make out the words, but one stood out like a sore thumb.

Rape.

He gathered his belongings and bolted out of the cafe.

CHAPTER 82

For weeks, Darrin had been moping and sulking around the house and there had been *nothing* that James could have done.

Until this evening.

After finding out that Michael had been taken to Fangsel, James had marched back home with determination in his step.

He had met with the MRAs and had gotten the go ahead to storm the court house.

They knew it was a death wish.

But Michael had been *one of them.*

He couldn't *possibly* have done what they were claiming he did.

James knew this in his heart.

Michael was being *targeted.*

Falsely accused.

How could that abhorrent woman ever *know* what rape *felt* like, when she had done *that* to him?

The fact that he was Draven Alec and had been in a consensual trade-ship with a girl who just *happened* to have a mother with political pull was too sensational for this *not* to be a targeted hit job.

He still remembered how Michael would open the door for his lady friend, and how she would gladly accept the gesture.

She would even *smile* at the politeness of it all.

He never showed *anything* but respect towards her. He was courteous and kept their affections for each other private, other than a peck or two on the cheek or lips in public around the MRAs.

And now she was accusing him of *rape*?

Fucking *preposterous.*

It just didn't make any sense to James.

"James, honey, is that you?" Darrin beckoned from the kitchen. "I made veggie fried rice."

James set his bag down on the couch and walked over to the half wall in the kitchen.

"Hi darling," he said.

He gave Darrin a peck on the cheek.

Darrin flinched.

"How was your day?" Darrin asked.

James found it hard to decipher which mood Darrin was in.

At least he was past the silent treatment phase.

"It was...*interesting,*" James said.

He grabbed the glass of wine already waiting for him on the counter.

"Oh?"

"Have you heard about what happened to Michael?"

Darrin turned off the stove on an impulse.

"You know I have no interest in your MRA stuff — "

"So, long story short, this woman that he was very much trading with pressed *charges.*"

Darrin began to stir in the soy sauce.

Clang. Clang.

"She claims he *raped* her."

Clang. Clang.

Darrin began scooping the rice into two bowls.

His hand trembled in mid-air.

He steadied it with the other.

Her.

James drank his wine while observing Darrin's reaction to it all.

Either Darrin came clean *now* about his history with Althea, or let it go and James *never* had to know.

"This is *exactly* why I kept telling you that you shouldn't get involved with *those* people," Darrin said.

"What are you even *talking* about? *This!* This is the beginning of the *revolution!* I'm not going to just *stand by* as one of us is falsely accused and sentenced to *die.*"

James put the glass of wine back on the counter.

He hugged Darrin from behind and pressed his entire body against his back.

Darrin felt James get hard against him.

They hadn't had sex in who even *knew* how long.

At first, after the heroin slip up and the night in jail, all that Darrin had wanted to do was just have mindless sex.

Darrin had stopped putting the rice into the bowls.

He was clutching the marble counter top tightly with both hands.

James kissed Darrin on his neck.

"James, *no.*"

He stopped and turned Darrin around.

"I love you."

"I love you, too."

"We *need* to storm the courthouse and show him our support. This is a *good* thing."

Darrin felt tears welling in his eyes.

James looked at the man he loved so passionately.

All that he saw was a man who had been broken by this awful world.

"I am sorry. I'm sorry. I know my being a part of the MRAs doesn't make you happy," James said, hugging him.

"I just need more time to process all this."

"I understand. I'm still trying to make sense of everything too. I just saw the press report in the evening that he was being accused of rape. In the afternoon, they were only claiming that he was being charged with distribution of sexist material."

They stood there for a long time just looking at each other.

Darrin figured this was as good a time as any to come clean about what he knew.

"James, there *is* something I need to tell you…"

"Anything, say anything."

"I know her."

"You know who?"

"Her, that woman who is claiming he raped her. I *know* her."

"Wait, WHAT?"

"I know her because she was my first…"

"Oh my god. *Her?*"

"…client at the house I used to stay at on Fredricton."

"Hang on, she was the woman that…"

"The one that screwed me while on her period? Yes."

James' eyes widened in shock and horror.

"I was writing my book at the cafe and I saw her face and I just knew, James, I just *knew* that she was lying. Her absolutely *abominable* face."

"I knew she couldn't be trusted! I just *knew* it!"

"I think I should tell you what happened after she was done with me. She knew that she was my *only* consistent client who made me able to pay for my place. She had her way with me, used me, and then threw me away. I was broke and miserable because I was so young and smitten by her. I thought she would take care of me, you know? I thought she *loved* me. So, I went to her apartment. She said she had just gotten out from under her moms and she wanted to have even more fun. She never even opened the door, but I heard her with a woman in there. I was homeless after that because *that* bastard let me go. For two months, I slept on the street near her apartment, hoping that she would at least glance my way when she passed me. She just hurriedly walked past me instead. Every day I begged on that street. It was so humiliating. I developed the habit then."

James pulled Darrin into his embrace.

He held Darrin as they both cried out of frustration, contempt, and nostalgia.

"I think you should tell your story to Michael's lawyer. I think you need to tell his lawyer what that abominable woman is like. The world *deserves* to know how she treats men."

"I...I don't know, James. What would come from it?"

"*Something!* We've got to do *something*! And that's why you've got to come protest at the courthouse with us. This is as much *your* battle now as it is mine. You have *got* to do this with me."

Darrin blinked, looking into James' earnest face.

He felt torn between what he *knew* in his gut he was: a weak, broken man, and what he *needed* to be right now, for himself, for James, and for the countless other men that she might have done this to: a *warrior*.

Breathe.

One.

Two.

CHAPTER 83

Magda opened her laptop to the last page visited.

She read the title again: LET MEN BE MEN

Even though she had read this one before, it was the last post to date from Draven.

She *had* to know the man who had been forced inside her.

She felt his hardened flesh inside of her.

She closed her eyes and legs instinctively as tight as she could.

> *"Look at her. Isn't she just beautiful?"*

The way his eyes looked at her. Pleading for mercy.

When she opened her eyes again, she was confronted with the words on the screen.

This might come as a surprise to many of you who, just like *me*, grew up in a society where we were told that heteronormativity had to be eliminated for the betterment of humanity:

Heteronormativity IS the NORM.

Over 90% of us *should* be heterosexual. Over fifty years ago, that *was* the norm.

How is it that in just under 50 years, lesbians went from making up less than 2% of the American female population to now *almost 50%?* While the rest choose to identify as bisexual.

The Women's Empowerment Bank has made it easier and easier for men to become *obsolete*.

All that they need from us now is our *sperm*. We've been reduced to the stuff that comes out of our *dicks*. And only if our sperm is *viable* are we ever considered even *remotely* valuable to society.

Our frustration has driven many of us who just *cannot* settle for homosexual relationships into desires to seek out *trade-ships*. The women who want these trade-ships usually get bored with us and toss us aside when they are done.

The amount of one night stands that I have had with women who don't want *anything* more with me after that...

It makes me feel like an *object*. Like a *toy*.

We deserve *more* than this. We should have the *freedom* to be heterosexual if we *want* to be. Wasn't feminism supposed to give women the freedom to *choose* what kind of relationships they wanted to have? We need to *end* this societal stigma against heterosexuality and stop glorifying *lesbianism* as the ultimate way for women to achieve happiness and fulfillment.

Perhaps this is my way to disclose that I am in a trade-ship with a woman, and she has opened her eyes to the possibility of heterosexuality.

There is still hope for the younger generations.

Until next time, for liberty, equality, and the brotherhood,

Yours,
DA

She smiled like a madwoman.

These are the things he was thinking.

The thoughts that she had *never* been exposed to.

Thoughts that enraged Natalia, but which Magda now *craved* to read.

As she browsed through the rest of his blog posts, she noticed that she hadn't read one of them before.

She couldn't believe her eyes.

Days of secret rendezvous with his website and there was *still* one more!

Another post that she could consume while Natalia was none the wiser.

Yes!

It was about suicide rates amongst men.

She and Natalia knew their own fair share of men who had taken their own lives rather than face living in this world.

Natalia called them *cowards*.

Magda wondered if she could somehow help them.

Before she could read it, she heard footsteps coming towards the bedroom door.

She slammed the laptop shut.

She wasn't expecting Natalia to come home so early.

Luckily, it was password protected.

When she opened up her laptop again later that night, long after Natalia had fallen asleep, the page was gone.

Blank.

Blacked out.

She tried on her phone instead, but she was met with an error code.

404: Not Found.

CHAPTER 84

They yell outside my bedroom door, day after day.

Don't they know I'm tired of their endless *screeching*?

I feel like I'm sixteen again, hearing them fight and not knowing if that meant one of them was going to leave me with the other.

Locked in.

Shut out.

The window doesn't open wide enough for me to sneak out.

There is no tree to help me climb down to freedom.

Out there.

I clutched my bed sheet towards my chest.

And even if I *tried* to escape, I would probably just end up institutionalized for mental instability or put on more hormone stabilizers.

It feels like a million hours pass by for every *second* of boredom that I clock in.

I must have counted every hair on my head.

Then counted it again, just to split apart my split ends.

I had refused food for the past few days until my stomach started eating itself and the bile came right up to my throat.

When I finally began to eat, I ate so much that I threw up.

Michael.

I've stopped thinking about him as much.

I tapped into my fight or flight.

I paced around the room.

I felt resolute.

No way out.

I had no options left.

I screamed into my pillow.

I knew I couldn't do a damn thing to change the outcome of this.

Their presence was wearing me down the longer I stayed in this place.

They told me that I should be *institutionalized* to find my femininity again.

I convinced them that this self-imposed confinement in their home will be better for me.

They forced me to see a therapist every damn day instead of going to the hospital.

With them in the *same* damn room.

They met me half way.

I was *not* crazy.

I was not.

Wanting to have a dalliance with a man, *any* man, is *not* crazy.

Even if that man was Michael.

It *shouldn't* be.

It *wasn't*.

But it *was*.

They keep telling me, and I keep accepting it.

They tell me I was *never* in love.

But I *was*.

I shook my head from side to side, grasping at chunks of hair on either side.

No, I *wasn't*.

Infatuation.

I was *played*.

My *heart* was played.

I didn't follow my *gut*.

Since I *acted* like a reckless teenager, they say that I should be *treated* like one.

They told me that, and I accept it.

Accept it.

Accept everything that they say and I'll *get out*.

Maybe if I accepted everything they say, I might still be able to save him.

I suppose I'm not indifferent to him yet.

I needed to be broken in even more.

I surrendered.

CHAPTER 85

He was given ten minutes to put on the work clothes that the guards had carelessly thrown into his cell.

Work.

How could he have forgotten?

It was one of the many benefits for those *outside* of this hell-hole.

Be useful for the matriarchy.

"*You there!*"

The guard pointed at him and snapped him out of his thoughts.

He hung his head and clasped his hands in front of him as she approached.

"You're headed to the hatchery. No tools for you yet."

He hadn't thought about it ever since that day.

Suicide.

Tick, tick, tick.

He saw the culprit of the damn ticking on the guard's left wrist.

"That fucking wrist watch," he mumbled.

The first words he had spoken since he had been thrown into solitary.

"Did you say something, *boy?*"

Keep your head down.

She smacked him across the head.

Keep your head down.

"Move!"

Once he was in front of her, she whacked his ass with her baton.

He wailed in pain and fell to the floor dramatically.

She kicked him in the stomach.

Blood rushed to his mouth.

He covered it with his hand and clutched his stomach with the other.

The dramatic fall made him feel rejuvenated.

He still had *some* power.

His mind was *all* he had to control.

His *reactions* might have repercussions, but not his thoughts.

As long as they couldn't control his thoughts, he could endure *all* the physical pain they doled out.

"Move! Let's go!"

She shoved him through a large grey door.

CHAPTER 86

It was the *smell* that hit him first.

The pungent odour of a vinegar-lemon cleaning solution.

There was also the putrid smell of something else that he couldn't quite put his finger on.

Then there were sounds of little baby birds.

"Simon will show you what to do."

The guard took off his handcuffs and pushed him towards the man with the beer gut.

He rubbed his wrists where they had been cuffed.

Freed.

"Simon," a man twice the size of Michael said and nodded towards him.

"Michael," he offered in return.

"We're at this belt."

He pointed to the one closest to them.

"We're supposed to separate the males from the females?"

"Do as Simon says."

"Okay, do as Simon says."

He watched as Simon, without hesitation, tossed one in four of the newborn chicks into a pit beside the conveyor belt.

The chirping stopped as soon as they were thrown in.

Ground up alive.

Day *one* of their lives.

All the males.

Wiped out.

This was the most *humane* way to do it, Michael was later told. Sometimes they would also suffocate the male chicks in giant garbage bags.

That was the value of their life, simply because they were born the wrong sex.

The chirps began to subside as the population of the birds decreased by one fourth.

They didn't do the debeaking on that day, but Michael would soon learn that burning and branding was not just for the *male* prisoners in this place.

The next day, he was given two eggs sunny-side up and buttered toast for breakfast.

He was ravenous.

He didn't think twice.

CHAPTER 87

His stomach rumbled.

"Hey! Are you *listening* to me?" Georgina snapped at him.

Dear god, when would this woman *shut up*?

All he wanted was some rest.

It had been what felt like *days* since he had last seen anyone from the outside.

"Yeah, yeah, I'm listening."

Michael rubbed his eyes to get the sleep out of them.

"You've *got* to tell me what happened. The *truth*. I don't want *any* part of your story left out."

He looked at her intently.

Judging by the way she was talking to him, he figured she could be trusted.

She *still* didn't want the best for him, though. Of that, he was sure.

"They're recording this, aren't they?"

"Yes."

"Then how am I supposed to tell you anything?"

"I'm your *lawyer*. They bring up anything that we talk about here in court, and I can call it inadmissible."

"But that doesn't mean shit. They'll still nail me."

"They've *already* nailed you. It's your *balls* you should be worried about. *Those* are what I can still try to help you save."

He closed his knees.

"Look, I *wanna* tell you. I wanna *trust* you, alright, but I *can't*. Not with this info."

He leaned in, close to her face.

She smelled his day-old breath but didn't back away.

Leaning in even closer to *his* face, she said, "I'll ask the questions. You just tell me the truth."

"I wanna know everything they're charging me with, Georgina. I have the *right* to know. I heard rumours about rape. I didn't *rape* anybody!"

He bowed his head towards his hands.

"You're being charged with one count of possession and distribution of discriminatory material, one count of identity theft… and one count of rape."

"Who are they saying that I raped?"

"Althea Hayworth."

Michael's eyes darted across her face, looking for signs of deceit.

Shit.

She was telling the truth.

He closed his knees harder, bringing even more discomfort to his groin.

"I didn't…I didn't do that. We were in a *tradeship*."

"It wasn't official. There is no record of it at the WEB. She's set to be married to a woman, Felicity something."

"Yeah, I know about her. But I didn't do what she says I did."

He looked at all the different objects in the room that he could throw against the wall.

How much should he fly off the rails and risk getting put into solitary?

The thought of being unable to wipe his own ass again stopped that line of thinking in its tracks.

Georgina looked into his eyes, trying to scan them for deceit.

"What? You think I'm lying? You think I'm a bastard too?"

"It doesn't matter what *I* think. It matters what *they* think, out there, and what Althea Hayworth says. We have to fight it, but we don't exactly have the law on our side. If she *says* you did it, and there's enough circumstantial evidence that you two were intimate, and her testimony is believed by the judge, I can't help you much, but I *can*…"

She kept going.

There was no way Althea could have *willingly* done this to him.

Does she know?

Does she know what her mothers did to me?

He tuned Georgina out.

"Are you listening to me?"

"Yeah, yeah. I am."

He tuned her out.

What the hell, Al?

CHAPTER 88

This is how it felt.

Like a million knives had *stabbed* me in my gut and every time I tried to take one out, another one would carve a new wound into my already bloodied stomach.

I was *done* caring about him.

Every time the therapist gave me a pill, I felt *instantly* better.

Then, I wasn't.

Then, I was again.

Every time I wanted to *stop* caring about him, I closed my eyes to refocus on myself, but *there* was Michael's face, *staring* at me, *taunting* me, making me feel like *I* was the evil one.

My eyes shot open.

Ma's eyes were glaring into mine.

"His lawyer won't press if she knows what's good for him. Unless his lawyer is a *shark*, then she *might* try to come after the DNA evidence, but that shouldn't budge the judge by a lot."

Mom yelling at us, telling us that we needed to be *fixated* on getting him into prison and *keeping* him there, was just a passing sound.

Our voices were always drowned out by Mom's.

Mom paced around the room.

"Easily move from one scene to the other. Practice it in your head everyday until the trial. You got that?"

Both Ma and I had to fall in line, or else…

Or else *I* would go to Fangsel for sympathizing with an MRA.

Or else *I* would be put into a crisp, white-walled, sterile hospital room, doped up on medications until I could be a *good* woman.

A good *wife*.

The threats had gone on and on.

Michael would be hung.

That was his destiny.

That was what she told me, anyway.

Did I *want* to join him?

I would be separated from Felicity and Aibek forever.

There would be no redemption for me.

> "There's no point in being a martyr, *Al*."

> "Leave that to the Draven Alec's of the world, *Al*."

> "Trust me, you do *not* want to lose this life, *Al*."

Shut up.

There were never any repercussions for the *mighty* Natalia Hayworth.

She stood tall above me, yanking my jaw up to her face.

Her eyes gleamed with ferocity.

I looked at her with contempt.

Is that what *I* looked like to Felicity? Standing above her? Holding her weak face in my hands?

> "Are you *listening* to what I'm saying, Althea?"

Just fucking shut up.

> "Yes, Mom."

Yes, Mom. My new fucking mantra.

"Good girl!"

She pet my head as though I was a dog.

I shoved her hand away.

I had to testify against a man, and he would lose his manhood and his life.

All because I had decided one day that this guy with his dick was worth the several months of a pleasure party that I had twisted into some sick, romanticized montage of self-revelation.

It was through Michael that I wanted to find myself.

Only *he* would help me do that.

I should have left him the *fuck* alone.

I shouldn't have gotten involved.

I shouldn't have...

I should have...

What the hell was the point of the 'should haves' now?

Here I was, listening to my mom preach at me about all the virtues of what *should* be done, when she had committed the *actual* crime: accusing a man of *raping* me when *I* knew and *she* knew that he hadn't.

But was that even a *crime* at all? Our legal system certainly didn't think so.

Believe all women. A *woman* would never lie.

Trust her testimony, trust her *story*, above all.

And even if a woman *did* lie, she would have good reason.

She would be doing it for the greater good of womankind.

The *end* would justify the means.

The rapists of the world, the *men* of the world, have gotten away with it for *too long*.

Not anymore.

That's what Mom would say.

Is that what I would say?

Is that what I *should* be saying?

Just one look at her told *her* story: she was enjoying the power trip.

Savouring it.

But if I *did* this, if I just *committed* to her insanity, I could get *everything* that I deserved.

That was the problem, but that was also the solution.

I would finally be *free*, and my problematic, rebellious, past self would be forever quarantined with Draven the Deviant, and that would be that.

Just like that, I could have it all back.

Is this what it meant to be working for the good of womankind?

I took a pill off the night stand, put it in my mouth, and swallowed it without the help of any water.

"Yes, Mom."

CHAPTER 89

Sigmund was being dragged out of his cell. Drugged, as usual. Except this time it wasn't out of his own volition.

Michael decided to ask the one man he knew in the entire place.

"Simon, where are they taking him?"

"Same place Nameen went to, man."

"Organs? Again? How many do these women need? Fuck."

"Ya man. But hey, if you donate a kidney without a fight and they don't gotta kill you or nu'n they give you a thou man," Simon said, smiling at Michael. His two front gold crowns were staring Michael straight in the eyes.

"A thou. How do they give it to ya? Paper?"

He marvelled at how quickly he had picked up on the jail slang.

"Paper?"

He laughed for a good few seconds.

"Nah man, they try to make it so that you get the best room for recovery. They stitch you up with painkillers and shit man. If you fight it, they just leave you there, no pills, no n'un. They call it even when you get a nice ass room and make you come back here. It's worth it to not fight it man."

"I'm just new to the whole thing, eh Sai?"

"Ya man. Sometimes it really shows."

"How should I hide it?"

"Don't bring up paper, man. Only 'Zazel gets paper. And she's got a *lotta* paper."

"How much we talking here? In the thous or mills?"

"Up there man."

He pointed to the ceiling of his cell.

"What's she in for?"

Simon chuckled.

"No one knows, man."

He came close to the bars of his cell.

"But some say she just walked in one day man, and just *went* for it. She made herself a nice cozy little home and just *stayed*."

"Wait, so she could just *walk out* whenever she wants to?"

"Ya man, that's what I heard."

"Then why doesn't she?"

"No one knows and any'uns tried asking her has been beat in the night man."

"Hmm…"

"Ya man. That woman's *scary*."

Michael walked into his cell, the door shutting behind him automatically.

He felt a deep chill rise through his spine, hitting his groin on the way up.

He cupped his crotch protectively.

He looked at the cell in the corner.

The biggest one.

Azazel smiled up at the ceiling, laying on her memory foam mattress, hearing

them talk about her as though she wasn't listening to every word they said.

CHAPTER 90

The air outside got warmer by the second with the amount of people that had crowded around the entrance of the courthouse.

This was the perfect opportunity for the Cavaliers to make their mark.

Sigma felt her head pound with anticipation.

She wanted to actually *do* something about this man instead of just standing around gawking at the proceedings like a bunch of stupid knuckleheads.

Her heart swelled with pride for the sacrifice that she would be making for the women of the future.

The quicker that men like Draven Alec were eliminated, the better.

She had her pocket knife ready in her belt.

She was close enough to the front.

Draven's lawyer, Georgina Baer, walked out of her car and took one look around before quickly climbing up the stairs to the courthouse.

She had four male guards surrounding her.

She was booed and pawed at by the crowd on her climb up the stairs.

Some female guards with batons held the crowd back.

Sigma knew she would have been dead in an instant if she got her hands on Georgina.

But Georgina was a *woman*.

A *despicable* woman.

But a woman, nevertheless.

Sigma and the Cavaliers would be *despised* for doing that.

She looked around.

There was no other car nearby.

He wasn't going to come in through the front.

These bozos were all waiting for someone who they weren't even going to *see*.

She had to get to the side.

She tried to push through the crowd.

She *could* stab her way through the crowd, but there were some allies in there.

Goddess fucking damn it.

Right then, a plain white van pulled into the side of the building across the street.

Sigma would have *known* that this was the van.

If only she had *seen* it.

If only she knew that she could have had Michael's life in the palm of her hand.

He was pushed into the building.

The crowd outside the courthouse kept growing.

Michael finally saw the insanity of the crowd through the corner of his eye.

He wanted to run, but there was nowhere *to* run.

The prison guards rushed him through the doors and into the elevator.

His arms had become mostly skin and bone.

    "You're *hurting* me!" he screamed.

He could hear his voice getting more high pitched.

Whatever they had been injecting into him once a day was making him grow a bit more flesh around his chest and changing the sound of his voice.

He flopped down onto the elevator floor.

He rocked himself back and forth.

"Tick, tick, tick goes the clock," he sang to himself.

The female guards glanced at him sideways, rolling their eyes and smiling at each other.

The elevator stopped at the basement with a thud.

Michael could feel the bones in his ass against the ground.

He was yanked up by the guards.

8:02.

A.M. or P.M.?

Had he seen *sunlight*, or was that just the glimmer of a yellow light bulb in the hallway?

He only knew that they were dragging him and his feet could barely move.

Maybe it was the shoes that were dragging him down.

Or maybe it was the weight of the realization that he was dressed for a funeral in black tie, and yet he still had hope.

The time, the day, the month, the year — all these mundane facts seemed *useless* now.

In here, in his brain, he only knew *one* thing: this was *just* the beginning.

When they finally made it to the courthouse, Georgina was waiting for him with shoe polish.

He *hoped* she knew what to expect.

She had no *idea* what to expect.

CHAPTER 91

He had been waiting for his turn to go back out into the world.

But now that he was here, in the courtroom, he wished he could go back into the cell with the ticking clock.

When was the last time he had gone for a *run*? Increased his heart rate in any voluntary way?

Georgina sat next to him, itching the back of her neck right under her bun.

Itches were contagious.

He felt the need to itch his crotch.

He crossed his legs just to avoid an embarrassing display.

The desire built and built.

The thought that he *wanted* to itch but *couldn't* because of some stupid societal convention bothered him to no end.

He took that thought and ran with it.

He thought through all the repercussions of itching at such a private part in front of so many women of high societal ranking.

Georgina kept itching the back of her neck.

He thought about why itching his crotch would have *no* effect on the final outcome of this insane trial.

The dandruff flakes kept flowing from Georgina's nails onto the back collar of her dark grey suit.

The desire to scratch his crotch rose up to his elbow.

He thought about how he had protested, written, and argued for *so* long against places like this, and now he just had this *woman*, most likely biased against him anyway, *defending* him when she'd rather put him in Fangsel.

Georgina *had* gotten men like him out before.

Men *like* him.

But not *him*.

Men who were less sensational and less headline-worthy than he.

But not *him*.

What was the connection between his crotch, his elbow, and the back of Georgina's neck?

He wanted to itch all three until he drew blood.

"Order in the court. *Order in the court!*"

The voice of that shrill blonde, standing right in front of his face with her breasts at his eye level, snapped him straight out of his thoughts and back into reality.

Tick, tick, tick.

"All rise for Your Honour Karyn Heidelbaugh."

Everybody shuffled in their seats. This was the *perfect* opportunity for him to itch his crotch.

Karyn Heidelbaugh walked in.

Just like that, the itch was gone.

CHAPTER 92

The courtroom felt drier than the Sahara despite the dead winter air outside.

The heat engulfed every pore in my body.

My mouth felt like sandpaper.

I wasn't in the prosecution's bench.

I wasn't required to be there.

I would eventually have to tell them my version of events.

I didn't see what happened between Michael, his lawyer, my moms, Valentina, and the judge.

I didn't see his *face*.

I caught a glimpse of his back when I walked out of the bathroom.

He had a hunch now.

I walked back into the bathroom.

I searched my face in the mirror for an emotion.

I put my purse down on the counter next to the sink.

I scrunched up my face into a mimicked cry.

I tried to sob, but nothing came out.

I returned my face to a blank stare.

When Ma walked in to bring me to the debrief with Valentina, she found me reapplying mascara.

I just thought that I needed fuller lashes.

Ma looked at me with sympathetic eyes.

I sighed.

"Don't bother looking at me like that. I'm perfectly fine. See, I'm going to take my pill now."

When our eyes met in the mirror, I flashed the pill at her and shoved my head under the tap to drink out of it.

She averted her eyes.

She knew.

I knew.

Everyone in that courtroom had to *know* that this was all a farce.

Right?

They *must* know.

They *must* realize this is absurd.

Right?

Wrong.

This would inevitably make Mom even *more* credible as a Ministress of Female Well-Being.

Ha!

Karyn would have sent *another* man to prison.

Valentina would have *another* win.

I turned to face the mirror again to put on a touch of pink lip gloss.

"How do I look?"

I smacked my lips a few times.

"Beautiful, darling."

Ma reached for my hand.

"Don't."

I pulled my hand away from her.

I wasn't going to let her make me feel *anything*.

I smoothed any wrinkles from my skirt and walked out of the bathroom, grabbing my purse on the way.

That's how I walked into the courtroom.

Until I felt the dryness of my own mouth when I saw Valentina and Mom conferring, everything in me stayed composed.

"Val, don't *do* this. Don't go *through* with this," I wanted to say.

I had *so* much to say to her.

I wanted to ask her *who? Who came to whom first? Was it you or my mom that decided to do this to **him**?*

The only thing that came out of me was a sputtered, "I'm here".

I couldn't conjure the strength to say anything more.

Not then.

Not yet.

What the fuck is wrong with me?

What am I so fucking scared of?

Mom? Michael? Fangsel?

Those fears had all *flooded* through my brain and destroyed all of my conviction.

I would make sure that Michael *never* gets out of Fangsel.

They had tried to go for the death penalty, but the judge had ruled that Michael still had some physical utility.

That was this morning, after the judge had seen his youth.

Assessed his bodily worth.

Mom laughed out loud, *heartily*, and Valentina joined in.

I felt my teeth hurt from clenching them hard, trying to bite back words and screams.

I swallowed.

No saliva.

None was being produced.

I felt my tonsils and throat muscles ache.

"Water," I said, weakly.

"What was that, honey?" Mom asked between laughs.

"Can I have some water?" I said dryly.

Ma came up behind me and handed me her water bottle.

When I took it, she put her free hand on my shoulder.

I looked up at her with no emotion in my eyes.

I looked at the side of her face.

Why was she letting Mom *do* this to us?

Why couldn't she just *fight* her?

Why couldn't *I*?

I knew *why*, but I wanted to really *understand* it, *embrace* it, and make it *me*.

I opened the water bottle and gulped and gulped until I was just sucking the air out.

They kept laughing.

What the hell was so fucking funny?

I shrugged Ma's hand off my shoulder.

I pulled her down to the bench and forced her to sit next to me.

I put my head in her lap and closed my eyes for what seemed like *hours*.

Then, I was back home.

CHAPTER 93

The first day for him in the courthouse had gone by a little too slow.

The clocks hadn't helped in that department.

He had gotten a glimpse of where he was, as they took him through the metal detectors.

The Courthouse of the Lady of Justice.

He saw through the corner of his eye a little picture, hung on the wall, behind the judge's podium. A woman, blindfolded, carrying a scale, with a sword by her side. On the bottom, two simple words: *Matriarchal Justice*.

He didn't want to think about the other two women in the room when he was dragged in there.

"Everyone wants their mommy when they're being fucked."

He blinked hard, trying to push the memory of those women away.

At least they weren't going to be directly in his view.

He had tried searching for Althea, but she wasn't there.

When he sat down with Georgina after the fact, all that he could see was her tired face.

He knew it was time to be honest with her.

"I have to tell you something."

"Hmm?"

"I don't know how to say this…"

"Spit it out."

He felt his palms dampen.

"Well, here's the thing. I uh, well, Natalia Hayworth, Althea's mother, she...she *raped* me."

"*Excuse me?*"

"I really, don't even know, how…"

"No, Michael, *shut up*. You don't know what you're saying."

He tried folding his arms across his chest, but the handcuffs hindered him.

"Just a suggestion, take it or leave it: run DNA tests on the samples of human extracts left behind at my apartment."

She frowned.

"I can't promise it will lead to much, it might even be a waste of time, but better *that* than me not having opened my mouth at all."

When Georgina got the results of the fingerprint and DNA samples from his apartment later that day, she knew something was amiss.

The only place in his apartment that hadn't been wiped *clean* of human remains was the bed.

The mattress, to be more specific.

The sheets, brand new. The floors, windows, counters, fridge, and even the inside of the oven had been wiped so completely clean that there weren't even *fingerprints* on them.

The only DNA other than *his* found in his apartment was *Althea's*, on both his bed and his armchair.

He claimed he had had some of the MRA men over several times for drinks, discussions, and music.

But no trace of them could be found.

She went back the next day. Michael obliged her in recanting his experience with Natalia. She couldn't walk straight on her way back home.

She broke down in tears as soon as she entered her apartment.

The Hayworths wanted him *gone*.

Not for what he *did*, but for his *ideas*.

CHAPTER 94

A man with dark, curly black hair had been chasing Georgina for almost two blocks.

While she wasn't *normally* the type to try to outpace a *loon* trying to catch up, this past month had already given her all the crazy she could handle.

"Miss! *Miss!*"

She paused and turned around.

She looked him up and down.

Not a threat.

"Yeah?"

"You don't know me, but my name is…"

"I'm not taking new clients right now."

"I don't need an attorney. I wanted to offer my services."

She laughed him off.

"Not interested. I prefer *women.*"

"No, Miss, not like that. See, my name is Darrin Davis, and I have information that could help you with the Michael Nolan case."

"What kind of information?"

"I know things about her. The woman, Althea Hayworth."

Georgina frowned.

"What do you want for it?"

His heart raced in anticipation.

He hadn't wanted anything before, but now he wondered if he *should* be asking for something in return, to make the information seem more worthwhile.

"I don't know how much it's worth to you."

Georgina knew he was playing hardball. Besides, what could this *waifish* man even know about Althea?

The *Michaels* of the world were Althea's type, not whatever *this* creature was in front of her.

"I can't give you much, but let's hear it."

"She used to frequent houses, on Fredricton. It was a long time ago, and she was kind with her payments, but *not* kind with her, you know, *manner*."

"So you were a gigolo, a for-sale *dick*, and you expect me to believe whatever story comes out of your mouth? Get the hell out of here. You look like you were tossed to the road before the day you knew what an *orgasm* was."

She began to walk away from him.

He grabbed her forearm.

"Don't you goddessdamned dare touch me!"

"Miss, I just *need* you to listen to my side of the story. Please, trust me — what she's accusing *him* of, she's done to *me*."

Georgina saw his earnest eyes desperately looking at her.

She crossed her arms and raised an eyebrow.

"Okay. I'm listening."

"I was just *seventeen,* and I believed that I had been *saved* from homelessness by my Mister, Gary. She was my first…"

Once he had finished, Georgina stood there dumbstruck that a woman — of all people, a *woman* — couldn't understand asking for consent.

"Darrin, how can I believe you?"

"I have at least two men from my home that can corroborate my story."

Georgina rested her body weight on one leg, arms folded across her chest while looking the man up and down.

She nodded in understanding.

This ex-gigolo had *his* story, and if she had to trust Althea's story of Michael raping her, then surely, she had to trust this man's story of Althea raping *him*. That would be the right thing to do to ensure no double standard on her part.

Especially as a defence attorney.

"I hear you. I understand what you went through, but I can't use any of this against her. You have to understand…"

"You can't *understand* what I went through, but you *can* help *Michael*. You know what she's like now. That's all I wanted. I just needed *one* person to hear me. To *really* hear me."

"I hear you. I want to be able to use what you have given me, but I *can't*. The *courts* won't allow it. I'm just trying to play by the rules."

"Can't you at least go to the press? Something? *Anything*?"

"I can't. My hands are tied. I go to the press and they can put the death penalty back on the table. I wouldn't be able to live with myself if I let that happen to him. I'm trying to save his balls."

Darrin nodded solemnly in understanding.

"I guess, I suppose, I just *needed* you to know. She's *not* innocent."

Georgina nodded back.

"I can promise you that I will *try*. I will try my best to relieve his suffering."

"That's all I can ask of you."

CHAPTER 95

Valentina looked as composed as she had been since the day the trial had started.

"The prosecution would like to present the DNA evidence found at the scene of the crime. Specifically, the evidence found in Mr. Nolan's bedroom."

Valentina pointed to the projector.

I saw that all too familiar room.

That familiar bed.

It looked a little too staged in the photos, but I couldn't be confident of when these were taken.

I closed my eyes.

I could feel the sheets on top of my bare breasts.

I could feel him softly breathing near my neck, making the little hairs stand alert.

I felt my breathing become shallow.

I could feel his fingers inside me.

I could feel my hand guiding his.

'Slower, please,' I would say.

He knew what to do.

He would pause and taunt me until I couldn't take it anymore.

I could feel my hair brush against the side of my face as I turned to kiss him.

I opened my eyes to a picture of my face next to a number.

I closed my legs as tightly as I could.

I felt wet.

My underwear was soaked through.

What the hell is wrong with me?

"There is no doubt that the DNA found on the bed matches that of Ms. Althea Hayworth," Valentina projected to the bare courtroom.

That must have been from all our sleepovers.

Sleepovers, ha!

Thinking of our rendezvous now like I was a fucking *teenager* again.

"No other DNA was found at the scene other than Ms. Hayworth's and Mr. Nolan's. There were also traces of Ms. Hayworth's *blood* found on the bed."

That must have been from the time I had bled out on his bed because I hadn't tracked my cycle to the day.

"*That*, we suspect, is from the day of the rape, due to the severity of the penetration."

No it's not, you lying…

"Ma, can I have my pill right now?" I whispered into Ma's ear.

"Sure, honey, but this is your *third* one today, you should slow down."

I snatched it from her hands when she pulled it out of her purse. She didn't react, and faced forward again.

I gulped it down without any water.

I refocused, staring unblinkingly at the screen.

The ten people that were subjected to this audio-visual assault were myself, my moms, Valentina, Georgina, the Honourable Karyn, three guards, and Michael himself.

No one else.

The media were debriefed after the fact by Valentina, of course.

The man's lawyer *never* got any screen time.

Mom had explained that to me.

As though I were a child who hadn't seen this happen a *hundred* times before.

I hadn't.

That wasn't the point though, was it?

She just wanted to *patronize* me.

That was the point.

Prove that she knew *more* than me.

I looked to the right and saw the profile of her face next to Ma's.

Her hands were clasped together.

That stupid pinstripe suit mocking me with all the knowledge encased in it, inside of her.

I just wanted to *feel* what I had felt on that day.

I just wanted to go *back* to before *any* of this had happened.

I closed my eyes and felt myself in his bed, next to him, running my hands through his dark, wavy hair again.

I smelled his cologne.

I sighed out loud.

Georgina turned her head to the right to look at me.

I glared right back.

I saw a little sliver of his figure peek out from beside her.

I felt numb.

The pill had begun to work again.

Thank goddess for that.

Valentina went on.

I wish I *never* had to see him again.

I wish he could just be *gone* and then…

And then what?

CHAPTER 96

Georgina looked at her notes.

"Your Honour, I would like to present four questions in lieu of a rebuttal regarding the DNA evidence found at Mr. Nolan's apartment."

"Your limit is five questions. Are you withdrawing your client's right to present one more?"

"Yes, Your Honour."

"You may proceed."

"The primary question is one of evidence obtainment: was it the case that in the prosecution's collection of the DNA evidence, they were *only* able to find the DNA of my client and of the plaintiff?"

Valentina shuffled in her seat uncomfortably.

"Your Honour, I would like to address that question."

"You may."

"Your Honour, the State searched for other DNA but was not able to find any."

Valentina sat down again.

"Your Honour, this brings me to my second question. If there was no other DNA evidence found, my client has records on his phone, according to the State's examination of it, showing that…"

"Objection! Testifying on behalf of her witness."

"Sustained! Please, Georgina, don't make assertions."

Georgina looked frustratingly at her sparse notes for a few moments.

"Your Honour, I will rephrase. Was there any possibility of any other DNA found on the scene? That of his MRA cohorts, for instance?"

"Valentina, do you have any insight into this?"

"We did not search for any, Your Honour."

"And why not?"

"Because we did not see it as a necessity, seeing as this case pertains to Ms. Hayworth having been raped by the *defendant*."

Georgina perked up.

"Then, is it possible that…"

"Objection! Are you seriously asking Judge Heidelbaugh to speculate?"

Georgina sighed exasperatedly.

"Your Honour, I will ask a different question altogether of the State. Was there any other *female* DNA found in my client's apartment?"

Valentina stood up.

"No."

Georgina saw Karyn look at Valentina with furrowed brows.

She felt as though she had successfully demonstrated that her client may be a *one-woman* man.

Wasn't there virtue in that?

She knew it wasn't enough to get him to keep his dignity, but it was something to get Karyn to think.

At least *consider* the possibility that this was a consensual tradeship and nothing happened outside of that.

"Finally, I would like to ask the State if the blood on the bed was tested for menstruation?"

Valentina rose up with force.

"Your Honour, that is a violation of my client's and *any* woman's bodily sanctity. This question is absurd!"

"Your Honour, if the State could please answer the question. Was it, or was it not, tested for menstruation?"

"Answer the question, Valentina."

"No, it was not."

Valentina sat down with a huff.

"Thank you, Your Honour. No further questions."

CHAPTER 97

Moments after I heard Mom in a heated argument with Ma, she marched into my room.

I could feel her tense up as she shakily sat down on the edge of my bed.

"What is it? Mom?"

She smoothed out the comforter near my feet.

She dug her fingers into the edge, attempting to restrain her answer.

I heard Ma fly down the stairs. Her footsteps echoed in the silence that followed my question.

"Nothing, darling. It's nothing."

"Do you want a drink or something?"

I didn't know what else to ask.

"No."

"Well, *I* would like one. Could you make me some chamomile tea, Mom?"

I saw her stare blankly at the wall of my childhood photos.

I heard her breathing become shakier by the second.

Was she going to cry? Was she *finally* going to emote something other than rage?

In spite of all the terrible things that had transpired between us, she was still Mom, and I grew more worried by the second.

I sat up and touched her bare shoulder in an attempt to comfort her.

It was damp and cool to the touch.

"*Compose* yourself, Mom. Now is hardly the time to lose your cool."

I didn't know how I became like this, with her, but here I was, offering unsolicited advice, devoid of any sympathy.

She pushed herself up and off my bed, letting my hand fall limply where she had just been sitting.

"You're right."

A long pause ensued while she inspected my room.

I looked her up and down.

She was a strong-built woman.

I had never seen her as anything other than a *tyrant*. An aspirational matriarch.

But right now, she had become more like a meek hare.

In the deafening silence, she seemed to lack a commanding presence, let alone *self*-command.

I wished I hadn't had to be the one to deal with *this* version of her.

I wished so badly that I could just muster up the courage to say what I felt about her *right* in this moment.

Too much.

The silence was too much.

Too many words unspoken between us.

I opened my mouth to say something, but I closed my mouth again twice.

I felt the blood course through my veins faster than it ever had before.

Mom's blood pressure and mine must have been the same in that exact moment.

We could both hear our hearts beat loud enough to drown out the sounds of Ma filling up the kettle downstairs.

"Mom, what hap…" I started.

She cleared her throat.

"Your supervisor called, she's granting the six months' leave you had asked for, no issues. She was a very sympathetic woman. Very sweet."

"Was *that* who was on the phone earlier? Just before you and Ma had a fight?"

I could see her fold her arms across her chest defensively.

She cleared her throat again.

"You know Felicity has called a few times since this whole thing started. You should call her back. She's even left voicemails."

I blinked back at her.

Avoiding the question.

She was good at that.

"I…wouldn't know what to say to her."

Mom looked at me, exasperated by my lack of assertiveness.

"She's your *future*, Althea. You need to call her back, remind her what she means to you, confide in her, at least. She'll be there with you through the worst and the best parts of life from here on out."

Did Mom *know*? Did she *know* that the woman she was pushing me towards had ensured that the Hayworth legacy would be a *boy*?

"You know she adopted a son, right? Aibek…"

I tried to search for an inkling of contempt in Mom's face.

She stared back at me blankly.

Unfolding her arms, she walked straight out of my room.

"Ma will get you some chamomile," she mouthed, before slamming my door shut.

CHAPTER 98

Left alone with my thoughts again.

I drew the pillow to my mouth and screamed into it until tears poured down my face.

I hugged my pillow so hard that I thought it might explode and have the feathers come right out of it.

I was frustrated at myself for not being *numb* enough to everything.

I threw the pillow at the window.

It barely made a thud before it felt back on the floor.

That infuriated me even more.

I rubbed my already red eyes until I saw spots.

I rocked myself back and forth until I resigned to get up and pace around my room.

My room.

What a goddessdamned *joke*!

My room.

Ha!

What room?

This room?

This was the room that *Moms* thought I should stay in.

The one that *they* decided I should inhabit until the day I could go out again with my reputation *pristine*.

The entire country *knew* by this point that I was a victim.

And I knew victims got *all* the sympathy.

Something that Michael hadn't even offered me.

Not *once*.

Fucker.

I walked up to the framed picture of me in a pink dress with two pigtails, holding a chocolate soft-serve ice cream cone.

I stared deep into the eyes of who I once was.

I cocked my head in the same direction that hers was, staring straight into her.

Past her.

I was trying to see the landscape behind her.

I saw my happy face stare right back at me instead.

That day, I ate *all* the ice cream.

That day, I still had my innocence.

What would she think of me *now*?

Would she like the person that I have become?

I would understand if she despised me.

Because *I* hated me.

I *hated* this version of me — the pathetic, man-obsessed, non-womanist version.

How could I make her proud?

I took the frame off the wall.

I threw it at the window.

The window glass and the frame smashed to bits on the floor.

It felt cathartic.

I threw another one.

I smashed it on the floor.

I wanted that cathartic feeling to resurface over and over again.

But each time I threw a frame on the floor, the feeling slipped further into the recesses of my mind.

I ran towards the closet.

I pulled out all the clothes I had ever worn with that horrid *man*.

I tried to fit as many as I could into my hands.

I put them in a pile on my bed.

I opened the first drawer on my nightstand.

The very few times that I had deigned to smoke or light a candle had left me with a lighter that was half-full.

That'll do.

The problem was that it *would* do.

In such a desperate situation, all it would take was setting these things aflame.

A few more things first.

The underwear drawer.

Those stupid red panties.

I lit them first.

Almost burning my fingertips in the process.

I tossed them into my garbage can.

The half-full juice box that I had thrown in there earlier set ablaze before the fire alarm started shrieking.

I covered my ears and sat on the floor facing the door, rocking myself back and forth.

Embracing myself in the intense feelings of catharsis and chaos that I had managed to conjure with the arson.

I didn't even hear the footsteps march up the stairs.

Suddenly, Ma was banging on my door and opening it without a moment's hesitation.

"Althea? Al? *AL!*"

The madness in my eyes must have stopped her from stepping inside.

I scanned her face, searching for anything other than fear.

"*Are you afraid of me?*" I yelled.

She stood paralyzed, looking from my right hand up to my face.

The lighter was clutched so tightly in my palm that I lost feeling in my hand.

The glass from the frames strewn all around me made it harder for Ma to approach without harming herself in the process.

"Are you *finally* afraid of me?"

I sobbed uncontrollably into the crease of my right arm.

She quietly stepped into my room and extinguished the fire in the waste basket.

She moved some of the glass pieces out of the way and threw down one of my pillows next to me.

She sat on it.

She held me against the side of her body as I sobbed into her neck.

Empathy.

This is what I needed.

I cried until I couldn't anymore.

She guided me up and nudged me gently into bed.

I curled up into the fetal position.

She spooned with me all night.

I got what I had been craving — *comfort.*

CHAPTER 99

The alarm on her phone went off.

4:30 A.M.

Georgina turned off the alarm and laid back down on her single bed.

She hadn't slept a wink.

Instead, she had played with her eyebrow piecing for hours.

The day before, Valentina had presented even more forensic evidence that further complicated Michael's position.

Trace evidence of Michael's DNA was found on Althea, under her fingernails and inside her vagina. Then there was the video footage shot at his apartment and uploaded onto the Draven Alec blog, and the CCTV footage of him coming in and out of the internet cafe at the times when the last five blog posts were published.

Georgina had asked, *"When was this DNA obtained?"*

Valentina had responded, *"On September 24th, 2075."*

"And the alleged rape occurred on what day?"

"September 21st, 2075."

Georgina had hoped that it sparked some doubt in Karyn's mind about the timeline of events.

He was indubitably guilty of the crime of distribution.

There was too much evidence and not enough excuses for that.

Georgina worried about him in there.

In Fangsel.

The last time she had seen Michael, he had looked like absolute *shit*.

With a broken rib and a bruise on each of his arms where they had been tied down to give him conversion therapy.

Then there was the lack of outside human contact other than her visits.

Nothing that makeup couldn't cover up for court, but makeup couldn't hide the pain.

His mom and siblings had refused to visit because of how it would look.

They didn't want to be associated with a man accused of *rape*.

Georgina, on the other hand, had made a considerable attempt to visit him every day that she could.

At the very least, in spite of her initial reluctance, his mother had graciously agreed to provide a character reference.

She had wanted nothing to do with *Draven Alec*, but she had put those feelings aside for *Michael*, her adopted son.

She would speak to his nurture, but announced boldly that whoever his biological father was must have been a *deviant,* because *her* child would have *never* turned out this way.

The letter had been decent, but not *nearly* good enough.

The second reference had been *exponentially* harder to obtain.

> *"Other tradeship partners, even exes? Ones that you've been courteous with would be best."*

> *"Do you believe I haven't been courteous with all of them?"*

> *"No. I'm not suggesting that. I'm just concerned that if any of them have been irked by you in any way, it could affect the quality of the letter. Even something as small as not getting her off before yourself could make your character statement weak, you understand?"*

> *"Yes."*

> *"So, is there anyone?"*

He had gone quiet while Georgina paced around him.

*"There isn't **one** woman in your life other than your mama who would give you a reasonable character reference, Michael? What the hell?!"*

He had shaken his head and looked down at his feet.

How had this man gone through so many *years* of life without having made at least *some* respectable acquaintances with women?

*"**Seriously**? Not even a shop owner? A delivery woman? **No one?**"*

He had just shaken his head.

Maybe he really *did* deserve to be in Fangsel.

Maybe he really *was* a sexist asshole.

Georgina looked at her phone to check the time, in an attempt to shake off the memory of that conversation.

4:45 A.M.

She got up and read through another one of his blog posts that he had had printed out before the case had started.

She had to be aware *in detail* of what he had been saying, to get a sense of his character.

But she knew it was a dead end.

There wouldn't be *anything* in this stockpile of insane anti-womanist ramblings that could *ever* redeem him.

She remembered the man who had flagged her down.

Darrin.

Another hopeless dead end.

She couldn't use what he had said to annihilate Althea's character, even though Georgina felt herself get agitated every time she realized this double standard was *precisely* what disadvantaged innocent men.

The last possibility was one that she had been dreading.

It would be unusual.

Valentina would fight it.

But Georgina was left with no other choice.

CHAPTER 100

He had fought the woman taking him away.

This was sanctioned by Karyn, the guards told him, when he tried to cower in the corner.

He had been warned by Simon that this was coming.

It had come for *all* of them in this place.

He screamed, "I want to grind up the chicks! I want to grind them up! No! *Please*! I want to *work*!"

The guard had laughed while two others had dragged him up to his feet.

"It's *picture time!*"

A cheerful blonde with deep blue eyes batted flirty eyelashes at him.

He grunted towards her.

"Take off your pants and bend over, darling, and we can get this over with a *lot* faster."

She couldn't *wait* to stick her contraption inside him.

He bent over, but his asshole didn't unclench on demand, and that *infuriated* her prying fingers.

She whacked his ass.

"Unclench, you piece of shit."

All her cheery demeanour vanished.

He grunted more.

She yanked his balls down towards the floor.

"*Ow, fuck!*"

"I said, *unclench!*"

He finally relaxed as she prodded around in there almost up to his small intestine.

It felt like worms were squirming in and out of his stomach, irritating his bladder.

He pissed on his pants around his ankles.

"You're a disgusting piece of *shit*, aren't you?"

She was laughing while messing around in his insides.

He felt a hot flush of blood rush up to his face.

He was just another *thing* they could use for their sick, twisted amusement in this godforsaken place.

She yanked her hand out of his asshole.

He could smell the residual shit in the air.

As she dropped her used glove into the garbage bin, he heard another set of footsteps behind him.

"I'll take it from here."

This voice was softer than the blonde's, mellow and less assertive.

"Leave your pants off."

He still couldn't see her, but he just grunted in response.

"He's a piece of shit *caveman*, huh?"

They both laughed.

She walked in front of him and told him to follow her.

He was pushed down into the same seat as last time.

He felt the tiny rod enter his anus as he settled into the seat.

He was strapped in tightly by the woman, his head held back by a strap around his forehead and his hands tied to each arm of the chair.

He whimpered and groaned.

He was shown pictures of men.

Then shocked by the electrode into getting an erection.

Then shown a picture of a woman.

If his penis didn't go soft, they threatened to pour boiling water onto it.

He noticed how the guards would always deliberately wear tight clothes that accentuated their bosoms.

Their bosoms made it hardest to stay soft.

It was the *fear* that kept him erect.

They didn't appreciate that.

So, the boiling water was poured.

He screamed in shock and agony.

Then they gave him two minutes to get hard after showing him a picture of a naked man.

They would increase the intensity of the electricity shooting up his asshole.

Men just didn't do it for him.

They never had.

Scared gay.

Was he just the anomaly?

His biological responses were betraying him.

Where was his fight or flight response when he needed it most?

Why wouldn't his penis *fly* its way into an erection and just *listen* to his goddamn brain?

Once his body went limp from the shock of the conversion therapy, they tossed him back into his cell.

CHAPTER 101

Karyn looked down at her binder of papers.

It had been a week since proceedings had begun for the trial of the State of Massachusetts v. Mr. Michael Nolan.

She looked at the man sitting in front of her, trying her best not to hate him until the proceedings were over.

She had spent over two hours before bed reading his insane misogynistic ramblings, confirming her decision to send him to conversion therapy.

She furrowed her brows, deepening her wrinkles even more contemplatively while looking at Georgina.

Karyn couldn't *imagine* doing what Georgina did.

She nodded towards her.

"Your Honour, I would like to present the first character reference from the defendant's mother."

Karyn motioned for Georgina to continue.

The faster these were entered into the records, the better for everyone.

"Your Honour, I would like to make it clear for the court records that the plaintiff has chosen *not* to attend this particular reading, for mental and emotional health reasons," Valentina announced.

"Noted. The defence may now proceed."

"Your Honour, Michael Nolan's mother, Mrs. Patricia Nolan, has submitted the following statement regarding the rearing and character of her son:

To Whom It May Concern,

My son, Michael Nolan, was raised in a heterosexual household, as I chose to marry his father when we were just nineteen years old. He was the second of the three sons that we had adopted, and was raised mostly by me. As he was born merely a decade after the Revolution, his father still held a few conservative beliefs, but those were beaten out of Michael by me and his school teachers.

He was not taught to read or learn from anything that upheld the supremacy of men. We only kept books in the house that were from the great female writers of the twentieth and twenty-first centuries, like Margaret Atwood, Rupi Kaur, and Gillian Flynn. His father eventually denounced traditional gender roles and became a strong ally of the feminist movement until the day that he died in July of 2058. Those were the values that he ultimately passed down to his son.

Michael has never once in his life used his physical strength against me. We never taught him to use physical force in the face of disagreement. We also taught him to use only polite, female-first language to communicate his personal feelings and opinions regarding any issues that he felt affected him.

As I am obligated to state for the sake of these proceedings, for the last two years Michael has rarely visited home, and he has been forgetful about calling me and his siblings. However, we believed that this was due to his difficulty in finding stable employment. He had voluntarily given up his claim to welfare in 2070 and since then has either had hard labour jobs or nothing at all. Ever since, I have sent him money and some other provisions for a few months to help him out, but that was the extent of our communication.

I was unaware that he was using the pseudonym 'Draven Alec' to distribute sexist and meninist material. I do not condone this behaviour, and neither would his father have.

As for the allegations of rape, we leave it to the discretion of the presiding judge to make the right judgement. But I do not believe that Michael had a single bone in his body that would have committed such an awful crime against womankind.

Sincerely,

Mrs. Patricia Nolan.

Karyn could hear the echo of the last *n* engulf the courtroom and settle into everyone's eardrums.

She noticed that Michael had been staring at the ground the entire time.

She took it to be a sign that he had disrespected his mother.

Valentina cleared her throat as she stood up.

"Your Honour, I would like to meet with Ms. Baer and yourself in your chambers, if at all possible?"

"Alright. Court is adjourned for the rest of the day."

CHAPTER 102

The next morning, the courtroom was silent with anticipation.

All eight people present patiently awaited the reading of the next character witness statement.

Georgina looked at Valentina and then back at Judge Heidelbaugh.

"The next character witness to be written into court records is from Ms. Georgina Baer herself. Ms. Baer, please stand and read your statement to the court," Karyn said.

"Your Honour, this is *absurd*!" Valentina exclaimed.

Georgina had been anticipating this *exact* reaction.

"Your Honour, can the counsels approach the bench?"

"Yes, you may."

Valentina fumed with rage as she marched over to the bench.

"Karyn, you *cannot* let her do this. Attorney-client privilege *restricts* her from doing this! She would…"

Karyn raised her hand to silence Valentina.

"This is the *one* way in which attorneys can defend their clients' character, Val. It's unusual, but it *has* been done before. Georgina is doing this by the book."

"This is simply *outrageous*! He basically gets to have a *spokesperson*, in the form of his *attorney*, speak on his behalf! This is *insane*!"

"Judge Heidelbaugh, I think we need to think about the implications of the outrageous allegations made against a respectable woman of the…"

Georgina smiled.

"Your Honour, I think Val is worried about *nothing*."

"Oh, *me*? I am worried about *nothing*, when you were making pointed claims about the mother of the victim just *last night*."

"You Honour, you have my *word* that…"

"*Goddess*, Georgina!"

"Okay! Both of you! That's enough. Georgina? Do you have *anything* related to what was said in private included in your character reference?"

Georgina shook her head.

Karyn looked at Georgina.

Her face gave nothing away.

Karyn wanted to make sure that there were going to be *no* surprises in Georgina's statement.

"Let's take this to my chambers."

Karyn banged the gavel.

Michael's head pounded as soon as the decibels hit his ears.

CHAPTER 103

Georgina raced behind the two women into Karyn's chambers.

While both of them were wearing flats, she was sporting three hundred dollar pencil-heels that left her unable to keep pace with them.

The door closed behind Valentina.

What a rude…

"Georgina Baer!"

Georgina struggled to open the door while carrying her stack of papers balanced in one hand.

"Yes, yes, Your Honour! I am here."

Valentina smirked, looking down and adjusting her bangs with her fingers.

"Okay, Val, what is the issue here with Georgina giving a character reference on behalf of her client?"

"Karyn…"

"*Your Honour* when we're dealing with a case, please."

Valentina cleared her throat and gulped down some phlegm that had come up.

She noted once again that she *really* ought to quit smoking.

"*Your Honour*, what Georgina is proposing is *absurd*! I need her *word* and a copy of that character statement to ensure that she *won't* bring up the story that Mr. Nolan concocted in private to his lawyer."

"I *won't*, Your Honour. I have *no* intention of bringing it up. Here, look at my character reference."

Valentina shifted on her feet, quickly scanning the five hundred word document.

She scoffed.

"*This*? This is *useless*."

"That's for Judge Heidelbaugh to decide."

Valentina laughed.

"The last time we had a lawyer do this was in the early fifties in State v. Johnathan Friel. Friel was sentenced to death anyway and his lawyer, that *woman*, was *suffocated* to death in her car. So why take the chance, Georgina? Why put your piece into public record? You'll have a *target* on your back!"

"He has the *right* to have two character references on the record. That's all he gets. I already *have* a target on my back, Valentina. Have you *seen* the men I have defended in the past?"

"But this man is *different*. *This* is the man who has been behind the *worst* crimes against womankind in recent history in this country. He *is* Draven Alec! *He* spread misogynistic material! *He* raped a woman!"

"That has *yet* to be determined, Val."

"Way to believe all women no matter what, Georgina!"

"I have to *defend* him somehow, Valentina. That is *my job*!"

"Okay, okay, *enough*! I have heard absolutely *enough*. Last night and now today. *Both* of you need to take some mental health days after this case is done."

Valentina and Georgina folded their arms across their chests in defiance, but nodded nonetheless.

"Now, Valentina, the precedence is there. This is one, *very* restricted way that Georgina can defend her client. She has a word limit for the reference. She has now stated that she will *not* be bringing up the accusations made by this man, and she is aware of the consequences of this for the man. So, I am moving to let Georgina read into the record her character reference for Mr. Michael Nolan."

CHAPTER 104

When they returned to their tables, Michael tapped Georgina on her wrist and nodded in approval.

She smiled in response.

"You may proceed, counsellor," Karyn said.

"I, attorney of law in the state of Massachusetts, Ms. Georgina Baer, write this in reference of Mr. Michael Nolan, client on the record. In the brief time that I have gotten to know Mr. Nolan, it has become apparent to me that the charges against my client have been put forth with malicious intentions."

Georgina paused and looked directly at Althea.

"The prosecution asserts that this man is culpable of committing the most *heinous* crime against a woman: allegedly *raping* her on a night when she was *nowhere* in the area. She was, however, seen by several eye witnesses and by street cameras to be entering and leaving Mr. Nolan's building on September 22nd, 2075. The day *after* the rape had allegedly occurred."

She saw Althea flinch.

In that moment, Georgina became certain of one thing: Althea Hayworth had been *lying*. Perhaps about the rape, perhaps about the aftermath, but most *certainly* about her feelings towards Michael.

When Georgina looked at her now, she didn't see a broken woman anymore, but rather a young and naive woman who had finally been *slapped* in the face with the harsh consequences of her tradeship with this man.

With *any* man.

"Having gone through the same schooling system that Ms. Hayworth has, I do *not* believe that she would have been *foolish* enough to get involved with a man who could have *ever* posed a threat to her bodily well-being. We are taught from a young age how to deal with *traditional* men, the ones who display pride, aggression, and toxicity. We are taught how to *defend* ourselves. And in case danger *does* arise, we are taught that we have *every* woman on our side. For *two* days after the rape allegedly happened, Ms. Hayworth did not come forward with a statement about this alleged rape. She did *not* confide in her mothers, her coworkers, or her *fiancée*. The *law* would have been on her side, the *police* would have taken her claims seriously, and the *media* would have *crucified* this man for raping her, with *no* doubt whatsoever. *Especially* given that he was *already* set to be tried for his role as Draven Alec."

Georgina looked at Karyn and saw a flicker of doubt flash across her face.

It was only momentary, but it gave Georgina hope.

"There is *also* the issue of no other DNA or fingerprints being found at the crime scene other than those of my client and Ms. Althea Hayworth. There was not one hair, one fingerprint, or even one *smudge* of a fingerprint found at Mr. Nolan's apartment, even though he claims that he has hosted many MRA meetings there."

All of the facts that she could clearly present were now out there for Karyn to consider.

Georgina just hoped that it would be enough.

"I would like to conclude with my perception of my client during our meetings. In all the meetings that we have had, I have not had to request a glass screen. I have been able to sit with him, in the same room, across a table from him, without *any* cause for alarm. I have not been threatened or harmed by anybody that he knows, or by himself. I have had *no* reason to believe that he desires power or has sexual deviances that would disallow him from being a well-behaved citizen of this country. I have no reason to believe that he is a *threat*, and for that reason, I have no reason to believe that he would *ever* rape a woman, in spite of his sexist ideas. But I will concede that he *does* have sexist ideas, for which he should be given treatment."

Georgina sat down.

The courtroom was silent.

Valentina glared at Georgina from the prosecution's table, but there was nothing that she could do about what had been said.

Character references only did so much, and fighting them was not a part of Valentina's plan.

"The prosecution has no questions regarding either reference, Your Honour."

"The defence rests their case."

Michael agitatedly tapped her on the wrist.

She nodded towards him in pity.

It was the most she could do.

He looked at her with complete contempt.

He knew that he would be back in the picture room that evening.

He *despised* her for that.

He despised *himself* for that.

CHAPTER 105

I sank deeper into my bed.

My eyes stayed wide open.

I hadn't anticipated the way that my stomach would *lurch* when I saw the bruises on his pale arms.

Even just a *shadow* of him was too much for me to bear.

A *shadow*.

That's what he felt like now.

The more time I spent away from him, the more he felt like just a *shadow* lingering in my past, shading my present in deep greys.

I shrugged off my pants.

They rolled smoothly down my thighs.

I ran my nails down my pantyhose.

My unkempt, jagged nails made a run down my right thigh.

I plucked at the loose threads.

They felt satisfyingly well-spaced under my fingertips.

One.

What was Michael doing?

Two.

It got caught in my nail.

Three.

Tug at both of them and…

Snap.

I jerked upright and pulled off the ruined pantyhose.

Then my plain, black, silky smooth underwear.

　"Make sure you wear one that doesn't show through your pants, Al," Mom had said this morning.

I remembered the oddest things at the oddest times.

　"Yes, Mom."

Between my bare legs, I felt the cool air in the room skim my labia just enough to make me want to cover it with my palm.

Protect it.

That was my instinct.

After all, I *had* been raped, hadn't I?

I let my fingers run over the dry skin covered with curly hairs.

I hadn't felt like grooming my pubic hairs since the last time I had…

I hadn't even felt a *single* sexual desire ever since that last time with *him*.

That was the frustrating thing.

I let my finger drift there, right above my clitoris, remembering Georgina's reference.

She *knew* I was lying.

The trepidation from that knowledge made my nipples taut inside my bra.

I began in slow, circular motions, trying to relax my shoulders deep into the bed.

I thought of Fess' beautiful face.

Blood rushed to the nerve endings in my clitoris.

I recalled her hair, the way that it would bounce in the cold wind, the coconut-y smell of it enveloping my whole body in a sort of tropical paradise.

When was the last time I even *spoken* to Felicity?

She hadn't been allowed in the courthouse because she wasn't immediate family.

Yet.

I was grateful for that.

I hadn't even been able to *think* about her through all this.

Except now.

Now, when I wanted a release.

I frustratingly tried to reminisce about her hair, the coconut scent, and paradise.

The image of her faded from my mind as quickly as I had conjured it up.

Agitatedly, I pulled at a clump of pubic hairs until they stretched into one taut rope.

A tiny acrobat could have easily practiced on these elongated strands.

I felt like an acrobat.

I just wanted to shut my eyes and *scream*.

I yanked at the hairs until their roots came out.

I noticed that the roots had the tiniest remains of blood.

It dried up quickly.

I sprinkled them onto the floor.

I climbed back into bed with my blouse and blazer still on, my bra underwire still prodding at my ribs, and my ass as bare as the day I was born.

I fell into a fitful sleep, only to be awoken by my frozen joints.

Twenty blankets stacked on top of each other wouldn't have been able to cure my internal frigidity.

Georgina knew.

I knew she knew that I was a liar.

My story wasn't even sane.

What have I become?

CHAPTER 106

9:45 A.M.

The clock on the far left wall ticked the seconds of my pathetic life away.

It was already time for me to face him again.

Once again, I was in the *same* room, at the *same* time, breathing the *same* air.

I would come face to face with him shortly.

How was I supposed to compose myself?

A spider behind the judge's podium distracted me.

This morning, I had been subjected to the usual pre-court screaming match between Mom and Ma that I had come to enjoy.

One would yell at the other to make coffee.

One would shove a mug in my general direction.

I would leave it in front of me untouched.

They would argue about the best costumes to wear for today's charade.

Mom would go with one of her many dark pinstriped pantsuits.

Ma would go with one of her many funeral-appropriate dresses.

They had to look *somber*.

They wanted to look portentously *dignified* for this facade.

Pretend like they weren't completely *ecstatic* to send this man to his demise.

Pretend like they hadn't both *conspired* and *coerced* me into telling a story.

I would have to tell that story today.

Rehearsal wasn't necessary, because the script had been read to my sleeping body in the early morning hours by either Mom or Ma for days.

It had become a part of my subconscious.

It had become a part of *me*.

The story made sense.

It was all cohesive.

So fucking *perfect*.

Flawless.

I had started to *believe* it.

You tell a lie often enough and it becomes the truth, right?

Memory was a submissive thing.

I looked away from the spider and down at my hands.

While I had zoned out and stared at my hands, he had walked in with his lawyer.

The back of his head looked greyer.

How could someone age so damn fast?

What had he gone through in that place?

I shifted in my seat, trying not to think about that.

I had forgotten to take my hormone stabilizers this morning.

Shit.

My heel clicked against the leg of the chair.

What I *thought* had been the loudest sound in the room had barely made a drop in the ocean of voices around me.

My heel was caught there.

I froze with panic.

What if I couldn't get it out when I was called up to the stand?

The panic made me shift even more.

No one cared.

No one.

Not about me.

Not about him.

All they wanted was another man, *this* man, behind bars.

They just wanted him *gone*.

They just wanted him to disappear for saying the wrong things.

For *being* the wrong things.

I rotated my neck, trying hard not to fixate on that.

Shit.

Tears threatened to fall down my face and I had to compose myself.

He hadn't turned around to search for me.

The main actors in a play *always* looked around to search for their loved ones.

It comforted them.

Didn't my presence *comfort* him anymore?

I remembered holding him when he had had one of his terrifying nightmares.

Didn't he *need* me anymore?

This was *insulting*.

I meant *nothing* to him anymore.

I suddenly felt *justified* in what I was doing.

I *am* justified in what I'm doing.

Fuck him.

I had to bury the overwhelming need to *scream* at him.

I knew that such an outburst would only make him *exhilarated* that I cared.

Turn around, goddessdamnit.

It's okay if he doesn't.

I *know* what he did.

I *know* what he is.

He did it.

He would have done it to someone else.

Someone else, inspired by him and his sexist *rhetoric*, would have eventually done it to me or some other woman.

I'm doing this for all of *them*.

For *me*.

For the greater good of *womankind*.

He raped me.

He *raped* me.

He raped...

Me.

CHAPTER 107

Ten minutes ago, as they were heading into the courthouse, Georgina had gotten egged.

Michael could smell the sulphuric residue of the yolk on her shirt.

His mind wandered to the little chicks that he had ground up earlier that week.

The female baby chicks smelt the same after their beaks had been burned to a crisp.

Even though he was pissed as hell at Georgina for having condoned conversion therapy, he knew she was doing the best that she could under the circumstances.

In that godforsaken place, he had been cut off from all television.

He didn't know what they had been saying about him to create the *mob* scene outside the courthouse every day of this godforsaken trial.

Inside the courthouse, when he saw the hoard of people packed like sardines behind him, he felt his heart race in panic.

From the corner of his right eye he caught a glimpse of *her*.

Maybe the picture room was *finally* working its magic, because he felt *nothing* when he imagined her perfectly brushed black hair flowing between his fingers.

Seven sessions since the start of the trial.

Seven times that his brain had been *Skinnered* into loving men.

He shifted uncomfortably in his seat.

His right ear itched.

He wanted to scratch it, but his hands were cuffed behind his back this time.

He tried to shrug his shoulder up to his earlobe.

The touch of the fabric against his skin satisfied the itch.

The satisfaction stopped when he heard voices laugh in his other ear.

He first heard murmurs.

Then laughter.

And then felt hot water *scalding* between his legs.

Where am I?

He grimaced and shut his eyes as tightly as he could.

His knees followed.

He crossed his legs and shifted in his seat until he couldn't feel his crotch.

The numbness was a welcome change from the burning, scabbing, and itching routine he had grown so used to.

　　"Are you okay?" Georgina asked.

Fuck.

That was the *first* time someone had inquired about his state of being since this *whole* ordeal had begun.

Am I okay?

He blinked hard, trying to focus on Georgina's face.

He looked down at his pants in horror.

They felt hot and wet.

　　"The judge hasn't walked in yet. Do you want to clean up?"

　　"Yes, please."

　　"Guards?"

　　"What the hell is it?"

　　"He needs new pants. Now!"

She looked at him sympathetically.

He gratefully accepted her kindness.

Under any other circumstances, Michael would have wanted *more* than just a simple exchange of gratitude between them.

The picture room *really* wasn't working.

CHAPTER 108

As Georgina waited for Michael to clean himself up, her mind drifted to the afternoon after she had presented Patricia Nolan's reference.

"We're willing to offer your client a plea bargain," Valentina had said.

Karyn had grabbed a KitKat, opening it hastily.

The wrapper had made a sound so obnoxiously loud that Georgina and Valentina had just stared at Karyn until she had taken the first bite.

"On a chocolate-only diet, ladies. Continue."

"Okay, what is it, Val? Make it good."

Georgina recalled how Valentina's bangs kept swooping in front of her deep green eyes.

Valentina had cleared her throat and looked down at her papers.

*"So, I have discussed this with Karyn already, and we have decided that this is the **best** course of action…"*

*"Of **course** you two have."*

"You can drop the attitude, Georgina. We're all trying to do our best here, given the circumstances."

Georgina looked at this old woman, with blonde curls in her hair, munching on that damn chocolate bar, trying absurdly to lose a few pounds. The whole thing was so cartoonish that had she not held as much power as she did, Georgina would have laughed out loud.

*"**No**, Karyn. We're seriously **not**. This entire thing is a bloody **joke**. For Goddess' sake! You **know** this. You **both** know this. He's goddamn **innocent**!"* Georgina had shouted.

*"That is **yet** to be determined, Georgina. And I'd like to remind you that **I** decide the outcome of this case. So don't you **dare** raise your voice to me in **my***

chambers. You two can smoke outside and have a showdown for all I care. In **here***, I'd like to keep things* **civil***."*

"Alright, so as I was **saying***, I have a proposition for you. Before I put Althea through her testimony and make life on the outside* **really** *difficult for Mr. Nolan if he gets out, let him plead guilty and go to Fangsel, with some cancer care, if he needs it, no mandatory organ donation, no media, no* **show,** *none of that. Do we have a deal?"*

"No."

Georgina had been adamant.

"What the hell, Geor…" Valentina started.

*"***No***, because I want the world to see Althea's testimony and decide for* **themselves** *whether or not she is a liar. Because this* **didn't** *happen."*

She had said this about *all* of her previous clients.

It was her job, after all.

But this time, she *meant* it.

"My client denies the assault was ever even **committed** *by him. He says that* **he** *was the one who had been assaulted,"* she had blurted out.

"Shit, Georgina. How **gullible** *are you? At this point the man is going to say* **anything** *for a get-out-of-jail-free card. You can't believe a fucking* **word** *that comes out of his mouth."*

"So **you two** *can make deals behind closed doors and Michael doesn't even get to speak for himself in court or in front of cameras? The court of public opinion has already hung him for his ideas. Not for his actions, but for his* **ideas***. You both won't even consider the* **possibility** *that he is a victim here. How the* **hell** *is that fair?"*

Karyn had stood up and slammed the chocolate bar on her desk.

"Stop acting like a petulant child, Georgina. We aren't here for **fairness***. We're here for* **justice***. You want fair? Go run for office and change it back to the way it was when the* **men** *were in charge. Do you remember what* **hell** *that was like? Only* **two percent** *of rapists were put behind bars. Do you remember* **that***?* **I DO***! Are you forgetting what else he's been charged with? Distribution of sexist material and hate speech. He's a* **menace** *to society. He's a menace to* **women***. Now, he needs a defence lawyer, that's* **fair***, but* **justice** *is a different story. The fact is, Ms. Hayworth has* **accused** *your client of rape. It is* **her** *testimony and the consistency of it that matters. So unless you can prove his innocence, justice* **will** *be served."*

Georgina rubbed her eyebrows, trying to ease the stress headache that was coming from recollecting this conversation.

*"Look, I only want the best possible outcome. As if enough isn't **already** being done to him in that hell hole. Let her say her piece, and then let's all set a precedent for a little **leniency**. Come on, Karyn, think about it, why did Althea wait to tell her story? Why wait a whole **three days**?"*

*"That's **victim blaming**!"* Valentina had interjected.

*"I'm not **blaming** her for what happened! Goddessdamnit! I'm denying **that** it happened. Can't you **both** see the difference in the two claims? For crying out loud!"*

*"You're a **disgrace** to women, Georgina. That you still **choose** to be in this line of work, defending these pieces of absolute **shit**, is beyond my comprehension."*

*"Death by hanging **is** off the table, as it has always been, because he is still physically useful. Maximum sentence will be life in Fangsel and, no, Georgina, I **won't** consider leniency, seeing as you're rejecting the plea bargain and counting on some sort of public character assassination of Althea to win him some publicity points,"* Karyn had declared.

*"An innocent man is going to go to that hell hole because of **you**. **Both** of you! And you don't give a flying **shit**!"*

*"I give a shit about the **woman** involved! That poor **woman** is going to go through the **hell** of a testimony because of **you**! What about **her**?!"*

"ENOUGH! Both of you!"

Karyn had kicked off her heels and sat down in her office chair again.

"Who does he say assaulted him?" Karyn had asked.

"Natalia. And her wife."

*"Do you even know what the **hell** you're saying right now?"*

*"Karyn, our Honourable Judge, **asked**, Valentina, so I **had** to answer,"* Georgina had said.

Valentina had shoved into Georgina's shoulder from behind.

*"You're lying! You're fucking **lying**! He tells you a story and you just fucking **believe** it?"*

She had noticed Karyn frowning.

*"Georgina, that accusation is bloody **outrageous**. You cannot expect me to believe that an upstanding citizen like Natalia Hayworth would have absolutely **any** reason to rape that man. Especially a man that her daughter was in a consensual tradeship with, by her own admission!"*

Valentina had been completely blocking her view of Karyn's face.

Georgina had seen Valentina's back shudder before she had erupted in laughter that filled the entire room.

Karyn had joined her.

Georgina had stood there, dumbstruck, looking at the rising and falling of Valentina's back.

Valentina had turned to face her, wiping her eyes of laughter-filled tears.

"Georgie, I'm glad you don't get to defend the man with your insane story. He would be laughed out of court and you along with him."

*"But I am **not** lying!"*

"Show yourself out, Georgie," Karyn had said, still chuckling.

Georgina had taken her bruised ego and managed to march herself out of Karyn's chambers with her head held high and her back taut.

She had heard them snicker as she walked away.

She remembered crying all the way home.

"I'm good now," Michael said, interrupting her thoughts.

"Let's go. It's time."

CHAPTER 109

The two women had met at the same cafe for years.

Rodger had *always* been happy to oblige, even though one of them seemed to want him *dead*.

He didn't mind.

More business, in cash, under the radar, meant that he could keep some men off the streets and give them jobs.

Besides, he didn't have to worry unless he crossed one of them.

One of them was fine with his lewd comments. She even liked sucking his dick once in a while.

That one, *that* girl, he liked.

She even tipped him handsomely for keeping his mouth shut about everything.

They sometimes didn't see eye to eye.

He knew that too.

He never minded the ruckus though.

It always ended with the dick-sucker wanting to get with him even *more*.

That was what he was looking forward to on this fine, crisp, unusually cold day.

"Liv, here girl, decaf."

Rodger slid over the coffee cup whose rim was stained with the previous user's lipstick.

She smiled, showing off all her teeth. Some silver, some white. All that he would have *loved* around his cock.

"Turn around, handsome, and shake that *ass* for me. "

She hooked her index finger into the belt loop closest to his left hip.

She drew him close until he almost tipped into her chair.

"Could you *not*?" Sigma scowled.

"It's just a bit of *fun*, Sig. Come on, loosen up a little. "

Olivia shifted her gaze from Sigma to Rodger.

"Well, Rodge, just the black coffee for this uppity…" she started and then laughed.

Rodger pretended to be offended before he turned around to walk away.

"Really Sig, you gotta loosen up about men a little. We know what you do for a living, but come on, don't you want a little side —" Olivia air-cupped Rodger's behind "— something?"

"Not *everyone* relies on men to get off, Liv. Some of us don't like our jobs, but we do it for the betterment of womankind," Sigma chastised.

They laughed.

They had a mutual loathing of their clients, who needed to hire their expertise for the progression of womankind.

"I appreciate your info on Nolan being that bastard Draven Alec."

"No problem. You owe me one."

Rodger interrupted their conversation with two black coffees.

Olivia kept her mouth shut about all the dirty details she knew about the Hayworths.

"The organs are coming in great lately. A lot more of them locked up in there."

Sigma scoffed in approving disgust.

"Bastards. At least they're useful for that *one* thing."

Rodger glanced sideways, noting Sigma's disdain for his kind.

He grinned, thinking about how funny it was that this woman with a buzz cut and her tiny tits who dressed like a man, hated *men*.

CHAPTER 110

It was as though in the blink of an eye I had completely lost control of the situation.

Today.

That's all I could fixate on.

Today.

Within the next few minutes, I would say my piece.

Fuck.

Then, Michael had soiled his pants and left the room.

It should have been easier not to care.

To be ready and focused on saying my piece.

All of it should have been *easier.*

But as with any performer going up onstage, it was nerve-wracking.

No matter how ready you were, or how well-prepared, or how many times you had rehearsed the lines, an audience *always* made the situation unpredictable.

Today.

Today, there would be at least a hundred of them, some with their cameras, others with their pens and papers.

Staring at me.

Pitying me.

Wondering how I could have *ever* involved myself with such a *monster*.

Waiting for me to speak and say all the words that they wanted to hear.

Condemning *him*.

As if I had something *true* to say about *him*.

Compose yourself.

Yes.

Mom.

The mantra *would* have worked, if I hadn't seen his figure in the corner of my eye settling into his chair again with fresh pants.

As soon as I had positioned myself on the witness stand, I saw *him* again.

Dead straight in front of my face.

Him.

He made me lose composure.

He made me sweat.

He raped me.

Yes.

Mom.

CHAPTER 111

Valentina called her sole witness to the stand.

Georgina shuffled through her papers to find a blank one.

Valentina wanted to throw a book at her head to make her stop the noise.

"Please state your full name for the court."

"Althea Hayworth."

"Do you swear to tell the whole truth and nothing but the truth, so help you Goddess?"

"I do."

Althea's head pounded.

In the brief silence that spread through the entire courtroom, she felt alone.

The loneliness crept in through the back of her mind and devoured her completely.

Somebody's feet shuffled.

Somebody cleared their throat a little too loudly.

She remembered getting her tonsils removed and having this feeling of wild *panic* right before the anesthetic kicked in.

How did we get here?

Valentina broke the silence.

"I know this is hard for you, Althea, but could you please recant the events of September 21st, 2075 for the benefit of the court records?"

"I can. Yes."

Her voice was already giving her away, but Moms had said that a quivering voice could be a sign of distress.

Nothing to worry about.

Especially in *this* courthouse, where the victim would *never* be cross-examined and her testimony could *never* be questioned, a quivering voice was a sign of *terrible* distress.

Valentina brought a box of tissues to the witness stand as she saw Althea tear up.

"It's *okay*, Althea. We're all here for you."

Her moms had coached her well.

The judge looked remorsefully at Althea. She had tried more rape cases in her career than she could count. But none had ever been *this* meaningful to her, with so much heated backlash and call for *blood*.

Not *one* person in the courtroom that morning chose to look the way of the defendant.

He was *guilty* of rape.

They *all* knew it.

Althea just needed to tell her story.

"Could you — " Althea started, with her eyes welling up, "— please ask the defendant to leave the room?"

She looked at him for what felt like a long minute, but quickly turned her head away in remorse when their eyes met.

Michael didn't avert his eyes for one *second* from the witness stand.

He stood up, balancing on his hands against the table.

"You have got to be *fucking* kidding me! Althea, look at ME! *Look* at me! I didn't fucking *rape* you. Tell them all the fucking *truth*! Tell them the *truth*, Althea. Tell them that you *wanted* to be with me. Tell them what you wrote in that letter. Be fucking honest, for *once* in your miserable fucking existence!"

Karyn banged the gavel.

"Mr. Nolan, I implore you to *not* speak out of turn…"

He was yanked away from his seat with such great force that he thought his shoulder might pop out of its socket.

"Tell them that you *wanted* this as much as me! I never touched a *fucking* hair on your *fucking* head unless you *asked* me to. Why the *hell* are you doing this? Did *they* put you up to this? Do you know *why* they put you up to this? Do you even *know* what they *did* to me?"

The gavel banged over and over, echoing in Althea's ears and drowning him out.

He looked at her one more time for any emotion.

Just *one*.

Any one.

She had her head hung down.

She had sold him out.

Georgina had sold him out.

The feeling of betrayal soaked into his bones as he collapsed onto his knees.

The guards dragged him on his knees.

"Get the hell up! Get the *fucking* hell up!"

His knees wouldn't let him.

"I need another guard!" Karyn boomed.

They lifted him up to his feet and kicked him in his stomach.

Everyone in the court room heard him scream in agonizing pain.

Several people in the courtroom gasped.

Althea screamed back, emboldened: "You'll say *anything,* won't you? *Just* to get out of this!"

"*You* deserve this more than *me*, Al. When you find out the *truth*, you'll be sorry."

Karyn's voice echoed after the door closed behind Michael.

"Given this...*spectacle*, I proceed to call a recess to give the victim the chance to regain composure of her mind."

She banged her gavel.

Althea had been given another hour to regain numbness.

CHAPTER 112

Valentina shakily took out a cigarette.

"One coffee please."

The vending machine poured out the black liquid while she impatiently tapped on her cigarette.

Althea rushed to the bathroom in search of a free stall before retching into the sink instead.

Valentina *felt* like retching.

Was there any truth to what he was saying?

They were both consumed by this question, but neither one of them could convince themselves to stop the proceedings now for long enough to think things through.

His fervid assertion of his innocence had left a bitter taste in both of their mouths.

What if...

Althea heaved until she felt like she was about to throw up the inside of her stomach lining.

Valentina felt unsteady as the ground beneath her shook.

Althea pulled a pill out of her purse and swallowed it.

Valentina firmly planted both feet on the ground and drowned her coffee in one gulp.

They both sighed.

They were both tied to the same fate: *live with it.*

They made their way back into the courthouse.

CHAPTER 113

"Order in the court. The Honourable Judge Heidelbaugh presiding."

She took her seat at the front of the courtroom.

"Please sit."

She didn't feel like she deserved the recognition.

Today was *not* about her.

It was about Althea and *her* story.

She didn't want a *moment* of attention to be taken away from Althea's opportunity to obtain *justice*.

Her glasses sat on the bridge of her nose, but she scrunched up her forehead and glanced over the rims to be able to see in the distance.

She had a bad habit of biting her pen when she was stressed.

The entire room was tense, and that made her almost want to swallow the plastic pen cover sitting innocently on her table.

"Let us begin," Karyn said.

Valentina cleared her throat. The nicotine had thickly coated her tonsils this morning.

"I know this is going to be hard for you, Althea, but could you please tell the court what happened on September 21st, 2075," Valentina said, with all the sympathy she could muster.

"Yes, I can."

Althea furrowed her brows with sadness and darkened her gaze.

"Go ahead, dear," Karyn said.

"Yes, thank you."

Althea cleared her throat.

"On September 21st, 2075, I willingly walked to Mr. Nolan's home at around three in the afternoon. We had been together in a consensual trade-ship."

The entire courtroom gasped.

"Order in the court! Right this instant!"

The whispers quieted down.

"Could you explain what you mean by "consensual trade-ship", Ms. Hayworth?" Valentina asked.

"Of course, yes. By "consensual trade-ship", I meant that I was engaging in intercourse with him on a regular basis, and I did not mind."

"Thank you. Please continue with the rest of your testimony, without interruption from the courthouse. This is already hard enough for you, and we know that."

Valentina put her cold palm on Althea's shivering hand.

When their eyes met, Valentina pulled her hand away swiftly.

The look they shared made both of them recoil in disgust.

Althea composed herself, nodding solemnly and sniffling.

"But that afternoon, something was *different*. I went to his place as usual, but it was one of the first times that I thought something may have been wrong, because he was more *stern* than usual. I ignored my gut feeling and went inside anyway. "

Althea paused, shakily picking up her glass of water and drawing it to her lips.

One sip.

Two.

Gulp.

Her throat felt as dry as it had on the first day that she had walked into the courthouse.

"I went inside and he was sitting on the chair in front of his double windows."

She paused, scanning the room, tears obscuring the silhouettes of the strangers in front of her.

"He had been reading, by the looks of it. One of the pamphlets by the crazy MRAs up in Europe. He was in one of his 'traditional' moods and I had only consented to dominating him. That's how we had always done it."

The courtroom seemed to be eating her story up. The slew of female journalists in the front rows nodded and sighed in collective, kindhearted understanding.

"Midway through intercourse, he overpowered me, dug his nails into my back, and rammed some sort of pill down my throat."

Several people started crying. Some women gasped in horror towards Georgina. The few men lingering at the back of the courthouse hung their heads.

Georgina stared directly at Althea, unmoving, unflinching, and unblinking.

Althea cleared her throat, looking away and back towards Valentina again.

"When I woke up, I was on my back."

Karyn frowned in contemplation.

After this, Althea knew *exactly* what she wanted to say.

She had rehearsed it enough times in front of her moms.

It was Mom-approved.

Yes Mom, Althea thought.

"I asked him to get off of me because I felt so confused, I hadn't said yes to this, and he said… " she burst into tears.

A tall woman stood up suddenly at the back of the courtroom.

"*Please!* We don't need to hear anymore! He is *guilty!*"

"Order! Order in the court! This is just for public record, Althea. You don't have to tell the court *anything* that you are not comfortable with. You can tell me in private if you'd like, okay?"

Althea mumbled between sobs, "I would like to continue."

Magda stared at her feet in horror for not daring to look up *once* at her daughter.

Natalia looked stoically at Karyn with furrowed brows.

"Only if you want, dear," Karyn nodded.

"He said, 'I knew you *cunts* were good for something.' "

Althea sobbed uncontrollably this time.

The entire courtroom *erupted*.

A few women leapt to their feet and screamed at the judge.

"*Enough!* We've heard *enough!*"

"That's when I picked up my clothes and left and went straight to Moms' place and told them everything."

"Did you go to the police right away?"

"No, I did not, because I was in shock. In absolute *shock* at what had happened."

Magda shifted uncomfortably in her seat.

She switched her top leg from left to right and tried to ignore the itch lingering deep between her thighs.

The razor had left a scab about an inch long.

She couldn't *wait* to itch all over.

She was snapped back to reality when Natalia dug her nails into her thigh.

"... I trusted my moms. I knew they would come to you and that you could help me."

CHAPTER 114

"We need *order* in the court, this *instant*!" Karyn's voice boomed over the microphone.

Valentina proposed, "I think this calls for a clearing of the court."

"I will have to second that motion," Georgina echoed through the chaos.

"Guards, remove all those in the audience at once." Karyn banged her gavel.

The guards were swift.

People threw purses and shoes towards Georgina at the front of the court before being escorted out.

A woman in the middle row hesitated before getting up.

She was staring at Althea in absolute horror.

"Ma'am, you have to leave."

"I'm her fiancée."

"You have to leave."

Felicity looked to Althea for support.

Althea turned her head away to look at Karyn instead.

"I need my moms."

"What's that, dear?" Karyn asked.

"*I NEED MY MOMS!*" Althea shouted through tears.

"Dear, don't worry. It's okay. It's okay, dear, they're going to stay."

Magda went up to Althea and held her while Natalia escorted Felicity out.

A few doors down, Michael sat on the floor, handcuffed, in a dusty room.

CHAPTER 115

He could hear voices outside the room.

Tick.

He hugged his knees to his chest, rocking himself back and forth to the sound of the clock.

Tock.

What in the actual *hell* was Althea doing?

Did she *know* what had been done to him?

She *had* to have not known, or else she wouldn't be doing this to him.

The more he thought, the faster he rocked back and forth.

Tick, tock, tick, tock.

He heard voices come closer to the door.

"*Damn it!* Martina and I had a *deal!*"

"Ma'am! Ma'am! You *can't* go in there. That man is off limits!"

"She gave me a goddessdamned *job!*"

He scooted away from the middle of the room towards the back wall and cowered near it.

He put his hands over his ears.

NO!

"Come on, be a goddessdamned *WOMAN* and let me in!"

He quickly got up and walked to the middle of the room.

He put his fists together and drew them up to his face to protect it.

The days of starvation, shitty food, hard labour, and conversion therapy had made him weak, but right now he kept his posture sturdy.

He wouldn't go down without a fight.

The woman's voice was hoarse and deep.

"Come on, just *one* minute," the same voice said.

"The judge would have your *head*, you fucking hear me? She would have *our* heads!"

There was more scuffle.

He began to hear the sound of his heart beating instead of the scuffle outside.

Tick, thump, tick, thump, tick, tick, thump, tick, tick, tick, thump…

BANG!

Thump, thump, thump, tick, thump, thump, thump.

His heart rate increased tenfold.

The footsteps marched away.

CHAPTER 116

Sigma was frustrated.

The two female guards had clear instructions to keep the asshole safe from any intruders except his lawyer.

But she and Martina had a *deal*.

She was the one who had given Sigma his damn name.

For Goddess' sake!

She walked outside the courthouse in a hurry, narrowly scraping past anyone who was in her way.

There had to be a window into that *damn* room with that *damn* man.

There just *had* to be.

She wasn't going to stop until she found it, broke through it, and took his fucking *balls* as souvenirs.

She wanted to finish the damn job that she had been hired to do.

Every damn window and door was bolted and guarded.

Goddess fucking damn it!

Martina hadn't held up her end of the bargain.

She was *supposed* to clear the way for Sigma to go in and *finish* that bastard. She was *supposed* to control her stupid fucking colleagues.

Sigma had killed Martina's dad like she had demanded.

What more did that woman want?

This wasn't going to bode well for her in the coming months, especially if she wanted someone dead.

Sigma shook her head in disgust.

There may not be any other chances to give this man the *justice* he deserved.

She knew that much.

She would have to get someone on the inside to do the job *for* her.

That could take *months*.

She didn't run with any women who were insane enough to get themselves locked up in a place like that.

The Cavaliers were respected for a *reason*.

This is what she got for being just *peachy* with the damn chief of police.

Goddess fucking dammit!

CHAPTER 117

Felicity stood on her balcony sipping on a cup of coffee.

The second one this morning.

The last few weeks had been an absolute *nightmare*.

She would sleep for one sleep cycle and then wake up drenched in sweat.

From the days of not being allowed in the courthouse, the nonexistent communication from Althea, the inescapable press coverage of her trial, and the insanity that had transpired at the beginning of Althea's testimony, Felicity had *barely* been able to think straight, let alone sleep restfully.

Magda and Natalia had insisted on postponing the announcement of their wedding in the online papers until later this year.

Once the press from the trial had died down.

Valentina had been quick to condone the decision.

At least the sentencing was tomorrow.

Felicity had managed to shield Aibek from all of it.

He was the *only* bright spot in her life right now.

"Mommy! Mommy! Look at what I found!"

He brought her an old picture of her and her moms from when Felicity had been around his age.

She bent down to his level.

She didn't have to bend as low anymore.

He had grown.

"Those are your grandmas and me when I was about eight or nine."

Aibek was still lanky.

Not because he wouldn't eat enough.

He ate more than *she* did.

He just played it all off.

During the court case, she had enrolled him in a school that took boys his age.

It was almost an hour drive away, but Felicity made sure he got to school on time, every single day.

Another event Althea had missed.

She had been missing a lot.

Unlike all the little girls in Aibek's class who busied themselves with desk work, he ran around and played off his energy.

They schemed.

He explored.

His teacher suggested putting him on ADHD medication to calm him down.

She had refused, so now she had to find an all-boys school for him by end of January.

She looked into his curious little face.

There was something different about him now.

A little less...*innocence.*

She wondered what he had heard from the other kids about his soon-to-be Mom.

She looked at his little hands, dirtied with playdough.

"I think it's time for a bath, Aibek."

"But I wanna play more with the playdough, Mommy!"

"Bath! *Now!*"

He ran off before she could pick him up.

"Aibek! *Aibek!* Get back here!"

"You'll have to catch me!"

She chased him all the way to the bedroom and into her closet.

"Where did my little baby go?"

He giggled in the closet.

She went to the closet and tickled his stomach like he was the Pillsbury dough boy.

He giggled some more.

She picked him up.

While he wriggled against her to get free, she dropped him into the bathtub.

"Bath. *Now.*"

Her stern face *always* did the trick.

She kept the door ajar as he began to undress.

She wanted to make sure that he turned on the tap and *actually* bathed himself.

It was always a chore with him.

He had a habit of playing in the sink with his toys while completely undressed and dirty, instead of plopping into the bathtub.

This time, she had hidden his toys in her dresser.

When she heard the click of the plug, the movement of the tap, and the rush of the water into the empty bathtub, she opened the door wide enough to see him.

He was completely undressed now.

"You want your toys?"

He nodded.

"Okay, put the soap in."

"But mommy! I want my toys *now*!"

"Then you'll just have to *wait* for your toys."

He stood in there with his feet submerged in water.

"Okay mommy, look. Look, I'm going to do it."

He squeezed the bottle of shower gel into the bathtub.

She watched his supple behind jiggle up and down as he jumped around in the tub.

This was the first time that she had noticed how his body had started to develop muscle.

She admired the strong, muscular shoulders that he was beginning to develop.

She stood there observing every line in his small back.

She wanted to feel his soft skin for as long as it remained that way.

Before she knew it, he would be a *grown* man, and she didn't want to miss a *moment* of this beautiful boy's growth.

He turned around to look at her.

"Mommy! My toys! I want my *toys!*"

His exclamation snapped her back to reality.

She was *his* mommy.

She felt a surge of pride in asserting that to herself.

She brought him his toys and put them in the bathtub.

As she placed one of the action figures into the water, her hand touched his soft belly.

He giggled.

She moved her hand further down and pointed between his legs.

"You have to make sure to wash down here too, okay?"

"Where, mommy, where?"

She wanted to make sure he was hygienic.

Boys were different. They needed to be *shown* and not just told. At least that's what her parenting books had told her.

"Right there," she said.

He looked at her with trusting eyes, and nodded.

She let her fingers linger just above his thigh, for a moment, before she tickled his stomach submerged in the soapy water.

She pulled her hand out of the water, got up, and wiped her wet hands on the hand towel.

She watched as he played with his toys before completely closing the door to give him his privacy.

She put her palm on her stomach, wishing so badly that he had been inside her, created of her own flesh and blood.

CHAPTER 118

"Order in the court, Honourable Judge Karyn Heidelbaugh presiding."

"Please, everyone, sit."

The murmurs gave way to pin drop silence.

No one scratched, moved, or dared to blink.

They didn't want to miss a thing.

Karyn slipped the bailiff a piece of paper, declaring that she had made her decision.

"Would the counsel, Ms. Georgina Baer, and the defendant, Mr. Michael Nolan, please stand," the bailiff said.

Georgina stood up first.

Michael pushed his chair back with his chain-bound feet.

The screeching sound echoed through the courtroom.

I held my head down.

I braced myself for the verdict.

He adjusted himself into a tense upright position.

Karyn sternly looked over at both of them.

"The defendant has submitted two character references to the court for consideration, as is allowed by the State of Massachusetts. Upon hearing both of the references, I have not been able to conclude that Mr. Nolan is verifiably capable of reformation. His mother herself made *no* mention of that, and neither has his legal counsel. Ms. Baer was allowed to question the veracity of the evidence presented by the State, and she made a reasonable attempt at arguing for the gap in the DNA evidence collected from all parties that were present at Mr. Nolan's apartment. However, that does *not* supersede the facts of the case. As the facts stand, Ms. Althea Hayworth's testimony regarding the events that transpired on September 21st, 2075, confirms that she *was* indeed raped by the one Mr. Michael Nolan. Hence, in the case number 398706, Michael Nolan v. State of Massachusetts, I hereby declare the defendant *guilty* of rape in the first degree."

The crowd inside erupted with applause.

Mom ejected herself out of her seat to join in the standing ovation.

"We did it! We *did* it, Althea!"

She bent down and kissed my face.

Ma gave me a solemn look before Mom yanked her out of her seat to join in the applause.

Those watching the live coverage of the verdict cheered in their homes, on the streets, and outside the courthouse.

Sigma stood with the women near the back of the courtroom and clapped.

I noticed some MRAs had gathered in the back. They stood against the wall with their arms still folded across their chests.

They were carrying the same masks with the logo I had seen before.

"Order in the court! Order! *Order*!" Karyn shouted.

The gavel banged as the noise died down.

"On the count of distribution of sexist and provocative materials, I declare the defendant *guilty*."

More cheering.

The gavel banged again.

"For court records, I will now read the sentence. In the case number 398706 Nolan v. State of Massachusetts, presiding judge Karyn Heidelbaugh sentences Mr. Michael Nolan to physical utility lifetime in Fangsel, Plymouth without parole until death. He is to be used for organs, manual labour, and experimentation as needed for the betterment of womankind."

The gavel banged again.

"Mr. Nolan will be committed to nine hundred hours of conversion therapy. In continuation, Mr. Nolan is sentenced to receive castration as reparation, with no chance to preserve sperm for future procreation in the WEB."

I stayed in my chair.

"He is disallowed from having *any* female visitors or intact male visitors."

I almost choked on my own tears.

"Disallowed from contact *with* or contact *from* the Hayworths."

I looked towards Michael as he stared at the ground.

The growing crowd in the room chorused with applause.

"Denied cancer care."

What have I done?

"Denied death with dignity to end physical or mental suffering."

I noticed Georgina gripping his shoulders and mouthing 'sorry'.

I don't think he heard her through his loud sobs.

Today, justice had been served.

Then, chaos ensued.

CHAPTER 119

Sigma had come into the courtroom along with the last few women and lingered there.

She was determined to get to *that* man.

She saw Olivia's burgundy coat in the middle of the courtroom.

She nodded in approval to herself.

A few of her Cavalier women were interspersed in a perfect V shape aimed towards *him.*

They all had their weapons hidden and ready.

She had to get to him before he was taken off to Fangsel.

Karyn was reading his sentence.

"…or mental suffering."

The courtroom was erupting into applause.

She saw a man in the back shuffle and pull out something.

She went towards him with her pocket knife out.

They began chanting in unison and marching towards her, aiming to get to the front of the courthouse.

"No sentence without a fair defence! No sentence without a fair defence!"

Sigma sliced into the man she came across first.

"No sentence without a fair…"

Darrin screamed.

"JAMES! NO!"

James fell to the floor clutching his side.

Darrin flung himself onto James' body as men, guards, and women stomped on his back rushing in all different directions.

The men kept chanting and walking towards Michael.

"NO SENTENCE WITHOUT A FAIR DEFENCE!"

Olivia pushed some women towards the left exit as they screamed in panic. She was determined not to get caught in the ruckus.

"Move, move, *move*! We've got to get the *hell* out of here."

At the front of the courtroom, Felicity clutched onto Althea's hand and tugged her towards the exit on the right side.

Karyn banged her gavel.

"Order! ORDER!"

"No sentence without a fair defence!"

"Guards! ARREST THEM!"

"No sentence without a fair defence! No sentence without a fair defence!"

The men were met with the Cavaliers near the front of the courtroom.

Some of the men got into fist fights with the women, while others were slashed in the arms, legs, torso, and face by pocket knives.

Then the guards pulled out their batons and began hitting any male body in sight while trying to move the women aside.

Sigma ran towards the rest of the Cavaliers, who were trying to get to their target through the crowd and guards.

Darrin picked James up, adrenaline making his strength Herculean, slinging James' arm over his shoulder and slowly, but steadily, walking out of the courtroom with nary a guard standing in their way.

CHAPTER 120

Martina shoved past Valentina, seeing Sigma run towards Michael.

Sigma had her pocket knife out in front of her.

She had been given *one* target, and that target needed to be killed.

"Move! MOVE goddessdamn it!" she screamed at all the women dispersing.

Any men in her sight were sliced.

Suddenly, Martina was in front of her.

"Martina! Move the *hell* out of the way!"

"Stop! *Justice* has been served, he's going away for *life*! Didn't you hear what Karyn said?"

"Not *nearly* enough. That poor woman and her family deserve to know he's *permanently* gone. Now, MOVE!"

Martina didn't budge an inch.

"You could have let me do this *days* ago, and instead you had your *guards* stop me."

"Karyn promised *justice*."

"I'm the *only* one who can serve the *right* kind of justice."

"You can't do this to *him*."

"Why the hell not? The bastard deserves to die!"

"He is still useful to womankind. *Alive*!"

Sigma looked past her at her target.

He was slowly moving towards the exit with Georgina by his side.

"You gave me a job. The bastard *is* Draven Alec."

"I didn't know it at the time that Draven Alec and Michael Nolan were the same person."

"So goddessdamned what?! He is a *rapist*."

"He is also my *son*!"

Sigma looked at her in bewilderment.

"Why the *hell* would you want to protect *that* man? He has the same DNA as your goddessdamned *father*!"

"But he's still *my* son!"

Sigma's eyes shifted back to her target.

Keeping her eyes squarely focused on him, she shoved the knife deep into Martina's abdomen.

Martina clutched her stomach as Sigma pulled out her knife.

She rested her chin on Martina's left shoulder as Martina slumped onto it, still keeping her eyes on her target.

"You're just collateral damage," she whispered into Martina's ear.

She pushed Martina onto the ground while wiping the knife on her shirt.

She raced towards her target, slicing and pushing through any flesh that stood in her way.

She no longer cared if it was a man or a woman that she was harming.

She had to *end* that man.

At the front of the courtroom, Natalia swiftly marched towards the right side exit, following Althea and Felicity.

As soon she had gotten out, she noticed that Magda hadn't been following her.

CHAPTER 121

"No sentence without a fair defence!"

"Order! ORDER!"

Magda noticed Georgina steering Michael towards the front exit on the left side.

"No sentence without a fair defence!"

"Guards! ARREST THEM!"

As the men came towards Michael, Magda tried to race towards him.

"No sentence without a fair defence! No sentence without a fair defence!"

Valentina and the guards held her back.

"Magda, we've got to get the *hell* out of here!"

"You can't go that way! Get out through those doors, ma'am!"

"Don't touch me! Don't *touch* me!"

"No sentence…"

"Order!"

"Michael!! Michael Nolan!!"

She saw him turn around to look at her.

"I'm sorry! I'm *sorry*!"

He didn't react.

Not even a nod of acknowledgement.

Georgina pushed him towards the exit, even further away from earshot.

He turned his head towards the left side exit and began to shuffle out, with the chains on his arms and legs limiting his motion.

"Michael, I'm sorry."

Magda cried into her palm, attempting to muffle her sobs.

Valentina screamed as she fell to the floor with Karyn by her side. Both of them had been engaged in a fist fight with some of the men's rights activists.

Two guards pushed Magda towards the exit.

Her breath caught in her throat all the way out of the courthouse.

She ran towards the exit on the right side and straight into Natalia's arms.

She inhaled and exhaled in rapid succession, trying to catch her breath from the shock of seeing his deep blue eyes looking straight into her own.

Natalia grabbed Magda's arms, digging her nails into them and shaking her.

"What the fuck were you thinking, Mags? MAGS? What the *fuck* were you thinking?"

"I'm telling Althea *everything*."

CHAPTER 122

Darrin wrote furiously.

His journal had been filled up almost to the last ten pages.

December 30th, 2075. ——

Althea never turned around. She never saw me standing hand in hand with the man who had saved me from the months of irreparable damage that she had caused.

I waited and watched and heard what her lawyer had to say to the press. I waited and waited until the last day. Until the day that Michael had his dignity taken away, I waited.

I swear I saw her see me through a side glance one time. She never fully acknowledged my existence, my breathing the same air in the same room. The two men whose lives she had made utterly miserable, and she didn't even care to look at us.

It was mighty haughty of her to sit there and soak in the attention she got after having successfully put a man behind bars for doing what she did.

She had done that to me. She had taken me. Raped me. I know no one would believe me. I know that I would be laughed at, balked at, and made into a joke, but I know what she did to me. It took me until that last day in the courthouse, when she could have retracted what she said. She had all the opportunities in the world to do that, but instead she let him be thrown into that place.

And Georgina. I know she tried her best to get him off. She tried everything she could. James even said that she really did poke all the holes in the evidence that she could, but that awful woman's story, that's all it took for the world to believe Michael was a rapist worthy of the hell in that place.

My husband, stabbed! Stabbed because we tried to do the right thing. To free Michael.

I know what I have to do. I know who I need to support. As much as my mind tells me that getting involved with these radical men could be dangerous. I must fight.

CHAPTER 123

"I tried calling Ma, but Mom said she's not feeling well."

"That's to be expected."

She wasn't in the mood to talk.

I wasn't in the mood to speculate about what was going on between my moms.

Ma hadn't spoken a word to me since the madness at the sentencing.

Mom had sent me a text asking me if I was okay.

I had responded with 'Yes, Mom.'

And that had been that.

I slid under the covers.

"I *need* you, Fess. I need you like I have never needed anyone before."

I let the frustrated tears fall down my face.

She scooted towards me, facing me, brushing my tears away with her soft thumb.

"Come here, Al. Come here and lay on my chest."

I heard her heart beat in my eardrums.

Aibek watched us through a slight slit in the door.

When our eyes met momentarily, I saw him through the opaque tears as clear as a dirty glass.

I blinked the tears away and saw him smiling at me.

He quietly shut the door and ran into his room.

I snuggled deeper into Fess' hair.

"It's okay, baby. It's *all* going to be okay."

I fell asleep to her cooing the same line over and over again.

When I woke up, it was just past midnight.

Fess lay beside me, wide awake, staring at the ceiling.

"Fess, I am so grateful for you. You have been so stoic about all of this. I think you and I could really be amazing mothers to that boy."

She didn't say anything back.

"Here, with me, right now, I just…I really appreciate it."

I reached for her hand.

She pulled it away and clenched it close to her heart, grasping at the bare skin on her chest.

"I can't…I can't be what you want me to be, Al. I can't be *okay* with all of this and still marry you."

I propped my head up with my arm and touched her cheek with my other hand.

"It's over now. We're safe. No one is getting in the way of us being together anymore."

She turned her head to look at me.

"Do you promise that you will *never* do this to me again?"

I nodded immediately.

"I need to hear you say that you won't put me and Aibek through anything like this *ever* again, Al. I *need* to hear you say it like you *mean* it."

"I *know* I won't. He isn't worth losing you. Losing Aibek."

"I know he was an evil man. I can feel it in my gut, Al. Didn't you know? Didn't you *ever* suspect that?"

I pulled my hand back and grabbed a bunch of my blanket to my chest, trying to think of what to say.

I recalled the time that I had found his phone. The conversation where he had confessed that he was Draven Alec. And the aftermath, when we had never had the chance to talk.

All the stuff he had given me had been thrown in the trash, where it belonged.

My apartment lease ended.

Did he get my letter?

None of it mattered anymore.

I refocused on the woman in front of me.

"I didn't know. I swear it. He had me fooled."

It was the truth.

How can I be certain that he had *never* coerced me into giving in to his selfish desires?

Maybe I had been like a dog at a shelter — abused again and again until I no longer saw it as abnormal. Until I just saw it as something that I *expected*; something that I *deserved*.

Or maybe I had been like Eve, in the garden of Eden. Given paradise, and yet the snake had offered me something I just couldn't resist.

I just hadn't realized the *consequences* of the knowledge that he was imparting onto me until I had banished him from *my* paradise.

How much had I fallen under his spell?

How much of what *truly* happened have I misremembered?

How much of myself did I lose in just a *phase*?

Fess gulped audibly, interrupting my introspection.

It was *my* turn to hold her until she cried herself to sleep.

We spooned.

Things felt like they once had.

Before anything with Michael had ever happened.

CHAPTER 124

"Find Azazel! Find her and ask her to help you!"

The voice echoed in my ear as the last few images of Georgina flashed before my eyes.

I recalled seeing her get stabbed multiple times, and then there was a sharp pain when I was knocked across the head by a baton.

I felt the cool of my breath descend from my nostrils onto my upper lip.

I could feel the hairs on my moustache become matted against my face.

What have they done to me?

I felt every small movement my body made, as it shook off the drug-induced sleep.

Every blood vessel within my body surged towards the wound under my right rib.

"Fuck!"

What have I done to myself?

I remembered the crazy woman with the buzz cut that had been held back by the guards as I was taken away, drifting in and out of darkness.

She had managed to slice through the skin near my rib.

I recalled seeing the trail of blood as some of the women carried me into the bus.

The only parts of my body that I could move with any deliberate thought were my eyelids.

I cracked one open, only to be hit with a strong sense of regret.

A bright light gaping through the cracks.

My head pounded.

The blood rushed there.

I quickly closed my eye again.

I wanted to curl up into the fetal position.

I couldn't tell if I was already in it.

I blinked rapidly, trying to clear the opacity of sleep from the one eye that I had some control over.

I looked to my side, feeling the rough nylon sheet rub against my bare arm.

I was lying flat on something.

I tried to make out some more of my surroundings with the limited vision that I had.

It was pristine.

Clean.

White sheets, white walls, and that smell...

That awful smell of sterility.

I was in a hospital bed.

A sharp pain shot down from my heart into my groin.

The pain didn't linger there.

It just disappeared.

What have they done to me?

The pain skipped my groin and went into my aching toes.

I tried to wiggle them in vain.

Where am I?

If only I could open my other eye.

There was no chance of that happening.

The crust had glued it *shut*.

I tried to lift my head an inch.

It gave me a centimetre.

I tried with all the strength in my body to move my hand, deadened by sedation.

Inch by inch, my fingers crawled towards my thighs.

Like a wounded spider dragging itself home.

When I finally reached between my thighs, the index and middle finger tried to feel what was there.

Gauze.

A bandage.

Numbness.

Two cavities and loose skin flapping against my thigh.

My heart raced. Adrenaline shot through my veins as my open eye darted from side to side, trying to rack my brain for a way out.

I started heaving.

My lungs hurting with each breath I took.

I felt the pressure of my lungs against the wound near my rib.

I sobbed aloud, ignoring the pain.

The part that *they* hated had been *ripped* out of my flesh.

Fed to the goddamn dogs.

I hoped the fuckers enjoyed it.

I lay there, motionless, staring straight into the bright light through my one good eye.

I *willed* myself to be blinded by it.

How did I get here?

ACKNOWLEDGEMENTS

I want to thank my husband, first and foremost, to whom this book is dedicated. He is the reason I have a consistent breakfast every morning. My sister, to whom this book is also dedicated, for being my cheerleader and for challenging me on absolutely anything and everything, as teenagers do.

I want to thank Michele C., David D., and Keith M. for providing me with incredible feedback on an earlier manuscript; yes, this is the seventy thousandth draft. Keith M. in particular, for ripping my final working draft to shreds and helping me grow as a writer. I appreciate you seeing my vision, working with me, and writing the numerous comments that made this book what it is now.

I must thank my parents here, Mr. and Mrs. Joshi, for giving me the gift of life, without which I wouldn't be able to annoy them sufficiently as their favourite eldest daughter. Vasuky, for reminding me that everything in life can be satirical, your life-long friendship, and all the laughs that come along with it. Ebru, for the incredible cover art, your friendship and praise — you stroked my ego.

To all my other friends, Tisha and Dom L., Aisha S., Magdalena K. (also for letting me borrow your name) in particular, who have supported me through this incredible journey to writing my first novel, thank you.

Finally, I would like to thank all the people that taught me, debated with me, disagreed with me, and agreed to disagree. You keep me on my toes and motivated to keep learning.

ABOUT THE AUTHOR

Monica Joshi has a Bachelor of Arts in English and Philosophy from Queen's University in Canada. She self-published a novella, *Aria,* in 2014. She delved into political feminist fiction for her debut novel, *Matriarchy.* Joshi calls Ontario, Canada her home with her wonderfully witty husband and two adorably annoying cats. You can visit her online at www.monicajoshi.com.

CPSIA information can be obtained
at www.ICGtesting.com
Printed in the USA
LVHW110801260322
714479LV00015B/226